Song Girl: A Mystery in Two Verses

Keith Hirshland

James -
I hope you think this hits on the right notes
K

For information, or to order additional copies, please contact:

Beacon Publishing Group
P.O. Box 41573 Charleston, S.C. 29423
800.817.8480| beaconpublishinggroup.com

Publisher's catalog available by request.

ISBN-13: 978-1-949472-40-0

ISBN-10: 1-949472-40-0

Published in 2022. New York, NY 10001.

First Edition. Printed in the USA.

"And when you close your eyes
You can hear the music playing"
Pat Green

♪♫♪

Song Girl: A Mystery in Two Verses

Table of Contents

The Prelude

He sees…

A hospital room. It looks like every hospital room he's ever seen or in which he's ever been. Although when he stops to think about it, he admits that number isn't very many. This room strikes him as relatively new, at least recently painted, and surprisingly bright thanks to a large window that lets in the sun from another glorious Colorado Springs day. He thinks the room smells like a hospital room should smell, antiseptic, cleaner than clean. There's a table attached to the hospital bed that can swing in and out of the way for the use of the patient, the nurse, or the doctor depending on the needs of each. The only other piece of furniture in the roughly 9' by 11' room is the chair in which he finds his butt at the moment. There's a flat screen TV mounted to the wall and a half a dozen, by his count, machines, appliances and pieces of equipment monitoring vital signs and, he has to assume, keeping her alive.

She's in the bed. Flat on her back. Eyes closed. He thinks she looks so peaceful on the outside. He hopes all the technology, on which she is currently dependent, tells the same story about what is happening on the inside. He is certain he's seen her eyes flicker on more than one occasion. He commits it to memory each time and tells the doctor.

“She’s comatose,” was all the doc offers in response.

He has been there for the better part of 24 hours.

She sees…

A bed. It’s her bed but which one? The bed she slept in at the Haynes’s house? No not that bed. It’s her childhood bed, the one in which she slept before she had to leave that house. It’s comfortable, comforting. It’s her old bed but it’s not her old room. At least she’s pretty sure it isn’t. This room is bathed in soft white light. The images from inside the room are unclear. Is that a chair? Is there a person in the chair? Before she can give the thought more attention there is a knock on the door.

“Come in,” she says. Or did she. Was that her voice?

The door opens and she can see people, at least what appear to be people. They’re all shapes and sizes. Men, women, and children, lined up outside her door. Each one waiting to see her. In they come. One by one. They touch her hand, her face, her hair. They appear concerned but they are happy to see her. She thinks they look familiar but she doesn’t think it’s because she knows them. Then she realizes she doesn’t *know* them but she recognizes them all. They’re famous. They’re singers and songwriters. She’s seen them on TV, in music videos, on stages in concerts. She’s seen their faces on CDs, record album covers, cassette tapes. His, hers, her friends’, her parents’. For some reason she can’t understand why? Her heart hurts when she thinks of her mom and dad. The familiar strangers keep coming. Each and every one leans in and whispers something in her ear. She closes her eyes and opens her ears and hears words, they're the titles of songs they've written or sung.

She opens her eyes and another person is by her side. Is that Steven Tyler? The guy behind him looks like Springsteen, then comes Lady Gaga, Paul McCartney with John Lennon. *Isn't he dead?* She thinks. *Am I dead?* She wonders. But then there's Jason Aldean, Whitney Houston, Judy Garland, Paul Simon, Sir Elton John and on and on the line stretches. Out the door and down the hall.

♪♫♪

The First Verse: Before The Fall

Reginald Byrd and Stanley Byrd, Jr. were brothers. Stan a little older, Reg a whole lot meaner. Thanks to straight A's and a well-placed call from Stanley Byrd, Sr., the elder Byrd brother, was accepted to Colorado College in Colorado Springs. The younger Byrd also decided to go west a couple of years later. Not as a straight A student or the beneficiary of a well-connected father but as an attendee of Pueblo Junior College which would later become Colorado State University, Pueblo. The school just happened to be 40 miles south of the Springs. Reg chose PJC not because of the school's cool nickname — they were the Thunderwolves — but because it was one of the few schools that sent a congratulatory letter of acceptance. It also gave him the opportunity to be near his big brother Stan.

Colorado College was founded in 1874, two years before Colorado was admitted to the Union and became the nation's 38th state. Stan Byrd, Jr. was a decent high school hockey player and harbored the faint hope of lacing up his skates to play for the Tigers at the collegiate level. Colorado College had won National Championships in the sport, before Stan arrived, under the helm of its coach, a bull terrier of a man in shape and demeanor named Cheddy Thompson. The school's team, with Thompson calling the shots, made NCAA Frozen Four appearances six times. Thompson left in 1958 and the school remained one of college hockey's elite programs for a few more years. Then its hockey fortunes started to suffer and by the time Stan Jr. arrived the team was losing more games each year than it won.

In addition to school and hockey Stan Jr. went to work at the Antlers hotel. A landmark in Colorado Springs, the original building had burned to the ground in the fall of 1898. The new version, finished in 1901, featured 200 guestrooms, many with commanding views of majestic Pikes Peak, a gourmet restaurant, and a magnificent ballroom. Stan Byrd, Jr. was hired as a bellman.

Across the street was The Chief Theatre which displayed the current feature films of the day including *Midnight Cowboy* and *Butch Cassidy and the Sundance Kid*. On Tuesday and Thursday afternoons The Chief showed classics that remained popular drawing cards. A person could reminisce with *Bedtime for Bonzo*, *The Red Badge of Courage*, *The Day the Earth Stood Still*, *The Quiet Man*, and *A Streetcar Named Desire*. Stan Byrd had Thursdays off and watched them all, many more than once. Each time he went to the movies at The Chief he bought his ticket from Mary Virginia Hogenauer.

"Call me Ginger," she told a blushing Stan as he bought his ticket to *Viva Zapata* for the third time. The ticket giver and the ticket buyer became friends and soon struck up a romance. He knew it was getting serious when he would willingly sit through *The Prime of Miss Jean Brodie*, *Hello Dolly*, *Goodbye Columbus* and *Singin' in the Rain*, with, and for, her.

When his younger brother Reg came West, he did so in a classic 1965 Chevy Biscayne. It was two tone red and white and appeared to be all grill. It was more affordable than its very popular cousin the Impala and Reg thought it looked cooler too. It ran like a charm and proved to be plenty fast. He'd had it for less than a year when he crossed the Pueblo city limits. He drove it the entire time he was in Colorado but had somehow failed to remember to register it with the state Department of Motor Vehicles. That, however, would turn out to be the least of his problems.

Stan was thrilled when he first heard his baby brother would be close by. He promised they'd hang out, said they'd be "thick as thieves." But, of course, they weren't. Stan did mean it, in the beginning, when he said he hoped Reg would make the forty-minute drive north from Pueblo to the Springs. But, more often than not, when Reg called to say he was planning to do just that, Stan was working, or studying, or playing hockey or doing just about anything. Sometimes Reg came anyway and many times ended up too drunk to drive home, passed out on Stan's living room couch. On two of the trips he got arrested and thrown in the Colorado Springs city jail. Once Stan bailed him out, once he didn't. Stan and Ginger tried a few times to include Reg socially, setting him up with friends on several double dates. One of three things would always happen. Reg didn't like the girl or the girl didn't like Reg. Once in a while there was a mutual attraction but that never seemed to last. Usually, the second thing happened and Reg rarely cared whether the girl liked him. He did nothing to hide that particular fact to Stan or Ginger so they stopped trying to be matchmakers. The invitations became less and less frequent.

One Christmas they each received $1,000 cash from their parents. Stan did what he thought was the prudent thing and invested his money. Reg, as was his wont, was more rash. He decided to buy four new whitewalls for the Biscayne and several cases of beer.

The first thing Reg Byrd noticed about being a freshman in college was that nobody much cared that he was a freshman in college. For the first time in his educational experience the school day didn't start with an alphabetical call of the roll and a subsequent acknowledgement of attendance. After a few weeks of sitting in the back of the classroom, where nobody checked if he belonged there or not, he started skipping more classes than he attended. Instead of learning about philosophy and physics he found himself playing poker and pool in a dive bar frequented by a motorcycle gang called the Silent Commandos. Reg played football for a state championship winning team in high school and had stayed in shape so he wasn't intimidated by the bikers and they paid him little attention in return. At least in the beginning.

This particular motorcycle bunch claimed to have splintered off from another club which called itself The Market Street Commandos. That branch was a major disruptive force during the 1947 Hollister riots in California. In America in the 1930s and 40s the Fourth of July weekend was the time for annual "gypsy tour" events sanctioned by the American Motorcyclist

Association. The gatherings, including the one in Hollister, included races and social activities that translated mostly to partying and consuming copious amounts of beer. The Northern California town of approximately 4,500 people welcomed the cyclists every year with open arms. But in 1947 the arms of the town weren't big enough. After World War II the event was so popular that more than 4,000 motorcycle enthusiasts (gang members) doubled the city's population. At first it was one big party then, as most big parties tend to do, it turned ugly. The seven person Hollister police force was overwhelmed with rowdy, inebriated motorcycle gang members from all over the country. Gangs that included The Market Street Commandos. The event gained even more notoriety thanks to a short story titled "The Cyclists' Raid" written by Frank Rooney and published in Harper's Magazine.

After Hollister and the split to form a new gang, The Silent Commandos were led by a hard ass named Christopher Trent Mascaro. The gang called him C T. Reg Byrd would come to refer to him simply as Mr. M. One night, in the Pueblo bar, a couple of the bikers were playing pool and drinking shots when an internal dispute about a misplaced cue ball bubbled up. For reasons known only to him Reg Byrd stepped up to the table, slapped down a twenty-dollar bill, and challenged the winner. Sensing potential trouble, he also bought the two pool players, bikers he would learn were called Wizard and Lamaj, and each of their twelve friends another round. Tempers cooled, everybody shared a laugh, and word got back to C T Mascaro that a big friendly college kid who hung out at the bar was “good people”.

Wizard, Lamaj and Reg Byrd became friends. Reg asked about the origins of the nicknames and was told that Wizard’s given name was Harry Blackstone.

“Apparently there was a famous magician that went by that name,” Wizard said over a beer one night. “C T hung the handle on me. Thought it was a riot. I didn’t like it too much at first but tell you the truth, it’s grown on me.”

“He’s also been known to make things disappear,” Lamaj chimed in. “And by things, I mean people.”

“Shut up Lamaj!” Wizard spat accompanied by a dirty look.

“Really?” Reg asked. “You’ve killed people?”

“Hell no,” was the biker’s response but Reg saw Lamaj nodding his head in dissent.

“Wow,” Reg blew out a deep breath. He looked past Wizard to Lamaj, “What about you?”

“I never killed nobody,” he answered quickly. Reg thought about the double negative.
“OK. Good,” Byrd said, “but I was more interested in how you got your nickname.”

"Oh, that," Lamaj smiled, "not quite as entertaining a story as Wiz here," he slapped Wizard on the back. "My mama, God rest her soul," he crossed himself as he said the words, "named me Jamal. CT just reversed it."

On a subsequent night Reg found himself sitting at the bar alone, nursing a bottle of beer when the boss man sidled up next to him. Reg liked the biker boss and could tell the feeling was somewhat mutual. He was friendly, most of the time, but there was a layer of menace just below the surface that made Reg nervous. Small talk turned to a telling of the story of the split between the "Silent" chapter of the Commandos and the much more malignant "Market Street" chapter. Mascaro retold the Hollister story and added that Hollywood made a movie, *The Wild One,* based on the whole affair starring heartthrob Marlon Brando. He lamented the fact that despite having watched the movie at least a half a dozen times he found no reference to his role in the affair. After hearing the story Reg ordered another beer and a shot for his "boss" then looked over at the motorcycle gang leader and asked a couple more questions.

"Why Colorado?"

"Well Tweety," he had taken to calling Byrd the nickname based on a Looney Tunes cartoon character. Despite a couple of initial, indifferent, protestations the name stuck. "The situation with those Market Street a-holes was getting untenable," Mascaro said. "A bunch of those thugs wanted to join ranks with the Hells Angels to form a San Francisco chapter."

"That's a bad thing?" Byrd asked, taking a sip from his beer.

"Worse than bad," Mascaro said before knocking back his shot. "Hells Angels are the worst of the worst."

"Why?" Byrd wondered out loud. "I thought the Hells Angels was the gold standard of motorcycle gangs."

"That's the problem, Tweety," the biker boss said, punching Byrd's arm. "They think their shit don't stink. Hell, no pun intended," he stopped to laugh at his own joke. "Half those guys barely even know how to *ride* a bike let alone maintain one. They just want to drink and fight and scare the crap out of folks. Not what I'm, er we're, about. Besides we all hate San Francisco." He laughed again and waved at the bartender for another tequila. Mascaro finished the story by telling Reg they all decided to ride East and ended up in Pueblo. But before they left, they changed their name to the Silent Commandos and swore an oath to keep their mouths shut about what they'd seen and done. An oath that C T Mascaro had just broken.

During the next few months Reg got pretty good at pool, even better at cards, and became a de facto member of the Commandos. He didn't have a bike but the bikers loved his car. And C T Mascaro continued to take a particular liking to Reg Byrd. Despite his disdain for the classroom Reg turned out to be street savvy. Mascaro noticed that and appreciated it, then he took advantage of it. The head honcho found his latest charge to be tough and occasionally possess a biker's mean streak. But he also noticed that mean streak was conveniently wrapped in a package that looked the exact opposite of the way the rest of his caporegimes appeared. He showed Reg some "tricks" he had learned like how to bend a wrist a certain way to exert maximum discomfort or exactly where in the kidney region to punch someone to cause the most pain. He also gave Reg a gun, showed him how to handle it and made him practice at targets every day.

"You never know when this skill might come in handy," he told the young man.

It all made Reg a little uncomfortable. He welcomed the lessons, loved the camaraderie he had come to share with the bikers, but he couldn't help but feel that despite the fatherly tone set by C T Mascaro, the boss wouldn't hesitate to inflict some personal pain if Reg stepped out of line or put the Silent Commandos at risk. Mascaro also made sure his lieutenants knew exactly where Reg stood in the biker family hierarchy. They appreciated that first because Mascaro had always been a fair leader and second because they all liked Reg as much as the boss seemed to.

Byrd quickly became Mascaro's go-to guy for certain jobs and shakedowns. One of those jobs involved a punk who owed the Commandos more than he carried around in his pocket. Reg found that to be true the night he waited in a rear entrance alley behind the kid's building and the welsher literally ran into Reg coming out the back door of his apartment.

"You owe the Commandos money," Reg said as he picked the kid off the pavement.

"I know. I know," he stammered.

"Give it to me," Reg let him go.

"I was just on my way to pay Mascaro," the kid dusted off his backside.

"That's what you said last time," Reg grabbed him again and pulled him closer, "and the time before that."

"Look, big guy," the kid found some bravado, "he'll get it when he gets it. I'm good for it. Do you know who my old man is?" he asked as he tried to free himself from Reg's grip. Reg helped him by letting him go.

"Do you know who five finger Freddie is?" Reg asked lifting his right hand.

"Who!? What!? Are you a freakin' child?" the kid asked. "Five finger Freddie, good grief." He started to turn and walk away. Reg grabbed his shoulder and spun him around. Then he curled his fingers one at a time making a first with his right hand and knocked the punk out.

"That's five finger Freddie," he said walking away after taking every penny from the unconscious kid's pockets.

Reg did not know the mark, now lying unconscious thanks to five finger Freddie, was part of a family that had been Pueblo big shots for generations. His father was a prominent businessman and former town council member. The old man was well aware of his kid's bad behavior having had to bail him out, literally and figuratively, of difficulties more often than he wanted to admit. He settled his son's grievance and his debt with Mascaro privately. But at the same time, he didn't hide his displeasure with the severity of the justice doled out by Byrd. His son had to have his jaw wired shut which the father confided was actually a blessing in disguise. Mascaro told him he would speak to his enforcer. The old man nodded his agreement but as a backup he quietly mentioned, with some embellishment, that there may be a dangerous fella in Mascaro's employ to a few friendly faces in the Pueblo Police Department. They in turn passed the word, with further augmentation, to colleagues up north in Colorado Springs. Of course, the Silent Commandos had eyes and ears as well. Word got back to Mascaro, then trickled down to Byrd, that Reg was the subject of scrutiny. The bikers advised him to trust very few people and be extra careful whenever he was out alone. Which he just happened to be on Thanksgiving Eve.

♪♫♪

Wrong Place, Wrong Time

Reg had just come from his brother Stan's apartment. They were having Thanksgiving dinner a night early because the couple had made plans with Ginger's family on the actual holiday. That had already left a sour taste in Reg's mouth which was exacerbated by shots of Wild Turkey and the dinner conversation. Stan had expressed disapproval of Reg's lack of commitment to his education and continuing association with a group of what his big brother described as "biker thugs". None of it, the food, the booze, the lecture, sat well with Reg and he ended up storming out of the apartment before Ginger could cut the pumpkin pie. He spent several minutes driving around unmemorable blocks before pulling over to the curb to consider his options for the night. In addition to the bottle of booze he had brought to his brother's he also had his personal Wild Turkey fire water flask in his pocket. Now he reached for it, unscrewed the cap, and took a gulp. There were a couple of girls he knew in town but he had no idea if they were working, serving drinks to the lonely hearts who had nowhere else to be on Thanksgiving eve. He was also aware there were still a couple of places in Old Colorado City that could provide certain services if a person was so inclined. At the moment Reg wasn't. He had to make his way south to Pueblo eventually so he decided he needed neither another drink nor the companionship of a stranger. He blew out a deep breath and noticed headlights in his rearview mirror.

Officer Steven Churchfield was on duty that night, working an extra shift so a fellow patrolman could have an extended Thanksgiving holiday with his family. At 35, Churchfield was a five-year veteran of the Colorado Springs PD. He was happily married with three children. The night before Thanksgiving had already proved to be an interesting shift. An earlier call had come over the radio about an armed robbery in the vicinity of 1600 Wood Avenue and Churchfield had responded. Upon arriving at the scene, he found a male victim, a little worse for wear, but able to give a description of his assailant. He pointed the patrolman in the direction he had seen the robber run and, after making sure the man was okay, he called for an ambulance then took off in pursuit. An hour or so later he'd heard nothing, seen no one, and was about to give up the search and take his dinner break. That's when he noticed the two-tone Chevy parked, but running, on the street near the intersection of Bijou and El Paso.

Reg sat up a little straighter in the driver's seat. Another quick glance in the mirror told him the headlights belonged to a CSPD cruiser. He'd seen enough of the distinctive Plymouth Furys to know. The rooftop cherry lights were off but visible when the car stopped a handful of feet behind Reg's car. The first thing Byrd did was raise his palm to his mouth and exhale into it. Then he held it to his nose and sniffed hoping to tell if he could smell the Wild Turkey on his breath. He couldn't tell but, he thought to himself, he could never tell. Next, he checked the glove box and saw the .22 caliber pistol he'd been given by Mascaro.

"Just in case," the biker boss had said when he handed it over. Reg grabbed the gun and laid it on the passenger seat, *just in case,* he thought to himself. The AM radio in the car was tuned to KOVR, "the voice of the Rockies". The station played both current hits and what it called "the golden oldies". At that moment Steppenwolf was singing "Born to be Wild".

Officer Churchfield noticed the head of what clearly appeared to be a man in the driver's seat. From what he could see there was only one person in the car. As he watched, and pondered his next move, he saw the driver lean to his right. *Probably grabbing his registration from the glove compartment* thought the patrolman. Then Churchfield looked at the license plate. Maryland. Expired. Before he could call in a check the driver's side door of the big sedan opened.

Several things went through Reg Byrd's mind in rapid fire succession. The street was dark, his car and the cop car were the only two on the block. He'd been drinking, he was familiar with the Colorado Springs city jail, and he knew, thanks to his brothers in the Silent Commandos, that there were elements within the CSPD that were probably out to get him. He panicked. Byrd grabbed the gun and put it in his right coat pocket. With his left hand he opened the door and climbed out of the Plymouth.

Churchfield froze for a second. In his experience the people he pulled over respectfully waited in their cars. But he hadn't pulled this car over, he'd happened upon it. The driver, the person coming out of the Chevrolet, was a good-sized man.

The officer noticed he was wearing jeans and a jacket zipped up about halfway. His right hand was in the jacket's right pocket. Churchfield also realized the man was actually just a kid. Not 16 but probably not that far north of 20 either. Just a dumb, nervous kid whose parents hadn't taught him that he should stay in the car when in the presence of a police officer. That thought made Steven Churchfield relax a little. It also got him killed.

He rolled down his window and was about to tell the approaching boy to get back in his car but he never got the chance. He saw the kid's hand come out of his coat pocket. *Is that a gun?* He thought and tried to process the question. His own firearm was clipped in its holster. He knew there was zero chance he had time to get the window, which he had just rolled down, back up. Patrolman Steven Churchfield suddenly realized the night before Thanksgiving would be his last night on earth. He said a silent prayer that he had done enough in this life to secure a comfortable spot in the next.

Reg Byrd was acting on a combination of fear, anger, adrenaline and panic. He rushed the cruiser, pulled his gun leaned into the open window, and stared straight into the cop's eyes. Resignation was the word that immediately came to him. In that instant he also thought about his own circumstances. His brother, his father, his mother. How what he was about to do meant he could never see them again. How two lives were about to be different; one changed, the other gone forever. He noticed the patrolman's right hand inches from his police department-issued weapon, the cop's left hand was on the window handle, fumbling, trying in vain to grab purchase and roll the window back up. He wore his CSPD uniform jacket, the name tag on the left breast read Churchfield. His hat was on the passenger seat, on the other side of his gun, CSPD shield pinned to the front. *I've never killed a cop before* thought Reg, *hell, I've never killed anybody before.*

He pressed the muzzle of the revolver against the officer's jacket. It stopped when it came up against his chest. He closed his eyes and fired twice, opened his eyes then moved the gun to the other side of the jacket and fired two more times. This time he kept his eyes open. The noise from the shots wasn't as loud as Reg thought it might be even though the ringing in his ears had started immediately. The policeman gave Reg one last look, released one last breath, then slumped over the steering wheel. Out of embarrassment, hatred, or just plain anger at the feeling that he was forced into the situation, Reg mustered up a load of saliva and spat at officer Churchfield. The goo landed directly on the patrolman's badge. He then pulled away from the patrol car and looked around. No lights came on, no dogs barked. It was as if what just happened never happened at all. He walked quickly back to the Biscayne and climbed in his car. Les Paul and Mary Ford were singing *Vaya Con Dios.* Reg knew that meant "go with God".

He didn't waste another second getting back to Pueblo. Once there he put the word out that he needed to speak with C T Mascaro. The boss was less than pleased about having to leave the comfort of his home on Thanksgiving Eve but the pipeline had made it clear that this was urgent. Reg Byrd was in trouble. When Mascaro arrived at the bar he was greeted by a few of the Silent Commandos who were huddled around the jukebox, Byrd was alone at the bar. Alone except for a bottle of Wild Turkey and two shot glasses.

"Celebrating with some turkey a few hours early are we?" Mascaro said as he plopped down on the barstool next to Reg.

"Something like that," Byrd said finishing off what was left in the glass and refilling it from the bottle.

"That's enough," the biker boss said grabbing both the glass and the bottle.

"It'll never be enough," Byrd shot back, "Somebody is dead because of me. The gun you gave me, the lessons you showed me, I put them to use tonight," Reg admitted quietly. He didn't know how the boss man would react to his confession. Mascaro let the words hang in the air for a few seconds and then slid the glass of whiskey back Byrd's way. He also took a long swig straight from the bottle of Wild Turkey.

"You better tell me about it," Mascaro seethed. Reg could see his right fist was clenched. *Five finger Freddie*, he thought to himself.

"Not much to tell sir," Byrd held the glass with both hands. "I shot him."

“WHOA!, Whoa, whoa, Amigo,” he put his hand on the young man’s shoulder and squeezed, “Who, exactly, did you shoot? Where and when?”

“Tonight. In Colorado Springs. He was a cop,” Byrd answered the questions in reverse order.

At the sound of Reg’s last two words, a couple of the bikers that had gathered around the jukebox took a few steps closer to the bar.

“Jesus, Mary and Joseph,” Mascaro exclaimed crossing himself. “Wizard! Lamaj!,” he barked. Mascaro nodded in their direction and they headed for, and out, the door. He knew if there was any chatter about a cop killing in Colorado Springs the two who had just left would find out about it. C T didn’t want to think about what would have to happen if one of the two, or both, came back with bad news. He turned back to Reg Byrd. “Look at me, kid.” Reg did and he could see the undercurrent of menace that Mascaro always carried come to the top. It was in his eyes. “For God’s sake, why? Was there a fight? For your sake, son, this answer better be the right one. And the truth.”

“It will be,” Byrd continued to look into Mascaro’s eyes, “the truth.” He took a slug of the whiskey and followed it with a deep breath. “There might have been a fight,” Byrd shook his head, “but I didn’t let it get that far. I had pulled over to the curb, the cop came up behind me. I didn’t know what to do.” He put his head in his hands. “I knew I was a marked man up there. I didn't want to go back to jail. I guess I panicked, did what I thought I had to do. I'm sorry Mr. M. Truly sorry." Byrd stopped talking. He was either going to live another day or he wasn't. That decision would probably come down to whatever news his two friends could ascertain. Mascaro took another long swig from the bottle, set it back on the bar, and started to pick at a corner of the label.

"Who else knows about this?"

"Nobody."

"You positive about that?"

"I guess I can't be 100 percent but I'm as positive as I can be. It was really dark. There was nobody else on the street, no dogs barked, no lights came on and nobody followed me when I left." Mascaro nodded and hoped against hope that Reg Byrd had been as inconspicuous as he thought he was.

"Where's the gun?" the biker boss asked.

"Still in my car. Glove box," Byrd answered and took a drink. Mascaro turned to another one of the bikers who had heard every word.

"Go get it," he said to the biker who headed for the door. He passed Lamaj and Wizard heading back in. "You sure nobody saw you?" Mascaro asked Byrd one more time and saw the kid nod slowly. "You were up north visiting your brother, right?" Byrd nodded again. "Does he know about this? Did you try and call him?"

"I thought about it but I didn't."

"Good. Don't. Don't tell him now, don't tell him ever. Don't tell anybody."

Mascaro slid off his stool and met the two bikers halfway. After a few minutes of muted conversation, nods, and a pat on the back for each, C T headed back to Byrd and the bar.

"Looks like you were right. So far nothing in the wind about a cop getting killed in the Springs." He looked at Reg and noticed a tear rolling down his right cheek. "Don't worry, Tweety," he said with a much more sympathetic tone as he patted his young lieutenant on the shoulder, "We'll take care of this AND you." He could see the kid visibly tense up. "Not take care of you that way," he said reassuringly, "Take care in the way of setting you up. Somewhere else." He could tell Reg Byrd believed him.

"His name was Churchfield," Reg said as another tear appeared.

"You just try and forget about all of that," Mascaro said and he took another drink from the bottle.

♪♫♪

Reg Runs

It turned out C T Mascaro had a cousin who managed a bank in Raleigh, North Carolina. In exchange for a piece of a piece of one of the Silent Commandos' many pies he agreed to be a landing spot for Reg and give him a job. Back in Colorado the Commandos arranged for a new ID, enough money, and a trade. The Chevy, that would be sold off for parts, for a decent motorcycle, a helmet, and a pair of boots. So, in the dead of winter Reg Byrd, who now thanks to C T Mascaro went by Mike Breed, headed back east.

He settled in nicely to his job as a security officer at the North Carolina bank. The work wasn't difficult but it kept him busy. Kept his mind off what he'd done, what he'd become, and gave him hope that he could, once again, become something else. Someone better. At work he caught the eye of another employee, an internal auditor named Diana Phillips. Reg, now Mike, made it a point to introduce himself to her with a smile. She smiled back and told him all her friends called her Daisy. He said he hoped to fit into that category one day and she replied that she thought he would. And he did. He spent days, weeks and months discovering the things she liked and the things she didn't. Honey buns, from a bakery nearby, was one of the former and he started leaving one at her desk a couple times a week. One of the things he found out she didn't like was dishonest people but there was nothing he could do about that.

They started spending more time away from work together. Evening walks in the park, brunches on Sunday. He learned she had just finished school at North Carolina State, graduating with an economics degree. She was an only child of a rancher and her family, a couple of uncles in Kentucky, owned thoroughbred racehorses. He was impressed that she had been to the Kentucky Derby more than once. He did his best to keep the conversations about her and gave up as little information about himself as possible. It was hard enough to remember his new name was Mike. In fact, at times when she addressed him that way he wouldn't respond. A gentle punch in the arm or a kick in the ankle would bring him back to his new reality. When she asked what he was thinking he would simply respond, "nothing" or "you". Never the truth. Never the fact that he had forgotten his name was Mike Breed.

The years went by and he found himself spending more and more time with Daisy Phillips. He was also thinking about himself. He knew he had fallen for this girl and there would come a time when he would have to start telling her the truth. But how much? How fast? His life had taken a turn for the better. He had a job he liked well enough, he was making decent money, and he had a girl. More important in his mind was that she liked him back. He thought less and less about what had happened in Colorado and more and more about what might happen in North Carolina. He had, long ago, stopped calling C T Mascaro every day. Partly because Mascaro told him to stop but mostly because there was never any new information to impart. Apparently, the Colorado Springs Police Department had finished its investigation of the murder of patrolman Steven Churchfield. They had never looked 40 miles south to Pueblo for answers and Mascaro assured Reg, now Mike, that the grapevine was silent on that topic. He also reassured the young man that if anything changed, he'd be the first to know. Seasons changed again and again and again without a word.

Birthdays also came and went and Daisy was about to have another one. It was no longer a secret at work that she and Mike were a couple and he had planned a special evening. More and more their coworkers would ask when they might expect "exciting news" as far as the two of them were concerned. Mike smiled each time, Daisy blushed, but deep down she started wondering the same thing. Both had long ago stopped seeing other people. Mike, in fact, had never started. "I love you" had long since become part of their normal vocabulary. But every time Daisy asked about Mike's personal life outside of her, searching for details about brothers, sisters, parents, or where he grew up, he shut her out or changed the subject. She started to wonder and he knew it. The way he figured it he had three choices: keep putting her off, come clean and tell her everything, or come up with a mixture of truths, half-truths, and lies to put her mind at rest. All three involved running the risk of losing her altogether. The mental tug of war lasted until Mike decided it couldn't last a day longer. He would tell Daisy everything. Who he really was and what he had actually done. He'd put all his cards on the table and hope against hope that Daisy would still be there when he was finished. He even called C T Mascaro and told him of his decision.

"I knew it would eventually come to this," the biker boss said.

"I just wanted to give you a heads up."

"Look, Tweety," Mascaro used the nickname he had given Reg years ago, "I'm guessing you've been struggling with this for some time but stop. Nobody is coming after you. Nobody cares. And if they did come sniffing around here, we'd all just deny ever knowing your name."

"Really?"

"Really. Go live your life kid. Mazel Tov." And he was gone. Off the phone and out of Reg Byrd's life. So, his mind was made up, further cemented by Mascaro's advice. He would tell Daisy everything and decided that if she loved him, they'd get through it. *No time like the present*, he thought, so he'd tell her on her birthday.

Daisy was a sucker for the movie *My Fair Lady*. The rags to riches story, the handsome Rex Harrison, the music, but most of all Audrey Hepburn. She insisted they see it more than once together and she saw it half a dozen times without Reg. He had saved some money and for her birthday and his big reveal he bought her a pearl necklace like the one Hepburn wore in the movie. Throughout much of the film Hepburn was covered up to her chin by dresses with high necklines but there were scenes in which her neck was exposed and graced by the string of pearls. Three strands hanging down to the top of her cleavage. He purchased an identical-looking piece for Daisy.

The jeweler was impressed and Reg hoped his girlfriend would be too.

He made a reservation at a recently rebuilt restaurant on the outskirts of Raleigh just off highway 70 that was getting rave reviews. The Angus Barn was said to have the best steaks around and an impressive wine list. Reg and Daisy took advantage of both. They left the restaurant and headed back to his place. On the way home, getting more and more nervous by the mile, Reg explained he had a bottle of champagne, a birthday gift, and a confession to make, when they got there. Silently she admitted that she was hoping for a different word than confession, maybe one that started with a “p”.

Once settled in the apartment Reg popped the cork, poured, and toasted to their future. All the while hoping they would have one in about a half an hour. Next, he presented Daisy with the Hepburn pearls. It wasn’t an engagement ring but she was thrilled nonetheless and showed her approval with a hug and a passionate kiss. He put them around her neck and stood back to admire how beautiful they looked. How beautiful she was. Then he took her hand, sat her on the couch and told her everything. Almost everything. He did confess to who he really was, where he was from and how he had come to North Carolina with a new identity. When she pressed for details he got cold feet and decided to be less than truthful saying only that he “got into some trouble” in Colorado and friends helped him start a new life. A life, he said, that he hoped included her long into the future.

He knew it wasn't a proposal but he sensed a huge weight was lifted off of Daisy's shoulders. He still harbored some guilt at having kept so much from her for so long and still not coming all the way clean. But he was relieved that he could finally be Reg Byrd again and it appeared Daisy was there to stay. They had more of the bubbly and he asked if she would model the pearls with nothing else on. She complied which led to only one, unavoidable, result. Afterward they were together in bed and talked about the future which included whether or not to tell their colleagues about Reg. He mentioned the boss already knew his story and added that telling anyone else could open up a pandora's box. She agreed and they decided, at least at the bank, he would continue to be Mike Breed and not Reg Byrd. She fell asleep in his arms.

A little more than a month later she realized she was late for her menstrual cycle, a week after that she went to her OBGYN. That night she and Reg had the second "most important discussion of their relationship." He said all the right things, held her hand, cried along with her, and told her "of course they would get married." Relieved, she left that night and went home. The next day she went to work but Mike Breed didn't. He never showed up again.

Daisy carried the baby to term, never considered doing anything else. She told friends and family that the father was an old flame who was in the military stationed in Germany. He had come home on leave and they had celebrated. People at the bank accepted her explanation but thought they knew better. She and Mike Breed had been an item, she was now pregnant and Mike was long gone. They put two and two together but never blamed Daisy. As the time for delivering the baby came closer, she went back and forth about whether or not she could be a single mother. She thought she could then she thought no way, every day, sometimes multiple times a day. With the charade of a faraway flame long exposed, her mother encouraged her to speak with the family pastor. Her father encouraged her to hunt down Reg Byrd with a vengeance. He would take care of the rest once she located him. The pastor recommended she speak with someone at an orphanage and he knew just the person. A fellow parishioner named Blanche Avery. It was breaking Daisy's heart but after countless hours of tears and prayer she agreed to give the baby, a little girl, up for adoption. Blanche said she would help her through the entire process and she did.

♪♫♪

Detective Marc Allen and Teri Hickox

The city of Colorado Springs had changed a great deal in the decades since Reg Byrd left. Detective Marc Allen couldn't have known how much when he walked out the back door of the Police Department Operations Center building and popped an ear bud into each ear. The red brick structure stood guard over most of a square city block just south of downtown. It had been an uneventful day in the city that, since 1978, was home to the United States Olympic Committee. Allen was looking forward to it also being an uneventful night. But as he started his journey home, he couldn't shake the feeling that he was being watched.

He wasn't an inherently paranoid person although he'd had similar feelings before. He was reminded of something Nirvana singer Kurt Cobain once said, "just because you're paranoid doesn't mean they aren't after you." In Allen's career as a cop plenty of people had been after him so he knew many times the feelings had been for good reason. But he hadn't experienced them lately and definitely not since changing his life and moving 1,600 miles from Raleigh, North Carolina. It normally started out in his gut but the raised hairs he now felt on the back of his neck were an indication of something more urgent. He did a quick 360-degree spin but found nothing out of the ordinary. A line of long ago planted oak trees framed the cop shop parking lot entrance on Weber street. Two squirrels had stopped chasing each other long enough to stare down at the detective from the top branch of one of the trees. Allen half expected one of them to rear up on its hind legs and wave. Could the rodents be the cause of his consternation? He doubted it but wouldn't immediately rule it out. His gaze went past the squirrels and the trees to the row of cars parked on Weber facing East. Nothing peculiar there but he couldn't help but focus on an ancient, orange and white, Dodge van occupying a space between a Camry and some model of Buick. He'd noticed the van before. In fact, he'd seen it every day he came to work since taking the new job. Always right there, windows covered by a combination of newsprint and poster board. Handwritten statements, prophecies and proverbs adorned several other spaces on each side of the van. A propane tank and a bicycle with what looked to Allen like flat tires were attached to the rear.

Allen couldn't see in and he had no idea if anyone was inside looking out. He didn't think the vehicle ever moved and if it did it was only to maybe occupy a slightly different parking space on the street. Early in his tenure he brought up the subject of the van to the cops in the squad room.

"That's the champ's van," he was told by a beat cop.

"The champ?" he asked.

"Yeah. Guy named Larry Holm." Allen immediately understood the reference. "Older guy. Vietnam vet is what he told us. He's harmless." Allen thanked the officer for the information and decided he'd feel better if he assessed the degree of harmlessness for himself.

He realized on this evening that he had yet to get very far on that front. Making a mental note to rekindle that effort with some up close and personal inquiries he walked west on Rio Grande. He loved the days when he could walk to and from work and he used the time to listen to Sirius XM PGA Tour Radio or any one of a number of podcasts. On this night he chose the latter. It was called The Cooper Vortex and it usually featured a lively discussion about who legendary hijacker D. B. Cooper really was and what had become of him. He marveled at the technology and thought about what life must have been like decades earlier when the only thing people had to listen to was AM radio.

Down the street the woman Marc Allen had known as Teri Hickox stared out from behind her Tom Ford sunglasses. She wondered if he'd recognize her if they happened upon each other on the street, in the grocery store, or at a bar. As she pondered that question Allen hustled across the street ahead of a green light on Tejon and jogged out of sight.

At home, nursing a cold beer, he reflected for what seemed to be the dozenth time about the circumstances that brought him to Colorado. He had what he thought was a darned good gig. Job security in the detective ranks of the Raleigh P.D., a beautiful and talented girlfriend who worked as a camera operator/reporter for a local television station, and a life in an interesting, growing, fairly progressive city that he enjoyed.

Then he had come across Hank and Teri Hickox who had left a couple of dead bodies and, in Allen's mind, one very important unanswered question, in their wake. They did it all while being not so loosely associated with one of North Carolina's most notorious, completely corrupt, small-time crime families. As Allen was putting the pieces of the two murders together and zeroing in on Teri as the prime suspect, Hank blew his brains out with a shotgun, absolving his adopted daughter of any guilt by conveniently wrapping a confession to both murders inside a carefully written suicide note. Detective Marc Allen still wasn't buying it.

He sympathized with the families in the middle of the murders along with the ones on the periphery as they all tried to put the pieces of their lives back together. At the same time, it was hard not to notice Allen's own life was falling apart. The aforementioned girlfriend up and left for a new job, with more responsibility, in Nevada and Teri Hickox, his main murder suspect, was lying low. Raleigh had suddenly lost much of its appeal. He still had friends in the department including an officer named Eliza Starz but since there was little reason to expend time or resources following Teri he stopped and started looking for a new job. Maybe one closer to the Pacific Ocean than the Atlantic. Maybe one within driving distance of his departed girlfriend, Denise Clawsew.

Cops tend to do a decent job of taking care of cops so when word got out that Allen was looking for another job, he started to get information about certain opportunities from across the country. One such posting was for a detective job in the

Investigative Division in the Colorado Springs P.D. He liked that one for a couple of reasons. One, he would be closer to Denise and the other was that he had heard of the CSPD thanks to a TV show called *Homicide Hunter*. The star of the show was a retired head of the Colorado Springs Police Major Crimes Unit named Joe Kenda. According to the program the man had joined the force in 1973, spent 17 years in its ranks as a detective before eventually leading the Homicide Division. The show also said he had investigated 387 cases and solved 356 of them for an astounding 92% closure rate. That told Allen that there was some darn good police work happening in the city of more than 600,000 souls and there was more than enough of it to keep him busy.

The city's police chief liked what he saw on paper and what he heard from both Allen's superiors and peers. They offered to fly him out for a face to face and he accepted. The get together included the chief, the current head of the Violent Crimes Section of the Investigations Division, a guy named Dan "Call me Danny" Gutrich and his boss the deputy chief of the Investigative and Special Operations Bureau who appeared to be a tougher than nails looking veteran cop. His name was Steven James Paulson but, for reasons yet to be explained, everyone called him Dennis. The meeting took place at a noisy, downtown steakhouse; pleasantries were brief and the four cops got down to business. They clearly believed Allen had what it took to be a cop in their shop but questioned why he would move most of the way across the country. The detective was honest because he didn't know any other way to be.

He told them about the pride he carried for all the good work he had done, his regrets about the dozens of professionals he was leaving behind, the frustration he still carried because of the cases he was unable to put to bed like the Hickox matter and he told them about Denise. The men around the table said they appreciated his candor, his exemplary history and his concern about the unsolved cases he would be leaving behind. Then Allen brought up the subject of Joe Kenda.

"That blowhard," blurted the chief of police. Reacting, the deputy chief nearly choked trying to keep from spitting out the gulp of beer he had just taken.

"Sir?" Allen wondered looking at the head honcho.

"Joe Kenda is a pompous ass. Couldn't solve a case if the perp showed up on his doorstep with a signed confession."

"But according to the TV show," Allen countered, "he solved more than 90% of 380 plus cases."

"And according to the real hard-working men and women of the Colorado Springs Police Department," Allen noticed the chief sit up a little straighter as he said it, "Joe Kenda is full of crap."

Marc Allen liked these guys and was becoming more and more convinced that he wanted this job. Before the gaggle dispersed, they talked more about the history of the department, areas of policing concerns (it seemed the Springs had an ever-growing homeless population), responsibilities, the chain of command and money. Allen said he'd like to "sleep on his decision" and the cops around the table agreed that it was a good idea. They said their goodbyes and Marc Allen used the rest of the day to explore the city.

He found a municipality that was far bigger than he had imagined, at least in terms of square miles. He drove north on I-25 and couldn't help but admire Pikes Peak which rose to more than 14,000 feet and stood sentinel over the city. He knew Colorado Springs was home to the United States Air Force Academy and he noticed it right away as he drove north. He took an exit and looped around, now heading back south toward downtown. He checked out that area, as well as several blocks north, south, east, and west of the police station. It was easy to spot the homeless population the group of cops had mentioned earlier. He eventually turned west onto Lake Avenue which dead-ended at The Broadmoor Hotel. Allen had heard of it, was pretty sure they played some major championships on its golf course, and he found the structure and surrounds both beautiful and impressive. He parked on a side street and Googled "Colorado Springs weather."

More good news, he thought as he read what popped up. An average of 16 and a half inches of annual precipitation, "that's good," he whispered. Moderate winter snowfall that, according to Google "remains on the ground briefly because of direct sun." "Also good," Allen added. Then he found the kicker and read aloud, "The city has abundant sunshine year-round, averaging 243 sunny days per year. Sold," he said with a smile.

He would have loved to make one more phone call before making the decision, a call to his dad and mom but sadly for Allen that was impossible. His father, also a police officer, had been killed in the line of duty and his mother, either unwilling or unable to live without him, left the earth less than a year later. He thought of them, guessed they would approve and knew his decision was the right one. He still took the rest of the day and that night to "sleep on it".

♪♫♪

Teri Gets Rich

Months earlier Teri Hickox had spent a handful of days digging up the coffee cans she knew were scattered across her dad, Hank's, North Carolina property. All told, her hard work unearthed close to $450,000 out of the cans buried in the estate's dirt. Dirt, along with the house and the barn, that Hank had left Teri in his will. When she was finished, she arranged the cans in a makeshift memorial, a small hill of metal, left in tribute to Hank. She guessed there were a few more cans with bills still in the ground but she was tired of looking. Especially since she was fairly certain she had found every can Hank had marked on the map inside his safe. The massive metal box also contained all of her dad's guns which she decided to keep for herself. All his guns except for the Pedersoli Wyatt Earp shotgun. The gun the only father she had ever known had used to splatter his brains all over his bedroom. That particular firearm was still in an evidence locker somewhere in the basement of the Raleigh Police Department.

Hank had left two more items in the safe. One was a picture of him with his arms around her adopted mom, Betty Lou. Teri thought they looked so happy, all dressed up with clearly some place to go. Lying next to the photograph was a cashier's check, made out to Teri, in the amount of twenty-five thousand dollars. For a second she wondered if he left the check just in case Teri didn't have the energy, desire or wherewithal to find the money buried in the ground, then she flipped the check over and found the post-it note attached to the back. The handwriting was unmistakably Hank's and it contained five words, "To take care of Duke." Duke was Hank's rottweiler. His constant companion who had settled by Hank's side, after his master took his own life, and howled. When the medical examiner took Hank's body away both Teri and animal control tried to do the same with the heartbroken dog. Duke refused to leave the spot and continued to wail for two straight days. Then the dog simply stopped howling, rolled over and joined Hank in the hereafter. Teri peeled off the note, folded the check and stuck both in the back pocket of her jeans. "More for me," she said as she closed and locked the safe.

Hank had left her everything, which more than upset what was left of the Betty Lou Goochly clan. Everything included the house, the barn and the 45 acres of real estate just 25 minutes from downtown Raleigh. Teri got it all and wanted none of it. She contacted a realtor who told her he could probably get her well north of four million for it. She hid her excitement, told him "the thought of keeping the property hurt too much," and ordered him to bring her any offer that started with a four and was followed by six zeroes. He did.

Teri also found, wrapped inside many of the rolls of cash, more handwritten notes from Hank. Each one told a different story. Short, sometimes emotional, chapters of a life that included tales about his childhood, meeting and falling in love with Betty Lou, and of Teri as a little girl. But none of the stories were about Teri's birth mother, Daisy. One of the missives was about Hank, as a boy, believing then wanting to keep believing, that he was a descendent of the legendary Wild Bill Hickock. That one made her laugh out loud. Another one elicited the exact opposite reaction. It told the story of why Hank decided to take his own life.

"I'm sorry you felt like you had to kill that woman," Teri read the words written in Hank's hand, slightly shakier than the others. *"But I'm glad you murdered that no good son of a bitch Tanner Goochly. I know you did bad things but I refuse to believe you're a bad person. I can't and won't let you go to prison for the rest of your life or, God forbid, let the state of North Carolina put you to death."* The note ended with a poorly drawn heart and the word "Dad". The note made Teri cry and miss Hank all over again.

♪♫♪

Old Friends and Aliases

Another thing Teri read in the months after Hank had taken responsibility for the two murders Teri had committed was an article in the Raleigh paper with details about the detective that had investigated the case. It mentioned he was leaving North Carolina for a similar job with the Colorado Springs Police Department. It included a picture of her "old friend" Marc Allen. She looked up the central Colorado city on the internet and learned many "experts" considered it to be "one of America's most livable places." She thought *why not* so she cut and colored her hair, withdrew a couple hundred thousand dollars in cash from her burgeoning bank account, and followed the detective west.

Before leaving she also enlisted the services of one of Tanner Goochly's buddies to create a few new identities for her. She would receive a driver's license, passport and social security number and all it would cost her was a few hundred bucks and about 30 minutes of sex. While the forger was grunting and groaning Teri was thinking about her new name. Hank had fantasized about being related to Wild Bill but Teri felt more of a kinship with the outlaws of the wild west. She had read up on William Bonnie, John Henry "Doc" Holliday, Hoodoo Brown, Belle Starr and John Wesley Hardin. But in the end, she settled on Longabaugh, as in Henry Alonzo Longabaugh, the notorious "Sundance Kid," as her new nom de guerre. A little extracurricular activity and a couple more bills helped her secure two additional driver's licenses. She figured a little insurance couldn't be a bad thing and she already had the forger right where she wanted him. She chose the last name Parker for one, after the legendary Bonnie Elizabeth Parker of Bonnie and Clyde fame and Haroney for the other because she thought the nickname "Big Nose Kate" was funny.

So, with her new identities and a wad of cash in her purse, she bought a new car for the trip. She thought she wanted a Porsche because she read somewhere that Adam Levine looked super cool driving one. Maroon 5 was her favorite band and Levine was its lead singer. But then she drove one of the SUVs for herself and changed her mind. Instead she purchased a Baltic blue Range Rover, although she still loved Levine, and drove it across the country. Before leaving her past behind she decided to sell most, but not all, of Hank's firearms. She peddled everything but his, now her, Winchester model 94 Legacy 24" rifle because she thought it had a classic look, the Colt Peacemaker handgun because she read that both Butch Cassidy and Wyatt Earp carried one, the snub nosed .38 for fun, and a .22 with a silencer because why not. The sale of the rest put close to an additional ten grand in her pocket.

The one story about which she never learned, in Hank's handwritten notes, the newspapers, or anywhere else, was the backstory about her birth mother Daisy Phillips. It was a tragic tale that started as a love story, turned joyless thanks to a cowardly father-to-be, included a heart wrenching decision to give a baby girl up for adoption, and ended with three strategically placed bullets in a body that was left near a dumpster behind a Planned Parenthood in Raleigh.

♪♫♪

Rampart Haynes

One day, when Rampart Haynes was 8 years old, he walked home from Sunday School. The steps that filled the slightly less than a mile journey were fueled by rage, confusion and thoughts of revenge. His eyes were brimming with tears. When he walked through the sliding glass door to his house both his parents were in the kitchen. His mom immediately noticed the tears running down her little boy's cheeks. His father focused on the blood and mucus coming from Rampart's nose. Rampart looked up at both of them then looked away. He wiped his nose on an already saturated sleeve. He turned back to face his parents. Blood, sweat and snot coalesced into a mess of a mask that spread from cheekbone to cheekbone.

"What in the world!?" his dad said.

"My Baby!" his mother cried.

They both approached the boy who stopped them in their tracks with an outstretched arm.

"Why did you name me Rampart!?" he blubbered accusingly, "Why?!" he demanded. "I hate it!" He spat out the last three words and rushed past them, through the kitchen and up the stairs to his bedroom. Elizabeth and Lucas Haynes looked at each other as they heard a door above them slam shut. She took a step toward the stairs but stopped when her husband touched her arm.

"Let's give him a minute," he cautioned.

"Lucas, he's crying and bleeding!"

"I noticed, Beth," he said releasing her arm, "but please, let's just give him a minute." She couldn't. Standing at her son's bedroom door, Beth Haynes took a deep breath and knocked.

"Rampart? What happened honey?"

"Don't call me that!" the boy reacted from the other side. "I told you I hate it!"

"I know you did," she answered, fighting back more tears, "but honey."

"Just go away," Rampart said before she could get out another word. "Leave me alone." She placed her palm on her son's door and rested her forehead against the wood.

"I hate to say it," her husband said from the hallway, "but I told you to give him a minute." She turned away from the door and they both went back down the stairs.

Thirty minutes later they heard the boy's bedroom door open followed by the sound of running water in the upstairs bathroom. Lucas looked at his wife over the top of the Sunday sports page. She was staring out the window chewing on a fingernail.

"What do you think happened?" she asked without looking at him.

"I'll go find out," he said getting up from the table. By the time he got up the stairs the boy was out of the bathroom and back in his bedroom. The door was closed. His dad thought for a minute about what to say and then tapped on the wood with the knuckle of the index finger of his right hand.

"Go away *MOM*!" the boy called out. Lucas thought he sounded a little less upset than before.

"It's Dad this time," he clarified, "can I come in?"

"It's a free country," the boy offered. Lucas wondered where his eight-year-old had heard that before opening the door and entering the room. He saw his son still dressed, except for shoes, in his Sunday School best on top of the made bed. His head was propped up by a pillow. He was reading a book. Lucas noticed it was *Charlie and the Chocolate Factory* by Roald Dahl. It was one of Lucas Haynes's favorites as a kid and he recalled fondly the story of Charlie Bucket and his incredible adventure. Lucas and Beth had rented the movie, starring Gene Wilder, for Rampart and a few of his friends during a sleepover. Rampart was surprised to learn the story was based on a book and thrilled when he had received it as a birthday gift. Lucas was sure this was at least the fourth time the boy had cracked it open.

“Hey kiddo,” he said sitting at the edge of the bed. Rampart responded by putting the book, pages down, on his lap. He looked at his dad. Lucas’s heart ached. The boy’s eyes were still red from crying. His nose was also red and slightly swollen. *Not broken though*, thought Lucas as he noticed the boy had missed a bit of dried blood and snot on his chin when he had attempted to clean up.

“You up for telling me what happened?”

“Not much to tell,” the boy answered, “you named me something stupid and I got punched in the nose because of it.”

“Rampart,” Lucas started.

“Don’t. Call. Me. That.”

“It’s your name.”

“Why?” the child almost started crying again but he looked past his father and fought back the tears. “What kind of a name is that and why did you give it to me?” he said softly.

“Well,” his father smiled as he remembered the story, “I’ll tell you.” He waited a second as Rampart sat up a little straighter. “Your mother wanted to name you Harold after your Grandpa.”

"Oh Geez," the boy made a face, "that's even worse!" His response made Lucas chuckle.

"Yeah I wasn't too keen on it either."

"Thanks," the boy said. Lucas patted his stockinged foot and continued.

"So, your mom and I were in the hospital and you were starting to act more and more eager to make your entrance. It was, as you well know, January 24th and the 49ers were about to play the Cincinnati Bengals in the Super Bowl."

"Go Niners!" Rampart said with a smile.

"Go Niners," his dad echoed, then kept going, "you were our first…"

"And only," the boy interrupted.

"And only," Lucas nodded, "and we had no idea how long it was going to take you to come into the world. Since it was the first time the Niners were in the Super Bowl, I asked your mom and the nurse if we could turn on the TV in the room and watch the game."

"Did they say yes?" the boy said, looking expectantly at his dad.

“The nurse wasn’t so sure but your mom said, ‘why not?’” He noticed the boy nod approvingly. “Anyway, the start of the game was still a couple of hours away when your mom started feeling the labor pains coming more frequently. The activity in the room started picking up with more and more folks coming and going but the TV stayed on. Eventually Diana Ross was introduced to sing the National Anthem.”

“Who?” Rampart asked.

“It’s not important,” his dad said.

“O.K.”

“But what comes next is,” his dad said reassuringly.

“O.K.”

“You know how the song goes, right?” he asked his son, though he already knew the answer.

“Of course, silly,” the boy smiled and started to sing. “Oh Oh can you see.”

“Just one ‘Oh’,” Lucas said, stopping him.

“What?”

“Oh say can you see. Not Oh Oh,” his dad corrected.

"Really?" Lucas thought the boy looked sincerely puzzled.

"Really," he assured him.

"Are you sure?"

"Positive."

"Oh say can you see," the boy started singing again.

"Good job buddy," his dad said proudly, "I'd love to hear you sing the whole song but let me finish the story. O.K?"

"Sure," Rampart said.

"Exactly 57 seconds into her performance the top of your little head popped out!" That made the boy giggle. "Do you know what word Diana Ross was singing *exactly* 57 seconds into the song?" he asked. The boy shook his head. "Well it sure as heck wasn't Harold," Lucas said lovingly pinching his son's cheek. Then he watched as the boy was clearly singing the song in his head.

"Or the *RAMPARTS*!" he exclaimed.

"Correct!" his dad congratulated the boy. "But it's O'er the Ramparts. Like *over* but without the v." The boy looked at him quizzically. "Never mind," Lucas said.

"*That's* how I got my name?" Rampart asked with a smile.

"It sure is."

"Gee," the boy thought for a second, "I guess that's kinda cool."

"We thought so too," his dad said and then added, "good timing on your part, by the way, because your name could have been 'bursting' or 'rockets' or 'perilous'."

"Or *Harold*," the boy wrinkled his nose.

"Or Harold," his dad repeated.

"I want to learn how to fight, Dad," Rampart changed the subject. "I need to." Lucas Haynes was flabbergasted at the conversation's abrupt shift.

"Why don't you tell me what happened?" he said to his son.

Just outside the room Beth Haynes was listening. She loved hearing her husband tell her son the story of how they came by his name. She hated hearing the boy talk about a bully taunting him because of that name. A taunting on which Rampart pushed back resulting in a bloody nose. But her feelings were mixed when she heard the eight-year-old tell Lucas he wanted to learn to defend himself. In the room, Lucas listened intently to the entire story. He felt sorry for the boy but also proud because as he recounted the events from earlier that morning Rampart successfully fought back the tears that had flowed so easily then.

"The Roman philosopher Marcus Aurelius once said, 'the best revenge is to be unlike him who performed the injury,'" he said to his son.

In the hallway Beth whispered, "Never take revenge. Leave that to the righteous anger of God." She crossed herself after reciting the line from Romans 12:19.

The boy looked at his dad and said, "If you lose a big fight, it will worry you your whole life. It will plague you until you get your revenge." His father looked at him with a mixture of surprise and admiration. In the hall his mother's mouth dropped open.

"Who said that?" Lucas asked.

"Muhammed Ali," the boy answered. "I want to learn to box. Can I? Please?"

Lucas didn't know. He did know that Colorado Springs was the home of the USOC and USA Boxing but he had no idea if they, or any other organization, offered boxing lessons to children Rampart's age. His gut reaction was that eight was too young to start. Buying time before giving an answer one way or the other, Lucas told his son the words his father told him when he was about the boy's age.

"You can be anything you want when you grow up," Beth had entered the room and she sat on the bed next to her husband as he said it. "Except," Lucas continued after grabbing his wife's hand, "a hockey goalie or a boxer." Beth chuckled. Rampart did not.

"Why?"

"Well, a goalie is judged by the number of shots that get past him…"

"Or her," Rampart interjected.

"Or her," Beth agreed.

"And nobody is perfect," his dad, her husband, continued. "Even the best goalies get beat and even the greatest boxers of all time, like Muhammed Ali, get punched in the nose."

"Been there, done that," the boy said as he touched his tender schnoz. "I think I'd like to give them both a try," he added.

"Why am I not surprised?" his dad said looking at Beth.

♪♫♪

Rampart Picks a Fight

Growing up Rampart did try both along with basketball, baseball and golf. Soon after the Sunday School punch, and at the suggestion of his mom, he started telling all his friends to call him "Ramp." It stuck. He was smart, athletic, good looking and funny. He couldn't remember anyone ever giving him a hard time about his name again. He joined the Falcon Youth Hockey League and played as a "Mite" with kids his age before moving up to the "Squirts." He even suited up as a goalie but that was short-lived. He realized his dad was right on the money about that position. The kids who scored the goals were always celebrated more than the one who stopped them. Plus, the gear was so darned heavy and he sweated like a stuck pig inside it.

Boxing was different, like deep down he knew it would be. There was still heavy gear, 16-ounce gloves on his hands and headgear that covered his forehead and cheeks. He still worked up a drenching sweat but he found it liberating, cleansing really. And according to his coach, a grizzled Army vet and former Junior Team USA boxing coach, he was good at it. The gym was a little seedy and at first that bothered the boy.

"It's kinda scary," he said to his dad the first time they had a look around, "and it's stinky." He held his nose. It looked like nothing more than a storage garage with a concrete floor, one regulation size ring, a couple of speed bags and a rubber torso with a head to punch.

“My guess is this is the kinda place in which every great boxer got his start,” his dad tried to reassure the boy. “But if you want to leave, we can leave.” Lucas still wasn’t sure how he felt about his only son getting punched on purpose. Rampart gave the gym another glance.

“Nah, I’m good,” he said. “let’s go find the coach.”

Turned out that at his age it was more drills, and conditioning, and working on good defensive posture than actual boxing but he did get in the ring. There was training during which some of the older, better kids would come and spar with the younger ones. The big kids weren’t allowed to hit the little ones but the little ones were encouraged to try as hard as they could to get in a punch. Eventually there were competitions that consisted of three one-minute rounds that gave Ramp a chance to throw, as well as take, some blows. Most of the kids he fought against, especially in the beginning, came out charging and flailing at the sound of the bell. Ramp was more tactical. Sure, he caught an occasional punch to the gut or bop on the nose but he found those cleansing and liberating too. His Mom took him to every practice; his dad came to all the fights. Mom to none. She did, however, always want to know how he did, win lose or draw, when he got home. Even when it was obvious because of a slightly swollen nose or the ribbon, medal and trophy he held in his hands. Rampart lost the first fight he had but very few after that. There were always more trophies than bruises.

At home they set up equipment in the extra room. A kid's punching bag with an adjustable stand so he could work on his hand eye coordination and a treadmill on which to run. His dad drove home the point that the coach, Sarge, had made in the gym that stamina and quickness were key to avoiding blows and winning bouts. They even set up a trophy case to display his awards. Ramp pinned posters to the wall of his pugilistic heroes: Muhammed Ali, Sugar Ray Leonard, Oscar De La Hoya and Rocky Balboa. Under the Ali poster he added the revenge quote, written with a black Sharpie in his own hand. He was nine.

Then she came to live with them.

Hannah Hunt

Hannah Hunt was what her grandparent's generation would call a tomboy. She was 100 percent girl but she preferred digging in the dirt to dressing up, reading *Where the Wild Things Are* to *Madeline*, and her favorite doll was a Wonder Woman Barbie complete with a red, white and blue cape and a golden rope that Hannah got on her fourth birthday. When she was old enough to consider such things, she told her mom and dad, one night at the dinner table, that when she grew up she wanted to either be a fighter pilot or a pitcher for the Colorado Rockies. Both aspirations earned two thumbs up from her parents.

She went to The Colorado Springs School. Her mom, Hayley, was a teacher there. Her dad, Hamilton "Ham" Hunt was a full bird Colonel, on the way to becoming a Brigadier General or more, in the United States Air Force. That's why they lived in Colorado Springs. Her dad worked at the North American Aerospace Defense Command, 2,000 feet deep and a mile into the granite insides of Cheyenne Mountain which loomed large over their neighborhood. NORAD was constructed during the Cold War and was one of the world's most famous military installations. It was originally built to monitor North American airspace for missile launches and Soviet military aircraft.

In 1983 MGM released the movie *War Games* directed by John Badham and starring a 21-year-old Matthew Broderick as David Lightman. In the film Lightman comes across a computer with a program called Thermonuclear War while playing video games. He assumes it's another game and begins to play inadvertently toppling the dominoes that could lead to World War III. Much of the movie takes place deep in the bowels of Cheyenne Mountain. Just for laughs, the Hunt family kept a copy of the movie in a closet somewhere.

NORAD's mission evolved when the Cold War thawed and, almost ten years before Hannah was born, her father became part of a team put in place to combat illegal drug traffic coming into the country by tracking small aircraft operating within the U. S. and Canada. After she was born the operation, along with almost everything else that operated within the mountain, was consolidated and relocated to nearby Peterson Air Force base.

Hannah liked playing with girls but she thought the games boys played were more fun. She had plenty of friends and one "best" friend. His name was Rampart Haynes and she had known him for as long as she could remember. Their parents were best friends too. Her mom's favorite picture was one Ham had taken of the two kids. Hannah was about five and a mess. Her jeans and tee shirt were filthy, face mostly covered with dirt and mud. Her blonde hair, miraculously unscathed, fell just past her ears. Rampart was just as dirty, standing proudly in his number 16 Joe Montana jersey with a knowing smirk on his face and his right arm around the girl's shoulders. Hannah's right hand held his tight. They could have been brother and sister.

One night her mom and dad and Rampart's parents were supposed to go out. Dinner and a movie was the plan. They did that kind of thing a couple of times a month. Normally the couples would get one babysitter and alternate at which house the kids would hang out. But on that night Rampart already had a sleepover planned at his friend Lee's house. They were Little League teammates and had begun boxing together too. As a result, Hannah would have her house and her babysitter all to herself. A couple of hours before her mom and dad were supposed to leave the phone rang. It was Rampart's dad saying Beth Haynes felt like she was coming down with something and she didn't want Hannah's mom to catch it. Her or the children she taught at school. They were going to have to take a rain check. The little girl overheard her parents talking after that. It sounded to her like they were deciding whether or not to still go out. In the end they decided the reservation had been made and the new Clint Eastwood movie was one they wanted to see. Plus, the babysitter, who Hannah loved, had already been arranged. They kept their plans.

Later that night Hannah was in her bed, but not asleep. A warm bath had gotten the day's dirt off and her teeth were brushed. She lay reading one of her dad's old Archie comic books. This one was titled "Reggie and Me." She didn't care much for Reggie Mantle but she loved Archie Andrews and thought Jughead Jones was a riot. As she turned a page, she heard a car pull up in front of the house. Briefly, she wondered why her mom and dad hadn't pulled into the garage. Seconds later things made even less sense when she heard the doorbell ring.

She'd never seen the three people who came into her home that night. One woman and two men. One of the men wore a blue uniform like her dad's, the other she recognized as a policeman. The woman didn't wear any kind of uniform but she was the one that told Hannah her parents wouldn't be coming home ever again. The babysitter had retreated to the living room where she sat on a couch and cried. The woman asked Hannah if she had any brothers or sisters. She thought about Rampart but shook her head no. Then the lady wanted to know about her grandparents or aunts or uncles. Hannah just stared at her. The man in blue asked her if she had seen her dad talking to any strangers recently and the policeman wondered if either her mommy or daddy had started acting differently. She didn't really understand either question or the way they asked them made her not like them very much. She just shook her head and started crying too.

When they were finished talking the man in blue and the woman took her to the Air Force base where her dad worked. Nobody told her why she was there. She spent the night on a cot in the room where she had gone once or twice for day care. People kept checking on her and she asked each one of them when she could go home. Nobody gave her an answer. She cried a lot, slept a little and wondered what was going to happen to her next.

When she was older she learned the Air Force kept her overnight because they wanted to make sure the death of her father wasn't connected to the work he was doing on behalf of the United States government. It didn't take them long to place the blame squarely on a drunk driver who blew through a red light in his souped-up Ford F150 truck and smashed into the Hunt's Mini Cooper as they were heading home from *Unforgiven*. The custom-made commercial bull bar on the front helped serve as a battering ram. Ham and Hayley never had a chance. The next morning a tearful Beth Haynes picked Hannah up and told her she'd be living at their house from now on.

Rampart knew the girl very well. They played together at his house, her house, the park. His mom and dad hung out with her mom and dad all the time. He knew her dad was a soldier and her mom was a teacher. He thought her dad was a little scary. They shared toys, books, a babysitter and a first kiss. He told himself it didn't really count because he was seven and she had just turned six. They were playing on the slide at the park and he came down right after her. It just happened and it wasn't much. Just a peck, one second of her lips on his, but he never forgot it. Then one day she was in the foyer looking sad. She had one hand on the handle of a suitcase and the other grasped tightly around a Wonder Woman doll. His mom stood behind her with the saddest smile he had ever seen on her face.

The night before his dad had picked him up from his pal Lee's house and said there was an emergency. Ramp could tell his dad had been crying and he worried that something had happened to his mom. Lucas assured his son that wasn't the case. Beth was waiting for them both at the house. The emergency turned out to be the news that Hannah's parents were dead. Killed in a car crash by a drunk driver. They sat him down and told him about the news like he was an adult. They told him they felt sad, confused and more than a little guilty because they were supposed to be with them.

"If we had just kept the date," his mom said between sobs, "maybe it wouldn't have happened."

"Don't, Beth," his dad said. Rampart watched him put his arm around his mom.

"But maybe we would have stayed a minute longer at the restaurant haggling over who would pay the check or sat in our seats in the theatre to discuss what we liked about the movie." She couldn't help herself.

"Don't, mom," this time it was Rampart. Then his dad said they had decided that it would be best if Hannah came to live with them.

"We hope that's okay, son," his dad said. Rampart was old enough to realize he wasn't asking for the boy's permission. But even if he had, the answer would have been "yes." "Hannah doesn't have anywhere else to go, anyone else to go with," his dad added, even though he didn't have to. Rampart nodded.

Then his mom added that if something had happened to them, instead of Ham and Hayley, they would have wanted him to go and live at Hannah's house. He nodded again but this time wondered why his mom wouldn't want him to live with Aunt Sarah, Uncle Jack, or his grandparents. He didn't ask. His stomach ached and he was scared. He didn't want to live with anybody else and thought what would happen to him now if something did happen to them? A tear escaped and rolled down his cheek. He wiped it away as his mom asked what was wrong. He told her. They all hugged and his parents told him there was nothing to worry about. They promised nothing was going to happen. For the first time in his life he didn't believe them. He figured Hannah's parents told her that exact thing and *something* had happened to them. The worst something.

Hannah was part of his family now. He grabbed her suitcase and they went upstairs to what used to be the spare room. His mom said they'd move the punching bag to the garage and put the boxing ribbons, medals and trophies somewhere else but Hannah smiled and said it was okay to leave them. She told Rampart she thought they were cool. He smiled at her and started to take down the posters but Hannah stopped him.

"Leave those too," she said with her hand on his arm. "Especially Rocky. I love that movie." She pointed at the other three boxers. "You can tell me who these other guys are later." He promised her that he would.

♪♫♪

Reg Runs Again

Reg Byrd couldn't get out of North Carolina fast enough. He was sure he was in love with Daisy Phillips until she told him she was going to have his baby. The thought of being a husband was daunting enough but a father too? No way, Byrd told himself over and over again as he rode his motorcycle all the way back to Colorado. He was headed there because he figured he had no place else to go. He arrived back in Pueblo early one evening. He stopped at a Texaco station and filled the bike up with gas then wandered over to the pay phone and called the only number he had for his brother Stan.

He listened to the phone ring and ring and finally hung up. He got back on his wheels and headed straight for the familiar surroundings of the Silent Commandos' bar. It looked the same, smelled the same, and housed many of the same characters. Byrd smiled when he saw a person who looked to be Lamaj at the bar. He was older, his hair grayer, but Byrd had little doubt it was him.

"Lamaj?" Reg said as he approached. The man swiveled in his chair and greeted Byrd with a smile. One of his two front teeth was missing.

"Well lookie what the cat dragged in," he said, getting up and giving Byrd a hug. "Come sit. You can buy me a drink."

"I can and I will," Byrd answered slapping Lamaj on the back. They both sat. Reg ordered a shot of Wild Turkey and a bottle of beer. Lamaj held up two fingers indicating he'd have the same. The drinks came and Reg raised his shot glass.
"To the good old days," he tossed the whiskey back.

"Brother, I'll drink to that," Lamaj answered and drained his glass. Reg looked around the room.

"Everything okay, buddy?" He asked.

"Everything is a big word, my man," was his reply.

"Where is everybody?"

"Mostly gone," Lamaj replied, "joined other riders, drifted off, made new friends."

"The Wizard?" Reg wondered. He noticed Lamaj shake his head slowly. "Gone?" Reg asked.

"For good," his friend answered and took a sip of beer.

"When? How?"

"While ago now. Got in a fight and forgot to watch his back. Somebody blindsided him with a business end of a Louisville Slugger."

"Jesus," Reg said.

“Wasn’t around that night,” Lamaj said before drinking another sip of beer. “Or maybe he was,” he added.

“What do you mean by that?”

“Wiz was sick, man. Cancer. Probably didn’t have much longer to live anyway.”

“My God,” Reg gasped.

“There you go again,” Lamaj scolded, “God weren’t there either. Wiz didn’t tell nobody but CT said they found his body riddled with the cancer when they cut him open.”

“I bet the boss was sick about it,” Reg lamented.

“Not as sick as The Wizard,” Lamaj said as he crossed himself, “God rest his soul.”

“Amen to that.” Reg raised his bottle. “Where *is* CT?” he asked.

“He’s around but not around here much anymore. He’s a grandpa now. Daughter had a baby girl and brought it with her to Pueblo to live.”

“You’re kidding?”

“Wish I was,” Lamaj drank, "I miss the way it was.”

“Me too, my friend. Me too.” They both polished off their beers.

“You in trouble?

“Seems I’m always finding myself in some kind of trouble,” Reg answered honestly.

“I’m supposed to talk to him later tonight,” Lamaj said. Reg knew he meant Mascaro. “There’s still a little bit of business needing to get done around here. I’ll tell him you’re back in town.”

“Please do,” Reg said, “I got a room at the Round ‘em Up Motel. Number 116.”

“Know it well,” Lamaj said with a smile. “Know it well.”

The next morning a knock on the door woke Reg from a fitful sleep. He rolled out of the bed and took a peek out the window from behind the curtains. CT Mascaro stood at the door, hands in the pockets of his faded blue jeans.

“Open up, Tweety,” he called. “I know you’re in there, Lamaj told me. Plus, I see that old piece of crap motorcycle in the parking lot.” Reg obliged and Mascaro walked into the motel room. “What are you doing back here, Reg?” Mascaro asked before Byrd could close the door.

“Didn’t know where else to go.”

"How about your home, with the girl you told me was crazy about you?"

"Things changed," was all Reg said in response.

"As they often do," Mascaro said, "but if I remember correctly you weren't ever very good with change, were you?"

"Guess not," Reg admitted.

"So, what now?" his old boss asked.

"No idea. I guess I was hoping things could just pick up where they left off." Mascaro just stared at him for a good ten seconds.

"You're kidding, right?" he finally said.

"I wasn't," Reg said sadly.

"That train left the station a while ago, son," Mascaro said with his gaze still on Reg. "There is no more 'where they left off.' There's only where we are now. And where we are now is nowhere near where we left off." They both stood in silence until Mascaro broke it. "Look, here's 500 bucks and another new ID," he said pulling out a roll of bills and a plastic card from his pocket. He also dangled a set of keys. "And these are the keys to the old Commandos van. Take it all and get going."

"CT, you already done so much for me," Reg started to protest, "I couldn't take any more from you or the Commandos."

"You can and you will." It sounded like an order to Reg. "But this is it, Tweety. Nothing personal but I don't want to see your mug again."

"Understood," Reg said. "Thank you."

"Where is the key to the bike?" he asked and Byrd walked over to the bedside and grabbed it. He turned and tossed the key to the biker boss. In turn CT dropped the cash, the card and the van keys on the bed. "Godspeed, Reg."

"Thanks boss. Oh," he remembered The Wizard. "So sorry to hear about the Wizard," he said to Mascaro.

"Me too son, me too. That sucked." Mascaro turned and headed for the door. Before he got there, he turned back to Reg. "Harry," he said.

"Beg your pardon?" Reg said back.

"Harry. The Wizard's real name was Harry." Mascaro was out the door before Reg could tell him he knew. Seconds later Reg heard what used to be his motorcycle start up and peel away. He went back to the window. Parked in the spot next to where his bike was sat an old Dodge van. It was orange with a white stripe running along its middle. He closed the curtain and turned back to the items on the bed. He picked up the ID. It was a Colorado driver's license made out to someone named Larry Holm. The picture didn't look anything like Reg. That made him laugh.

He decided he had spent his last minute in Pueblo so he grabbed his stuff, threw it in the van and hit the road. The vehicle may have looked like an old bucket of bolts but it ran great and drove just fine. It got him to Colorado Springs in good time. When he arrived, he took a spin around town and couldn't help but be surprised by all the changes. The Chief Theatre was gone, replaced by a parking lot. The scene made him think of the Joni Mitchell song "Big Yellow Taxi." He wolfed down a couple of tacos at El Taco Rey and then, out of some form of morbid curiosity, he headed to the neighborhood where, years ago, he had shot and killed Officer Richard Steven Churchfield. That neighborhood had changed too, but not all that much. The trees were a little taller and the houses were a little older. Reg thought they looked smaller too. He pulled away and decided to call Stan again. He found a phone booth and parked. There was some change in the console of the van so he grabbed a few coins and got out. He pushed a dime in the pay phone slot and dialed. After three rings a voice Reg didn't recognize answered.

"Stan?" Reg asked anyway.

"No Stan here," the voice dismissed him.

"I'm looking for Stanley Byrd," Reg said before the voice could hang up, "he's my brother."

"Don't know who that is, sorry."

"How long have you lived at this number?" Reg asked.

"Don't see how that can be any of your business," the man sounded to Reg like he was about to hang up again.

"Look, I don't mean to be nosy," he said quickly, "I'm just looking for my older brother. He used to live at this number."

"Like I already said I don't know him. In fact, I'd be hard pressed to think of anyone at all I know named Stan or Stanley."

"How long have you lived there?" Reg asked again hoping this time the man would answer. He did.

"I don't know, handful of years I guess."

"Thanks. I appreciate that," Reg said.

"Sorry I'm not your brother," the voice said.

"Don't be," Reg said and hung up. No Chief Theatre. No Ginger Hogenauer. No big brother Stan. And no way he was calling his mom and dad. He climbed back in the van. "I guess

I might as well be Larry Holm now," he said as he fired up the engine and drove away.

He had nowhere to go and what was left of his life to get there he thought as he absentmindedly drove through town. Up one street, down another. The tacos he had recently devoured were making quick work through his system which necessitated a stop at the nearest men's room. He found one at the Salvation Army and he used it. Back in the car, he turned right on Cimarron and then left on Weber. At the next stop sign he noticed the building that housed the Colorado Springs Police Department. "Might as well hide in plain sight", he said to himself as he went through the intersection, turned around in the middle of the street and parked in a space right across from the red brick building. Reg killed the engine, closed his eyes, and dozed off.

♪♫♪

New Friends

Detective Marc Allen bought a puppy. He figured if he was going to start a new life, with a new job, in a new city he might as well go all in. He was a big dog guy, remembered having a German Shepherd, an Olde English Sheepdog, and a mutt that had to have Great Dane somewhere in its lineage, as a kid. He also wanted something that didn't shed much and had researched the fact that breeding with poodles was all the rage. He didn't want a Labradoodle because it was too common, instead he considered Newfiedoodles, St. Berdoodles, and Bernerdoodles. But he was most intrigued by a mix of a Standard Poodle male and a Great Pyrenees female called a Pyredoodle. He found a breeder near Nashville, Tennessee, knew that was along the route from Raleigh to Colorado on Interstate 40, so he picked up the puppy on the way.

It was a female and she was adorable. He purchased a soft-sided crate, some kibble, puppy treats, a chew toy and a couple of bowls for water and food and made room for it all in the backseat area of his Chevy Tahoe. He met the breeder on her farm on the outskirts of Tennessee's capital city and saw the puppy's Poodle father and Great Pyrenees mother. There were other Pyredoodle puppies running around, some older than his, and he couldn't help but notice the faces had various stages of what looked to him like moustaches and beards. He decided right then and there he was going to name his new companion Lettie Lutz after the Bearded Lady character in a movie he saw about P.T. Barnum's Greatest Show on Earth.

He told the breeder he was going to call the dog Lettie and left the rest out. She told him she thought that was "cute".

As they started the journey Allen noticed the poor thing was scared to death. The shaking, whimpering and peeing in the crate gave that away. But by the time they hit Albuquerque and turned north on Interstate 25 for the last 378 miles of the trip, the two were fast friends. Slightly more than half of those miles that were left were in New Mexico driving through, or around, Bernalillo, Sante Fe, Las Vegas and Raton where they stopped so both could relieve themselves and eat. After heading out they crossed the Colorado state line and saw signs for Trinidad, Walsenburg and Pueblo before arriving in their new hometown. With the help of some of his new colleagues at the CSPD, Allen had arranged to rent a place in a building near downtown. It overlooked Monument Park and had a great view of the mountains to the west, especially Pikes Peak. Another plus was it was dog friendly. Allen and Lettie would quickly learn a lot of places in the Springs were. As he and the pup were moving in, a door across the hall opened and a woman walked out. The detective put her age at a little younger than his. She smiled and introduced herself as Tatiana Rice but said her friends called her Tracey. She added it would suit her just fine if he did too. Allen countered by telling her his name was Marc and that's what his friends called him.

"And who do we have here?" she asked, squatting down to greet the dog.

"This is Lettie," he said. "Her friends call her Killer." Tracey looked up at him. "Just kidding," he admitted. She turned her attention back to the dog.

"That wasn't very nice was it?" she asked Lettie scratching the puppy's chin. Allen watched as Lettie's tail worked overtime.

"I think she likes you."

"The feeling's mutual," Tracey rose and said looking at Allen, "if you ever need a dog sitter or walker I'm available any time." Allen appreciated the offer although he thought it was a bit aggressive for a first meeting.

"Any time?" he asked.

"Absolutely," she answered. "I work from home so I'm pretty much always around."

"Good to know, thanks," he said and he meant it.

"You remind your dad, okay girl?" She addressed the dog whose tail hadn't stopped wagging. Tracey reached down and gave the pup one last pet. "Bye Lettie," she said and walked away.

♪♫♪

Road Trip

They had made great time and arrived in Colorado Springs on a Saturday. Allen didn't have to report for work until Tuesday so he and Lettie used the time to get settled. He didn't own much and didn't want much more than that. He left a furnished apartment in Raleigh and was getting settled in another one in Colorado. The CSPD team had set up his internet. He found a note taped to the fridge with the WIFI network name and the password. He fired up his laptop, logged on and changed both. They had also installed a security system, on the police department's dime, that included a video doorbell. Allen knew he could see what was going on outside the door but also wondered if somebody, somewhere, could also be watching what was happening inside. He made a mental note to ask about that.

The apartment had a retro vibe that he kinda liked. When he walked in the front door he could see all the way through the main living area of the unit from the kitchen to a sliding glass door. It provided ample light as well as the magnificent view. The slider opened up to a deck which was large enough for a bar-b-que and a couple of chairs. The first room was the kitchen, a little on the small side, thought Allen, but how big a kitchen did he really need? One wall featured the fridge, a four-burner gas stove and an oven. There was an island which had room for a couple of stools, a sink and a dishwasher. Next was a dining area that included a table with four chairs which led to the main living space. A glance to the right revealed a white couch placed against a gray wall. It faced a gas fireplace surrounded on three sides by an ornate white wood mantel. In between the couch and the fireplace Allen saw a zebra skin rug on top of the gray carpet; above the fireplace was a 50-inch flat screen TV. There was a coffee table and a chair but the only light came from the recessed bulbs in the ceiling. The detective figured he needed a side table and a lamp or two.

The place had two bedrooms. The master was on the opposite side of the wall from the couch. Allen thought the queen bed looked brand new and so did the bedside table. Again, there was no lamp but there was plenty of room for Lettie's crate. The closet was more than big enough as was the master bathroom. He really liked the fact that there was another sliding glass door that opened up to an additional section of balcony.

A four-foot-high wall wrapped around the entire outside space and a barrier separated it into two distinct areas. He opened the door and let the puppy explore. He knew she wasn't big enough to see over the wall now but he guessed at some point she would be. There were two patio chairs on the bedroom balcony and two chaise lounges on the living room side. There wasn't a bar-b-que so he added that to his list along with the lamps and a more permanent crate for Lettie. After a cursory glance he decided the guest bedroom was fine and wondered if anyone would ever use it. A hallway with a pantry and more than enough space for the dog's food and water bowls led back to the kitchen and the entrance to the unit. A placard next to the door revealed the building's fire escape plan and a notification that there was a laundry room in the basement.

Somebody had included additional instructions with a black Sharpie saying each resident was responsible for his or her own supplies. He added detergent to the list.

"Looks like we need a pet store and a Bed Bath & Beyond," he said to the dog. She sneezed in response.

After the errands were complete, he decided to stop by the police station to get the lay of the land there too. He parked on the street, rolled down each window an inch or two, and killed the engine.

"Stay here and be a good girl," he said to the puppy. "I'll be right back."

He gave the Chevy Tahoe's interior a long look to make sure there wasn't anything the dog could destroy and got out. Inside he stopped at the information desk, a placard indicated the officer on duty's name was Selena Nobilo so he introduced himself. An elevator door to his left slid open revealing Deputy Chief Steven James Paulson. The young woman immediately stood at attention and saluted.

"Dennis, uh I mean, Deputy Chief Paulson, Sir," she stammered. Allen watched as the superior officer smiled and returned the salute.

"At ease officer," he said then he noticed to whom she had been speaking.

"Detective Allen. What, pray tell, are you doing here? I believe my notes said you weren't 10-8 until Tuesday." Allen knew "10-8" was universal police code for "on duty."

"Your notes are correct, deputy chief, but I got to town a little early and thought I'd do a little recon." The man nodded and Allen continued. "If you don't mind me asking, sir, is it SOP that the deputy chief works Saturdays?" Paulson shook his head.

"One WF dead," he started. Again, Allen understood the police shorthand, "WF" meant "white female." Paulson continued. "Another unconscious, but alive, taken to UC Health. Happened up North at the Yorkshire Square Apartments sometime this morning. The details are still coming in but an initial canvas found a neighbor who said the dead woman and her husband argued all the time. The guy added sometimes it got violent."

"Incidents that required CSPD involvement?" Allen wondered aloud.

"We're checking on that too," Paulson added. "Why don't you come upstairs with me?" It sounded to Allen like more than a request.

"Not sure I can, sir." The response made the deputy chief cock his head. Allen noticed right away. "I mean I have a puppy in the car," he said quickly. "I can take her home and come back."

"No need," Paulson said, "go get her. She's potty trained, isn't she?" he added.
"She's eleven weeks old, sir," he said sheepishly, "she does okay but," he left it there and shrugged.

"Go get her," Paulson repeated, "Sweetness would love to meet her."

Allen had no idea what that meant but he went and got Lettie out of the Tahoe. He made sure she peed on the grass before carrying her into the building. Paulson was still in the lobby having a conversation with Officer Nobilo. Allen thought the two looked more friendly than professional and wondered about her earlier slip of the tongue. The deputy chief turned and the uniformed officer looked up when Allen walked in.

"That just might be the cutest thing I've ever seen," she said from behind Paulson. "What kind of dog is it?"

"She's a Pyredoodle," Allen said stroking the puppy's head. "Her name is Lettie."

"Let's go upstairs, Lettie," Paulson said, "and bring your master with you."

In the elevator Allen noticed the buttons. Three floors above the one they were on and two below. Paulson noticed that he noticed.

"Underground parking on one for department heads and higher ups, Jail on two. We're the star, obviously, and four, five, and six are a mishmash. You'll learn." He punched the button for the sixth floor.

The door opened into a hallway that went both left and right. Paulson pointed left, "COP," he said, indicating the office in that direction belonged to the Chief of Police. They went right. "Try not to go there much," he said to Allen.

"Copy that," Allen replied, setting the puppy down and letting her walk. They passed another office, the lettering on the glass indicating it belonged to the Patrol Bureau Deputy Chief, Dana Kirkpatrick. Allen committed the name to memory. He had always had great respect for the officers on patrol and wanted to let the ones at the CSPD know. "I'd like to meet him sometime soon," he said to Paulson.

"Meet who?" he asked.

"Deputy Chief Kirkpatrick," Allen answered, "pay my respects."

"No problem but he's a she."

"Beg your pardon?"

"Deputy Chief Dana Kirkpatrick is a she, not a he," Paulson clarified.

“Geez. Bad assumption,” Allen said as he felt his face flush with embarrassment.
“You aren’t the first,” Paulson said, “and my guess is you won’t be the last. I’m here, on the end.”

They went through the glass doors into a reception area. There was a desk with a computer on top of it and two chairs. Beyond the desk large wooden doors led to Paulson’s office.

“I’d encourage you to not spend a great deal of time in *here* either,” the boss said as they entered the space. Lettie followed Paulson with Allen bringing up the rear.

“Copy that too, sir.” Two feet into the room Lettie stopped dead in her tracks. Allen danced to his right to avoid stepping on her. “What’s wrong girl? He asked the dog. He looked around the room to see if he could identify what spooked her. There was a small conference table, Allen counted six chairs, in the corner in front of what appeared to be a wet bar. There were shelves filled with books on one wall and a 60” x 48” oil painting depicting an aspen grove in the foreground and mountains behind on another. It was filled with golden strokes, fiery reds and beautiful blues. Allen admired it for a moment.

“You like it?” Paulson asked.

“Very much.”

“It’s a Robert Moore, he calls it Fruition. The guy’s done a lot of great work. Several of his paintings are on display at the art gallery at the Broadmoor. Amazing thing is, he’s colorblind.”

“Yeah, right,” Allen thought his boss was kidding.

“I’m serious. You can look it up.” Allen admired the work even more. “By the way, detective, in case you’re wondering that painting and everything else in here,” the deputy chief swept his arm around the room, “came at zero cost to the fine citizen taxpayers of Colorado Springs.” Allen admitted to himself that he had wondered about that.

“The thought had crossed my mind,” He said out loud.

“The wife is an interior designer,” Chief Paulson said, “this is all from her.”

“It’s very nice.”

“And it’s all mine until one of her clients wants something. Then I have to give it up and she brings in something else.” The deputy chief laughed.

Next Allen took in his boss’s desk. It was as impressive as the artwork and took up most of the space in front of a large picture window.

“Desk too?” he asked.

"Desk too." Next to the desk, sitting like a statue, was a magnificent Belgian Malinois. Allen stared at the big dog which was staring at the little one.

"This is Peyton," Paulson said walking over to the beast. "But I call her Sweetness."

"Of course you do," Allen said, acknowledging the reference to the great Chicago Bears running back Walter Peyton. "She's gorgeous," Allen admitted, "she won't eat Lettie, will she?"

"Depends," the deputy chief offered, "is Lettie a perp?"

"No sir," Allen answered, "just a pup."

"Sweetness, go say hello," Paulson commanded. The dog stood and slowly approached Allen and the puppy. "Don't worry she won't bite. Unless I tell her to."

Lettie, perhaps sensing less danger than her master, took two steps toward the police dog and started to sniff. Peyton sniffed back and then plopped down right next to the puppy. Lettie took the opportunity to jump on top of the bigger dog. Relieved, Allen continued to peruse his surroundings. He noticed some photographs and what looked like framed newspaper clippings. He took a closer look. One was Paulson shaking hands with the Chief of Police. *Day he got promoted*, thought Allen. Another showed Paulson dressed in golf clothing standing next to a guy Allen thought he recognized as a PGA TOUR pro. Both men in the photo had huge smiles on their faces.

"That's from the Pro-Am at The International a while back," Paulson had come up behind the detective. Allen played the game so he knew of the tournament. It was held just outside Denver on a course called Castle Pines. "I made an ace on the 16th hole," Paulson said proudly, "a hundred and seventy-two yards for the amateurs. I flushed a six iron. Ended up being the difference in our team winning the darn thing."

"I bet it did," Allen said with admiration. He knew a six iron from 172 in a pressure packed situation meant Paulson was better than the average player. Better than Allen for sure.

"Read the caption," his superior said. Allen did and some things immediately fell into place. The picture had the golf professional on the left, the deputy chief to his right but he noticed the caption read, "from left to right: PGA TOUR player Steven James Paulson and Colorado Springs Deputy Chief of Police Dennis Paulson (no relation) celebrate the chief's hole-in-one during The International Pro-Am tournament at Castle Pines Golf Club". Allen realized the paper had mixed up the two men. Dennis Paulson had won the 2000 Buick Classic on the PGA TOUR. Steven James Paulson was a cop. A cop that had been called "Dennis" ever since.

The deputy chief's phone rang. He walked back to the desk and answered it. Allen looked back at the dogs. Peyton, or Sweetness, was on her back, Lettie was chewing on her left ear. Then Allen looked up at Paulson and noticed his furrowed brow. The boss listened for a few more seconds and then hung up.

"Our situation at the Yorkshire Arms is now a double homicide." Allen said nothing as a reaction. "It appears the older woman was the younger one's mother. Both are now gone." Allen shook his head suddenly saddened by the depravity in the world. "You want in?" Paulson asked.

"Only if I'm up," Allen answered knowing how most police departments handled the doling out of cases.

"Let's find out," Paulson said picking up the phone again.

It turned out since Allen wasn't even supposed to be there he couldn't be "up" or next in line for a case. But it didn't matter because he wasn't needed. It didn't take long for two of the department's veteran detectives to find the man responsible for murdering the mother and daughter. The husband of one and son-in-law of the other was headed to Wyoming when he decided to stop at a roadside diner.

"Numbskull still had blood all over his shirt," one of the cops had told the squad room, "waitress noticed and called the sheriff who just happened to be her old man. He turned around and called everybody he knew, including us." A couple of hours later Tommy Scott was safely behind bars, in a cell, on the second floor of the CSPD building.

Allen didn't have anything to do with that particular arrest but there were plenty of times he was "up" in the days, weeks and months to come. It didn't take him long to find a lot of things to like about Colorado Springs. Plenty of outdoor activities; in fact he couldn't think of a better place in the country for an energetic puppy to grow into an equally energetic dog. There were good restaurants, fun watering holes, enough culture to satisfy Allen, the Olympic Movement and a couple of professional sports teams. But, as a cop, he found more than enough not to like as well. Gangs, homelessness, domestic violence and corruption were just some of the dark elements that kept him and his colleagues busy. In those ways it had plenty in common with almost every other decent-sized American city.

♪♫♪

Teri Took a Different Route

Teri took a different route to get from North Carolina to Colorado Springs. There was no puppy to pick up but she did admit to herself that she always wanted to see Graceland, the shrine to Elvis Presley in Memphis, Tennessee. A friend had also told her about a luxury getaway outside of Knoxville called Blackberry Farm so she decided to go there too. She packed up her stuff, clothes, guns, a few keepsakes and some cash, in three separate pieces of luggage. It all fit nicely in the Land Rover. She made the drive to the resort, on the edge of the Nantahala Forest in the Great Smokey Mountains, in about seven hours. Once there, she spent two days and nights relaxing, riding horses, eating gourmet meals and thinking about detective Marc Allen. Then she hit the road again and headed toward Memphis. It took about the same time to make that drive. She'd left early enough to roll up on 3734 Elvis Presley Boulevard a little after lunch time. There was a long line to get into the mansion. *Strike one* she thought. She found a parking lot and pulled in, but not all the way in because it was going to cost her $20 to do that. She grabbed her phone, called up the Graceland website and tapped the tab for tickets. She discovered it was another 40 bucks for General Admission and a whopping $150.00 if she wanted the "V.I.P. Tour".

"Strike Two," she said even though she knew she had more than enough money. "I actually just don't like his music all that much, so strike three." The driver in the car behind her honked his horn. She rolled down her window, stuck her arm out and flipped him the bird. Then she turned the car around.

When she was parallel with the honker he rolled his window down and showed her *his* pudgy, middle finger. "Don't be cruel," she yelled as she rolled up her window and left the lot. Teri realized she was ravenous because she hadn't eaten breakfast so she stopped at Marlowe's Ribs and Restaurant for a bite. After lunch she headed North on U.S. Highway 63 through the rest of Tennessee, a good stretch of Arkansas and into Missouri where she went west on Highway 60 to Springfield. She was pretty sure she thought she could hear the banjo from the movie *Deliverance.* At Springfield she stopped to use the restroom, grabbed a diet Dr. Pepper and a bag of "Spicy Hot" beef jerky, then it was North on U.S. 65 as it alternated between two and four lanes through the towns of Buffalo, Cross Timbers and Sedalia. She hooked up with Interstate 70 in the town of Marshall Junction and headed west.

It was getting late and the lights of Kansas City were visible on the horizon. She booked a room at the Hotel Raphael because it sounded interesting. She left the car with the valet and headed straight for the bar. The bartender talked her into their signature drink, the "Heart of America" cocktail. It was a concoction of Absolute Vodka, Blue Curacao, lemon juice, honey and an egg white. All shook up it was poured into a Fizzio glass and garnished with a red paper heart. He pushed the glass her way. Teri told him he was "all heart" and mentioned she was on a road trip across the country. He wished her safe travels and smiled as she took a first sip. She drank the cocktail down and ordered a second.

A slight hangover meant a later than ideal start the next day as Interstate 70 took her through the heartland of the country and into Colorado. It was flat and it was boring so she drove as fast as she dared. She stopped twice for fuel and food but decided not to stop for the night. Teri Hickox rolled into Colorado Springs at just after six on a clear, blue sky evening. She thought it was as pretty a sky as she had ever seen. She found a hotel downtown, left the car with another valet, grabbed the bag that was filled with cash and left the suitcases with her clothes and her guns for the valet. She went inside to pay for a room. She gave the woman at the check-in counter enough cash to pay for six nights. She didn't think it would take her longer than that to find a place of her own. She did, however, think it might take her longer than that to find Marc Allen. She was right about the first thing and couldn't have been more wrong about the second.

On the morning of the first full day Teri found a realtor, a guy named Scott Ericsson. She called him from her hotel room and told him how much she wanted to spend. They arranged to meet in front of the building after lunch. He told her he'd be driving a silver Porsche SUV.

"You like it?" she asked the realtor, referring to his car.

"It serves its purpose," he answered.

As she got in Scott's car she thought the real estate business in Colorado Springs must be pretty darn good. Then she remembered that if her search went well, she was about to plop down a good chunk of change for a new place and a percentage of that would go to Ericsson.

They headed south from the hotel on Nevada Avenue and made a right onto Lake Street which brought them into the fashionable Broadmoor neighborhood. The first house was on a tree-lined street but Teri thought it looked "tired". Once inside she noticed it had a ton of potential but it, like most of the homes in this part of town, was way too big for her. She mentioned that fact to Ericsson. Next, they climbed into the hills overlooking the city and Scott showed her two more houses that he thought might interest her. Neither did so they got back in the car.

"I have to admit those were beautiful homes and amazing views," she said as she buckled up.

"But," Scott said starting the engine.

"But they're huge!" she gave him the but, "and like I said, it's just lil' ol' me," she said in her best southern accent. "What in the world am I gonna do all by my lonesome up here?"

"Something tells me you'd make friends," he answered, "but I get what you're saying. Let's head back into town." Where they headed was a section of Colorado Springs Scott called the Old North End. "This is one of the Springs's most sought after addresses," he said, "there's usually not a ton of inventory."

Teri saw wide, clean streets named Madison, Fontenaro, Jefferson and Wood. The houses were a mix of Victorians and Bungalows with a few cottages sprinkled throughout. In Teri's mind most of them looked either big, old or both.

"This neighborhood is the Springs's most historic," Scott continued, "one of the oldest in the city as many of the original homes were built in the late 1800s and early 1900s." He couldn't help but notice Teri seemed less than impressed. "But looks can be deceiving since most have been restored and/or remodeled."

Teri agreed that the area must be in high demand because to Scott's point she only counted three for sale signs as they crisscrossed through the area. They stopped in front of one. The house was a brown bungalow and Teri told Scott she liked the way it looked. A concrete walkway bisected a decent-sized, unfenced yard. The path ended at a porch which protected the front door. The inside was small, especially compared to the homes they had just seen but Teri noticed it was shiny clean and it had been recently redone. The best proof of that was the kitchen. It wasn't huge by any stretch of the imagination but it was well appointed with brand new, stainless steel appliances, a farmhouse sink and an island which included a gas range. Leaving that space, Teri found the hallways narrow and the bedrooms tiny to the point of being claustrophobic.

“It’s 1,760 square feet,” Scott said. “Four bedrooms, one and three-quarter baths, it’s well within your stated budget and you can walk to the restaurants, bars and shopping downtown.” A quick look in the back found a small yard, a detached garage and messy neighbors on the north side.

“You’re getting warmer,” Teri told the realtor, “but I just don’t see myself living here either.”

“Understood,” he said. “Just for grins let’s go look at a couple more.”

The couple more, another bungalow and a massive Victorian, turned out to be busts as well and Scott Ericsson ended the day’s search by committing to bringing her more promising options tomorrow. He dropped her off at the hotel and they said their goodbyes. The entire afternoon made Teri want to shoot someone, or, at least, some *thing,* so she went upstairs, logged on to her laptop and found a better than decent looking gun range. She holstered her pistol, collected her carry permit which was another one of the documents her half hour of work in North Carolina enabled her to procure, and called down to the valet for her car.

The place was more impressive than the website showed. Teri walked into a huge showroom with all kinds of weapons, both new and used, lining walls, cases and counters. There was also a notable collection of ammo and accessories. In the middle of it all stood a large counter manned by a friendly looking woman. Teri approached.

"Help you?" the woman said. Teri noticed her nametag read Abigail.

"Hope so, Abigail," she said, "I'd like to do some shooting."

"You new here?" Abigail asked.

"Not quite sure what that has to do with anything," Teri answered, "and besides do you ask every person that comes in?"

"Pretty much," the woman said, "I've been here most every day since my boys opened this place. Now, be that as it may, even if that wasn't the case, I do believe I would have remembered you," she added a wink. Teri smiled.

"Brand new," she said, "although I have been around the block a time or two." She winked back. Abigail laughed a deep, cigarette smoke-affected laugh.

"Got a weapon or do you need to rent one?" Abigail was suddenly all business.

"Got one," Teri said pulling her Springfield Armory 3" sub compact out of its holster.

"Nice gun," Abigail admired, "but put it right back in that holster and keep it there until the RSO gives you the okay to take it out." Teri had been to enough gun ranges to know an RSO was a "Range Support Officer" though they were rarely ever officers of any kind. "Permit?" Abigail asked another question.

"Wouldn't leave home without it," Teri said, holstering the pistol and pulling the permit from her pocket.

"It's twenty-five dollars for an hour, you can buy ammo or supply your own though we don't allow no steel core, green tip, orange tip, black tip, armor piercing or incendiary rounds. You good with that?"

"Good as gold," Teri replied.

"Then all that's left is for you to sign this waiver." She started to grab the form and stopped. "Unless you want to become a member."

"What's in it for me?

"Unlimited range time is the main thing," she answered, "but you also get guest passes, you can take advantage of member only sales here in the showroom, priority lane discounts and," she gave Teri a big smile, "you get a free machine gun rental on your birthday!"

"Sounds like an offer I can't refuse," Teri said. "How much?"
"32.50 a month plus a one-time registration fee of 49 dollars."

"Not fifty?"

"Not fifty."

Teri quickly did the math in her head and peeled off three fifty dollar bills from a wad she pulled out of her pocket. She set them on the counter in front of Abigail.

"I'm in for three months plus the 49."

"Great. It'll just take a sec to get you all signed up," Abigail said taking the cash and walking over to the register. She came back with three dollars and fifty cents and a membership form for Teri. "Can I get you a bottle of water while you fill that out?" Abigail asked.

After she completed the form and signed it Teri was led to a door at the back of the showroom by a twenty something kid in blue jeans and a flannel shirt. Teri wondered if he was one of Abigail's sons, or, more likely, grandsons but she didn't care enough to ask. The door indicated the range was on the other side because there was a sign plastered to it which read, among other instructions, "Ear and eye protection is required beyond this point." Thanks to her new friend Abigail she had both. She and the kid went through. Inside Teri counted off eight lanes separated by barriers that appeared to be about four inches thick. Flannel shirt said the lanes were twenty-five feet long and he pointed out a control box at each station which operated wooden backboards on which paper targets were placed. The targets depicted the shadowy frame of a person's head and torso with concentric circles on the chest. They looked like every target she'd seen her entire life. The kid showed her how to mount the paper onto the wood backing.

"Just let me know if you need anything else," he said before leaving.

Teri picked the second stall from the left and she noticed another customer five stalls further along the line. They were the only two people in the room. She put on her eye and ear protection, slipped a 13-round magazine into the pistol and assumed the stance Hank had taught her as a little girl. With light tension on the trigger and both eyes open she depressed the rear grip safety lever with the fat part of her thumb and fired. The power, the noise, the feeling sent a thrill over her. She hit a different button on the control panel and the target came toward her. When it stopped she noticed four bullet holes were perfect head shots, seven others were placed inside the smallest of the two chest circles. The remaining two were in the neighborhood of the right shoulder. *Probably misses*, Teri figured, *especially if the target had the wherewithal to run*.

"Wow!" a man's voice, that didn't belong to flannel shirt guy, said. "That's some damn good shooting."

Teri looked away from the target and toward the voice. It definitely wasn't the flannel shirt kid. This guy was good looking and the first thing Teri noticed was his eyes. They were brown, but not really brown, she realized. *More like a bright copper actually* and Teri thought they were the prettiest man's eyes she had ever seen. He had nice hair too. Brown, not curly or straight, more like bushy and he was smiling. It was a smile made more interesting thanks to a small scar that ran toward his cheek on the left side of his face. Teri liked it. She liked the whole package.

"You should see me when I get warmed up," she said trying to sound more friendly than conceited.

"OK," he replied, "I'm Jake," he continued, "Jake Holler as in 'if you need Jake, just holler.'" She didn't react. "Yeah, that line never works, I don't know why I keep using it," he said, shrugging his shoulders.

"Really? *That* line doesn't work?" she asked, "hard to believe."

"I know, right?" he admitted. "Anyway you know my name, what's yours?"

"Teri," she answered honestly. "Teri Longabaugh," she lied.

"Well Teri Longabaugh I'll let you get back to your target practice. It was a pleasure to make your acquaintance."

"Pleasure's mine," she responded and he walked back to his stall.
Jake had been there when Teri arrived so he was first to finish. On the way out he stopped at Teri's station again. She removed her ear protection.

"Look I'm not usually this forward but I hate to see any chance I might have slip away because I was too afraid to ask." *Oh boy,* Teri thought, *here it comes.* "But if you'd like to meet me for a drink, I would consider it a highlight of my life." He looked down at his shoes. Teri was actually touched at how sweet and sincere the invitation sounded.

"Now that's a much better pick up line," she said.

"Really? What exactly did I say so I can put it in the repertoire?" They both laughed.

"I'd like to have a drink with you, Jake Holler."

"I'd like that too," he said, "how about tonight? I mean, of course, if you have nothing better to do."

"I don't actually," she said, "tonight would be great."

"Great," he repeated, "Excellent," he added. Teri thought he looked like a kid on Christmas morning. She was flattered. "There's a cool bar called The Rabbit Hole. I think it's on Kiowa Street."

"I'll find it."

"Good, good. Great," he said again and started for the door.

"Jake?" she said and he stopped.

"Yes Teri?"

"What time?"

"Oh. Geez, of course," he shook his head, "How about 7? Does that work?"

"Works just fine. See you at 7 at The Rabbit Hole." Jake Holler smiled and left the range.

♪♫♪

A Memorable Day

The day had been an interesting one for Allen. It began, like most of them lately, with him dropping Lettie off at Tracey's apartment. She told him when they first met she worked from home but since then he had learned exactly how she supported herself. She was fluent in four languages: Japanese, Mandarin Chinese, Spanish, and Farsi, so she served as a freelance translator for several paying customers including the U.S. government. She also made jewelry and sold those creations through her own web-based store.

The third way Tracey made money, and the one Allen found most interesting, was her work as an online juror. She said a lawyer friend had gotten her started. Allen knew there were law firms that recruited and paid people to serve as mock jurors for trials but he never knew anyone who had done it. Tracey explained that her job was to be a "mirror image" of someone actually selected to serve on a jury. They were privy to the arguments and rulings made in court and her reaction to those helped lawyers, sometimes for the prosecution but mostly for the defense, form strategies for the trial. Allen was shocked to learn that she could sometimes earn as much as a hundred dollars a day for a trial that lasted weeks. And she could do it all from the comfort of her living room.

He had, at her suggestion, gotten a dog crate identical to the one in his apartment and placed it in hers. Lettie marched right to it. The dog was growing but remained just as cute, Allen thought. Her tail had curled up and met with her haunches. The hair was long and fell from a center part. It made it look like the dog had a tiny Lhasa Apso or a mini Cousin It from Addams Family fame riding on her butt. Lettie's beard and moustache were also taking shape. So much so that Tracey told Allen he should have named her "Fu" as in "Fu Manchu". Allen thanked her for the advice. He had spied on her a couple of times early on and watched as she took the dog around the Monument Park trail twice a day. There was also a baseball/softball field nearby which provided the perfect spot to let Lettie off leash so she could run and play fetch.

On this particular morning Allen had an idea as he headed to the police station. He went through a Dutch Bros. drive-through coffee stand and got two large ones. He asked for cream and sugar to go. He parked his Tahoe in the station lot and, instead of going right in, he carried the coffee across Weber Street to the curious looking orange van. As he had noticed previously the windows were covered from the inside, some with cardboard, some with poster board and some with newsprint. He set one cup of coffee on the roof and knocked on the driver's side door. Seconds later he got a response.

"Get lost!" a booming voice said from inside the van.

"Mr. Holm? Larry? It's Detective Marc Allen from across the street. Can we talk?"

"I don't give a rat's ass if it's Woody Allen with Mia Farrow in tow. Get lost." Marc thought the reference was funny.

"I brought Dutch Brothers coffee," he said stifling a chuckle.

"Their coffee is crap," said the voice. Thirty seconds later the door opened wide enough for a weather beaten, wrinkled hand to reach out.

"Crap coffee first, chit chat after," the voice said. Allen handed him a cup.

"Cream and sugar?" he asked.

"With this stuff there's no other way," he said, extending his palm. Allen dropped the packets of sugar and creamer containers in it.

Five minutes later Allen was on the inside of the van sitting in the passenger seat. He turned to size up the cargo area and was astonished. The bench seat, which he assumed had once been there, was long gone. Instead, he saw a cot with a thin mattress on one side of the van and makeshift shelving filled with cans of soup, stew and chili on the other. Next to the shelves were stacks of newspapers and books. The back of the van featured a counter, also homemade, upon which sat a hot plate that was connected, by a black hose, to the propane tank that sat on the other side of the back doors. Allen was overwhelmed, not only by the quantity of the stuff crammed into the space but the quality of the smell emanating from the inside of the Dodge. Some of the odor, maybe most of it, he attributed to Mr. Larry Holm.

"I hear they call you the champ."

"Took a real genius to come up with that one," Holm said, "Larry Holm, Larry Holmes, hard not to make something of that. Anyway, everybody's got to be called something. What do they call you?"

"Allen, usually. But I've been called a lot worse."

"I'll bet," was all the man said.

"So, you live in here?" the detective tried his best not to sound too dismissive. "Where do you…?"

"Thanks for the coffee," Holm said, cutting Allen off at the pass. "I'm sure you have someplace more important to be." The emphasis was on the 'sure.'

"Guess I do," Allen acquiesced. He opened the door to get out. "Same time tomorrow?" he asked.

"Free country last time I looked," Holm said as he grabbed the door handle and shut Allen out.

"Yes it is," Marc said to the door.

"The coffee shop on Nevada is better," Holm yelled from inside. "Next time bring donuts! And tuna fish! I'm out of tuna fish!"

Allen entered the station and was immediately met with a buzz of activity.

“What’s up?” he asked a uniform walking by.

“Don’t know much,” she said, “heard something about a kidnapping.” Allen thanked her and started walking away. “Detective Allen is it?” he nodded. “You kinda smell.”

“Allen!” Lieutenant Danny Gutrich yelled from across the room, “my office tout suite, you’re up!”

Allen dumped his coffee cup in the nearest trash can and hustled for the locker room. He kept a second set of work clothes in there and quickly changed into them. He dumped what he was wearing in a plastic garbage bag, sealed it as tightly as he could and set it in the locker. On the way upstairs he stopped by his desk, grabbed his notebook and a pen and headed for the fifth floor. He entered the elevator and joined a young man which Allen would have described as a hipster, at least what Allen thought a hipster would look like. He wore tight fitting black jeans, a white short sleeved shirt and had a neatly trimmed mustache and beard. Around his neck hung a lanyard which identified him as Tucker Booth and the detective saw he worked in the IT department.

“Hey,” Allen said. Booth nodded. “IT huh?”

“That’s correct.”

"I'm Detective Marc Allen," he said as he extended his right hand. Booth shook it.

"Tucker Booth. Nice to meet you. You're the new detective, right?"

"Pretty new, I guess. How'd you know?"

"I installed the security system in your apartment."

"Did you?" Booth nodded as an answer to the question. "Can I ask you a question about that?"

Of course." Just then the elevator stopped at the fifth floor.

"Humor me for a second," Allen said getting out. Booth followed. "Does every detective get the spy treatment or just the new ones?" He asked when the doors closed.

"Everyone detective level and up," he answered. "And nobody is being *spied* on. It's purely a safety measure."

"I guess that makes me feel a little better. The equipment looks pretty sophisticated, how many cameras?" Booth looked at Allen for a moment and then smiled.

"Don't worry, Detective; like I said we're not voyeurs. The cameras are located in what we determined were the access areas to your unit and they're directional. We can only see the first couple feet inside those areas."

“Good to know. How many?” That made Booth think again.

“Four, I think.”

“You think?”

“No, I’m sure. There are four. Font door, both patio doors and the guest bedroom window. Four.”

“Who’s watching and when?”

“Again, there’s nothing to worry about, Detective. All the cameras, in all the detectives’ homes, go into one location. That’s where they’re monitored by a handful of officers but not full time. The cameras ARE recorded full time but the officers only spend an hour or two in the room at a time.”

“How do you, or they, know when or if there’s a breach?”

“The system is wired to send an alert if it detects any unusual movement or sounds like breaking glass. Do you arm your alarm, detective?”

“Mostly,” he answered honestly. “I also have a dog.”

“We know.” Booth said as he pushed the button to call the elevator.

Gutrich’s assistant waved Allen through when he got to the office. The room was directly below the one occupied by

Deputy Chief Paulson but the detective noticed immediately that it was smaller and appointed in a far more spartan manner. The Lieutenant sat behind his desk; another detective occupied one of the two chairs on the other side. Both men looked at Allen.

"Lieutenant," he offered looking at Gutrich.

"Marc, you're here. Great. Thanks for coming right up."

"I took 'tout suite' to mean tout suite, sir," he said.

"This is detective Carl Paulson," was the Lieutenant's response. Allen stared at the detective as Paulson rose to greet him.

"Are you…?" he started to ask.

"Related to the deputy chief?" Paulson finished the question. "Not even a distant cousin," he extended his hand and Allen shook it.

"I guess twin sons from different mothers then," he said.

"Dan Fogelberg and Tim Weisberg," Carl said. "I loved that record."

"Sit gentleman," added Danny Gutrich, "let's fill Allen in."

He learned two high school teenagers had disappeared from a party in Colorado Springs three nights ago. The parents had waited until this morning to call the police. Paulson said he and two patrol officers went to the school where the teens were students and started asking questions.

“Turns out they didn’t leave of their own volition,” Paulson added.

“Kidnapping?” Allen asked remembering what the officer downstairs had said.

“More like abducted.”

“Distinction without a difference?” asked Allen.

“Technically,” it was Gutrich, “there *is* a difference. According to the reports I’m reading several of the high schoolers who were at the party remember the two being taken against their will. But according to the parents…”

“Who waited *three days* to call us,” Allen interrupted.

“We try not to judge, detective.”

“Copy that, sir” Allen replied.

“Anyway,” Gutrich picked up where he left off, “both sets of parents say there hasn’t been any contact with the abductors. No ransom, no demands of any kind.”

“And we believe them?” Allen asked.

“Judging again?” Gutrich came back.

“Not at all, sir,” Allen got defensive, “just asking questions detectives should be asking.”

“Fair enough,” the Lieutenant said.

“Look Marc,” it was Paulson, “can I call you Marc?”

“Up to you,” Allen said.

“Look Marc,” he said, “I met these people, talked to them, looked them in the eye. They’re not bad folks and their kids are missing.”

“You’re right Carl. I apologize.”

“No need. We’re all on the same side.”

“Did the students say who took them?” Allen asked.

“Most didn’t get a good enough look.” Carl answered, “A couple did but said they didn’t recognize them.”

“Them?” Allen wondered. “More than one?”

"More than one," said Paulson, "and we were able to get a couple of decent sketches. The one thing most of the kids agreed on was that they were gangbangers."

"Why'd they say that?"

"The cars mostly," Paulson answered, "souped up Honda Civics. They're the preferred ride of the 13s.

"13s?"

"The thirteenth letter of the alphabet," Gutrich chimed in. "M. It stands for 'Mexican Mafia.'"

"Gang related," Allen started thinking out loud, "two teenagers, three days." He looked at both cops, "My experience tells me the chances are slim to none that those kids are still alive and slim left town." A silence fell over the room. Gutrich broke it.

"You're probably right, Detective, but it's our job to find out for sure. Okay gentlemen, let's get to it." The two detectives got up to leave. "Marc," Gutrich said, "hang back a second." He did as Paulson exited.

"What's up?" Allen asked.

"Go easy on Carl. He's a good cop."

"Hadn't thought otherwise," Allen responded.

"Not as good as you, but good. He came to us from Pueblo. Grew up there. His mom was a cop, made him want to be one too."

"Okay," Marc said not sure where Gutrich's story was going.

"He's got a bit of a chip on his shoulder. Wants to prove himself, especially in front of the new guy from Raleigh." Gutrich chuckled.

"The only thing he has to prove to me is that he takes this work seriously." Allen said, "if he's as good a cop as you say he is that's not going to be a problem."

"Appreciate that, Marc," Danny Gutrich slapped him on the shoulder. "I think we are all going to like having you around."

"I wouldn't be so sure of that," Allen said only half joking. "But I am happy to be here."

"Go help Carl," Gutrich said as he headed back to his desk.

Allen and Paulson immersed themselves in the case the rest of the day. Allen learned that the teenagers were Roderick Greer, an African-American male, 15 years old, that the kids called Roddy, and Natalie Cano-Peralta, a 16 year old Hispanic female. The two detectives took copies of the sketches to show the students back at the high school as well as both victim's parents. Some of the students said that Roderick and Natalie were friends, the parents confirmed that fact. A couple of the high schoolers told Allen that Peralta was also running with a gang. A group of troublemakers called the Young Threats. Neither of them thought Greer was a part of it.

“He had it *bad* for that chica,” one student, a friend of Roderick’s, said. “Lil’ Roddy couldn’t think or talk about anything else.”

Nobody could put a name to any of the faces in the sketches. Each hour that passed cemented Allen’s feeling that the teenagers were dead. He and Paulson decided to call it a day and start again fresh in the morning. They had already worked an hour past their shift. Allen hated picking up Lettie late so on the way home he called Tracey to apologize.

“Hey,” he said after she answered, “so sorry I’m running late but I’m on the way home.”

“No worries,” Allen thought she sounded genuinely unconcerned, “You do realize that this beautiful girl is now half mine, don’t you?”

“Those are terms with which I *refuse* to agree,” Allen shot back.

“See you when you get here,” she checked off.

He got home, got his girl, fed her then himself and sat down on the couch with his notebook ready to go back over the case.

A knock on the door interrupted that. He grabbed his phone clicked on the security app and saw Tracey. More precisely he saw someone he assumed was Tracey holding a piece of paper in front of the peephole. "Can Marc come out and play?" the words read. He smiled, got up, and went to the door.

"What's up?" he asked her after he opened it.

"Come over," she said, "we're playing Trivial Pursuit and it's so much better with four than three."

Allen was beat but he appreciated the effort and he liked playing Trivial Pursuit. Plus he thought it probably wasn't the worst idea in the world to get his mind off two surely murdered teenagers.

"Give me 5 minutes," he said.

After changing into jeans and a fresh t-shirt he put Lettie in her crate with a couple of dog biscuits and went across the hall. Tracey let him in and led him into the living room. Allen noticed a book sitting next to the game board. It was blue and had a sketch of a drum kit on the cover.
"Good book?" he asked Tracey who had plopped down on the couch.

"Not bad," she said, "it's clever." Allen picked up the paperback.

"*Murphy Murphy and the Case of Serious Crisis*," he read the title, "that's redundant."

"My guess is you'll find it clever too. I'll drop it off when I'm finished with it."

"Okay," Allen set the book back on the table. "I thought you said I'd be the fourth." Just then two people, a man and a woman both younger than Tracey or Allen, walked out of the kitchen. He had a serving tray with veggies and some sort of dip, she carried a bottle of red wine and four glasses.

"These are my friends Rampart and Hannah," Tracey introduced them to him, "and this is my neighbor Marc Allen," she introduced him to them.

"But not your friend?" Allen asked pretending to be hurt. Then he looked at the man. "Rampart. Now that's an unusual name."

"Rampart Haynes," he said extending his hand, "folks call me Ramp." They shook.

"Never been to a place where so many people get called something other than their name," Allen blurted. "And what do they call you, Hannah?" he asked.

"Hannah," she answered.

"Praise the Lord," he said looking at the ceiling.

"You a boxing fan, Marc?" Tracey changed the subject.

"Some," the detective answered honestly. "Why?"

"Ramp here is an Olympian," she said proudly. "He won a silver medal!"

"Almost," Rampart clarified. "I mean I *did* win a silver but it was in the Pan Am Games, not the Olympics. I never made the Olympic Team," he admitted.

"That's still awfully impressive," Allen said because he thought it was.

"Show him your medal, Ramp," Tracey said excitedly. Rampart patted all the pockets in his jeans.

"Must have left it in my other pants," he said it like he'd said it a hundred times before.

"I *love* that joke!" Tracey cried. "One of my favorite lines." Rampart looked at Allen and shrugged his shoulders.

They ended up playing two rounds of Trivial Pursuit. Two-person teams and Rampart and Hannah won both.

"We owe you guys a drink," Tracey said as she put the game's pie pieces into a Ziplock bag. "Let's go to the hole."

"The hole?" Allen asked.

"The Rabbit Hole," Tracey said, "you've never been?"

♪♫♪

Teri Makes a Discovery

Teri arrived at the Rabbit Hole twenty minutes early. She wanted to get a feel for the place before Jake Holler got there. The entrance had the look of a New York City subway portal. From the street you went down a flight of stairs covered by a glass canopy plastered with posters and one small sign with an arrow that indicated the way to the restaurant. It was impossible to tell if it was inviting or the exact opposite. You had to go through the door at the bottom of the stairs to find out. Inside it was dark but Teri could make out a lot of brick, some tables, several booths and a bar. Teri counted ten stools, half of them occupied by what looked to her like young professionals there for an extended happy hour. She took one of the empty stools and asked the bartender for a Tito's martini.

"One olive. Very cold," she directed.

"The olive?" he asked with a smile.

"Why not."

She thought the room had good energy and a lot of young people. As she looked around her eyes lit on a corner booth occupied by two girls and two guys. One of the guys was Detective Marc Allen.

"Holy crap," she said without thinking. She knew he was in Colorado Springs and she was hoping to find him. She just wasn't prepared for it to be so soon. She spun back around just as the bartender was dropping off her drink.

"You okay?" he asked.

"Sure, why?"

"Don't know," he shrugged, "you just look different than you did a minute ago."

"I'm thirsty," she said, "and to tell you the truth I'm *better* than I was a minute ago." The bartender nodded. *He must think I'm talking about the drink*, Teri thought but she knew the real reason. She grabbed the glass and took a nice long sip. "Delicious," she said and she meant it. The bartender looked from Teri to another customer.

"Hey Hannah," he said.

"Hey Dirk," Hannah answered. "can we get another round?"

"Sure thing," he said and he walked away.

"Dirk?" Teri said to the girl.

"That's what he says but I have my doubts. Looks like a Geno or a Vinnie to me."

Teri laughed.

“I’m T,” Teri said offering her hand. Hannah took it.

“T?” she asked, “and you thought Dirk was weird?”

“Touché,” Teri said.

“I’m Hannah.”

“I heard,” Teri answered, “pleased to meet you.”

“Likewise.”

“I happened to notice you’re with a group,” Teri looked at Hannah.

“Yep.”

“Which one is your boyfriend?” Teri asked. Hannah laughed.

“Neither. One guy’s my brother, the other guy I just met tonight. He’s a cop.”

“Really?” Teri acted surprised.

“Yeah. He’s actually a nice guy.”

“I think he’s kinda cute,” Teri said.

"Do you?" Hannah asked just as Dirk showed up with the drinks. She carried them back to the table. Teri gulped down what was left of her martini.

"Hey Marc," Hannah said setting the drinks on the table, "you have a secret admirer in here."

"What are you talking about?"

"The girl I was talking to at the bar. She thinks you're cute."

"What girl?" Allen asked looking toward the bar.

"That," Hannah turned and pointed to the stool on which Teri sat. It was now empty. "Girl," she finished. "I swear she was right there."

"You're such a tease," Tracey said. Hannah left the table and went back to the bar. Dirk met her there.

"What happened to the girl I was just talking to?" she asked.

"No clue. She put a fifty on the bar and bolted," Dirk said showing Hannah the bill.

"Weird," she said and went back to her friends.

Teri sat in her car. She had a little buzz going thanks to the adrenaline rush of seeing Marc Allen and the speed with which she had guzzled three ounces of top shelf vodka. She angled the mirror so she could see the entrance to the restaurant. She looked at the digital clock or her display. 3 minutes to 7. Her eyes went back to the mirror and she saw Jake Holler, looking all clean and cute and excited, bound down the stairs to the Rabbit Hole.

“Prompt,” Teri said, “I like that.”

“Was there really a girl that thought Allen was cute?” Inside, Tracey asked Hannah.

“You say it like it can’t possibly be true,” Allen chided her.

“Didn’t mean it like that, Marc,” she said as she raised her glass.

“Yes, there was,” Hannah said. “she was pretty, short hair, I think it was purple. Said her name was T.”

“T?” Rampart asked, “like the letter?”

“T. E. A.?”, Tracey spelled it out, “like the drink?”

“T?” was all Allen said.

“That’s what she told me,” Hannah replied, “I didn’t pry.”

Thirty minutes later Jake left the bar the way he had come but much less enthusiastically. His hands were in his pockets and his head was down. Teri watched him go. She felt bad but she was certain she would make it up to him. She was impressed that he waited a half an hour for her before leaving. She liked the fact that he didn't think it was worth staying without her. Three minutes after Jake left, the group of four including her new friend Hannah and her old friend Marc Allen exited the restaurant too. Teri started her car. She watched as they all got into a Chevy Tahoe, Allen behind the wheel. She was happy that she would be able to follow him all the way to his home.

Allen pulled away from the Rabbit Hole and drove a couple of blocks north on Tejon Street. Teri eased in a few car lengths behind. She followed as he made a left on Monument Avenue, went through the intersection at Cascade and cruised down the hill to where the street dead-ended. She stayed far enough back to remain inconspicuous but close enough to observe. She killed her SUV's engine. Two people got out from the backseat of Allen's vehicle, Hannah and the guy she said was her brother. She wondered about that then and did the same now. They were about the same age, maybe a couple years apart at most, but he was African American, she was clearly not. *Not uncommon*, Teri thought, *but not typical either*. They waved goodbye to the two still in the car and then said their farewells to each other with a hug. *A sibling hug for sure* was Teri's impression. The young man hustled across the street unlocking a Jeep on the way. He climbed in.

Teri's attention went back to Hannah and she watched her unlock a gate that was part of a black Aspen style three rail fence. She went through, turned and gave a thumbs up to the two in the Tahoe and was gone behind the building. The brake lights of the Tahoe flared red and Teri watched as the white reverse lights came on next. Allen turned the SUV around and the Jeep took up its place directly behind the Tahoe. Teri ducked down before they passed then rose and quickly started the Land Rover. She performed a U-turn of her own and was right back where she wanted to be, tailing the Tahoe. She noticed the Jeep make a left on Cascade but Allen made a right so Teri stuck with her main target. She didn't have to follow for long. Three blocks later Allen turned right at the light on Boulder. Teri could see there were a couple of houses and then another apartment or condo complex with an entrance to a parking garage. The street stopped at another dead end so she pulled over on Cascade and watched Allen steer the Tahoe inside the deck. She decided it was too risky to follow and told herself she'd come back another time to get a better look around. She made another U-turn and went back to look at Hannah's building. It new, upscale and interesting. She grabbed her phone and called Scott Ericsson. It went to voicemail.

"Hi Scott, it's Teri Hic," she stopped herself mid-word, "it's Teri Longabaugh," she cursed herself for the slip of the tongue, "I hope it's not too late to call," she really didn't care but she said it anyway. "I did some looking around for myself after you left today and I think I may have found an interesting option." She looked up at the building again. "There's what looks like a condo building on West Monument, down the hill, at the very end of the street. I wonder if there are any units available? I hope it's not apartments because I want to buy, not rent. Okay, check it out, will you? Thanks and see you tomorrow." She disconnected and headed back to the hotel. "Pretty eventful evening," she said as she turned up the radio.

When Allen and Tracey got home they parted ways at his door.

"Thanks," he said to her back. She turned.

"For what?"

"I don't know. The wine, the Trivial Pursuit, the company, new acquaintances," he stopped and thought for a second. "Just for tonight," he added, "thanks for tonight."

"You're most welcome Marc. Any time. You know where I live."

Inside his apartment Lettie was excited to see him. He let her out of the crate and watched her dance, and shake, and bound around the room. He marveled at how happy she could be. They went outside so she could sniff, growl at a couple squirrels, and relieve herself. Satisfied, they went back inside and that's when Allen noticed the blinking red light on his phone answering machine. He played the message.

"Allen, it's Paulson," he recognized the voice of the detective, not the deputy chief, "we caught a break in the kidnapping case. I'm down 705," he said referring to police headquarters.

"You mean the murder case," Allen said out loud as he reached for his mobile and punched in his colleague's numbers.

"Paulson."

"Hey Carl, it's Allen. Just got your message."

"Good deal. We got lucky."

"Why didn't you call my mobile?" Allen tried not to sound as annoyed as he felt.

"The guy's downstairs," Marc heard his colleague and thought he sounded a little defensive, "he's not going anywhere."

"I'll be right there." Allen called the dog and they went across the hall. He knocked on Tracey's door and she answered almost immediately.

"That was a little quicker than I expected," she said with a smile.

"Hey," he said missing the implication, "uh I hate to do this but,"

"Let me guess, duty calls," she finished for him. "It's perfectly fine. I was just about to make a bracelet and some earrings for a client. I could use the company." She petted Lettie on the head. "Come on girl," Lettie loped inside.

"Thanks," Allen turned to go.

"Marc," she said and he stopped. "If it's too late when you get back just let her sleep here and come by and get her in the morning." He nodded and wondered how late "too late" was.

He was only a handful of minutes from the building on 705 South Nevada and when he arrived he saw Detective Paulson in the break room shooting the breeze with two uniform police officers.

"Carl," he called.

"Hey Allen," Paulson looked at his watch, "you made good time. This is Stupples and Foltz. They grabbed our guy." Allen looked at the patrol officers and saw that Stupples was female, Foltz was not.

"Nice work. Tell me what happened."

"Pulled the guy over about an hour ago," it was Foltz.

"For a busted taillight of all things," Stupples chimed in. "I know it sounds like a cliché but it's true."

"Classic blue light special," Foltz picked up the tale. Allen knew he was referring to police slang term for pulling someone over. "He stopped, we stopped."

"Next thing we know," Stupples again, "the guy comes flying out of his car with his hands in the air yelling 'it wasn't me that killed those kids!' Foltz put him on the ground real quick and I Mirandized him. Then we brought him down here."

"I was still here," Paulson spoke, "cleaning up some paperwork." Allen looked at him and nodded.

"Let's go talk to the guy."

The guy was a gangbanger named Diego Alarcon and he sat on the floor of his cell with his back against a concrete wall. Allen noticed his head was shaved and he saw several tattoos on his scalp and neck including a large, black number 13. "Get up," he said. Alarcon rose to his feet and stared at Allen.

"The fuck are you? I know this limp dick," he pointed at Paulson, "but I never seen you before."

"I'm the new kid in town."

"New from where?"

"Right now I'd say your nightmares. What kids didn't you kill?"

"What the hell are you talking about?"

"You told the officers that arrested you that, and I quote, 'it wasn't me that killed those kids,' end quote. What kids didn't you kill?"

"B.S. I never said that, why would I? I never killed nobody." Allen wanted to slap the defiant look off Alarcon's face.

"Oh you said it, tough guy, and I think you meant it."

"Prove it mister *new kid from my nightmares*," he spat at Allen's feet.

"Ask and ye shall receive, asshat. It's all recorded thanks to the body cameras the two officers were wearing. We have you acting like a pussy in stereo." He thought he saw the color drain from Alarcon's face. He sensed the bravado disappear with it.

"You're lying!" He screamed at Allen as the detective walked away. "And I want a lawyer!"

"Comin' right up," Allen said as he raised his arm and extended the middle finger of his right hand. Paulson hesitated for a step or three then turned and caught up.

"What are you doing?" it was Paulson as soon as the detectives were out of Alarcon's earshot. "This department doesn't employ body cameras."

"I know that and you know that" he said to Paulson, "but that shitbag in there doesn't. Let's go talk to the officers."

They found them, still in the break room, seated at a round table and Allen asked got right to it.

"You guys good to go if we need your statements in court?" Officer Stupples looked up at the detective, Foltz looked at her.

"For fuck's sake detective what's that supposed to mean!?"

"Stupps," her partner cautioned.

"Apologies for the 'f' bomb detective but that was more than a little insulting," she said staring a hole in Allen.

"You're right officer, it was. Please accept my apology."

"Accepted, grudgingly," Stupples shot back, "but I'd appreciate it if you didn't let it happen again."

"It won't," Allen assured them both.

"Of course, we're good. That guy confessed." Stupples said, Foltz nodded.

Convinced he was caught on tape and faced with the prospect of spending the rest of his life in prison Alarcon gave everything up with the hope of getting a better deal and maybe even some sort of protection on the inside. He told Allen and the District Attorney he was one of about a dozen members of the 13s who showed up at the party to grab the 16 year old girl, Peralta. She was giving up information about their group to a rival gang, hers. Alarcon said the boy was just collateral damage. He said another gangbanger by the name of Marco Garcia Dawson was the ringleader and the shooter.

"He made her kneel on the ground and beg for her life and then he shot her execution style. The other kid pissed his pants and started screaming so Marco shot him too, just to shut him up."

This time there were two cameras in the room and the entire thing was recorded. There was also a stenographer present who wrote down the confession verbatim. When he was finished talking, she left for a minute or two to print it out, then came back in the room. She gave it to Allen who gave it to Alarcon's attorney. He wasn't positive the gangbanger could read. The attorney read it over, nodded and handed the paper to his client. Alarcon signed it. The whole process made Allen chuckle inside thinking of all the shows and movies he'd seen where cops hand the criminal a yellow legal pad and tell the thief, carjacker, rapist or murderer to "write it all down" when talking about confessions.

For his part in the brutal crime Alarcon got 35 years in prison which paled in comparison to Garcia-Dawson. Allen and Paulson got the collar and both, as well as Stupples and Foltz, testified at the killer's trial. The jury came back and recommended the death penalty even though many in state government hoped Colorado was moving away from capital punishment.

After hearing Alarcon's confession Allen went home. On the way he thought that nights like these are what made him both love and hate his job. He decided it wasn't too late so he woke Tracey up and retrieved his dog. He figured he'd let Lettie sleep on the bed that night but she preferred the crate.

Teri met Scott Ericsson in front of the hotel for the second straight day.

"Good morning. I trust you slept well," he said. Teri appreciated the ebullience but thought he bordered on being a little too cheerful. Despite that she smiled and nodded. "I've got three places set up this morning," he said as she buckled up.

"Is one of them in the building I mentioned?"

"One is," he said with a smile, "and your timing is impeccable. Those condos rarely become available."

"Born under a lucky sign, I guess."

"We can't see it for another hour though. Owner is a late sleeper." So they looked at the other two houses. Both had more fabulous views of the city but neither held much interest for Teri. On the way back into town Scott checked his messages and discovered the coast was clear for them to see the condo.

“It’s three bedrooms, two baths, and just over 2400 square feet. Fifth floor.”

“How many floors are there?” she asked because she couldn’t remember.

“Five.” Teri liked the thought of no one living above her. “But the first floor is actually parking so there are four floors with units. This one faces west,” Scott continued, “so you’ll get the great views of the park and the mountains with the afternoon and evening sun to boot. You’ll pay a little more because it’s on the top floor. There are two parking places on the ground level. One is covered, in the parking garage, the other is a visitor space in the outside lot. It *is* on the park which means joggers, runners and cyclists but it’s gated. You need a key to get in.” Teri didn’t say that she already knew that part. “Oh, and one other thing that might be considered a draw back,” Scott shot her a look.

“What might that be?”

“The traffic and the coal train. Interstate 25 and the tracks are just on the other side of the park, it can get noisy sometimes.” Teri thought she actually found that a plus. She didn’t mind the sound of traffic and she liked trains. Found the thought of riding the rails romantic.

"So what's the deal with this place? Why is it suddenly available?"

"Owner's a kid named Juan Crevallos; he plays for the Sky Sox. Truth be told, he just lives in it, his parents own it. They bought the unit for him and for them when they come visit?

"Sky Sox?" Teri asked, "baseball team?"

"Yep. Triple A affiliate of the Rockies. He's a twenty-year-old shortstop from the Dominican Republic."

"How do you know all that?"

"Google. Anyway, he just got traded to the Cincinnati Reds so he's headed to Louisville to play for their farm team the Bats. His old man has something to do with a big resort at home. Rumor has it he's worth millions."

While talking they had reached the destination. Scott parked the Porsche in almost the exact spot Hannah's brother had parked his Jeep the night before. The realtor led them into the building and Teri stopped for a moment to stare at the names listed on the roster near the main entrance. She saw "J. Crevallos" next to number 501 and then noticed an "H. Hunt" by unit 310. She didn't want to appear too interested so she lingered just a moment longer. In that time she didn't see any other "H's" so she hoped "H. Hunt" was Hannah. They rode the elevator to the fifth floor and entered the unit. It was bright, clean, new and well appointed.

"How much?" Teri asked after they had been inside for less than a minute. Scott looked at his notes.

"They bought it five months ago for 710 thousand. It's listed at..."

"Call whoever you have to call and tell them I'll give them $950,000 for it," Teri interrupted. "Cash. But that includes the furniture." Scott Ericsson pulled his phone out of his pocket and made the call.

♪♫♪

Reg Reconnects

After several months, motivated by loneliness, guilt or some combination of both, Reg Byrd broke down and called his parents. He waited nervously, with his finger on the disconnect lever, in case Stan Sr. answered. He didn't.

"Hello," Gloria Byrd said. Reg opened his mouth to speak but couldn't get a breath. "Hello?" his mother said again.

"Mom," he finally found the word.

"Reginald? Is that you, son?"

"Yes Mom. It's me."

"My God! Are you alright? Where have you been? Where are you now? Are you sick?" The questions came fast.

"I'm fine, mom."

"Where are you?" she asked her son again.

"I'd rather not say. I just wanted to call and say that I'm alive and doing okay."

"Well you don't sound okay. Are you in some kind of trouble?"

"No mom. I'm not in any trouble. I told you I'm fine. Listen I have to go but I'm going to write you a letter and catch you up on everything. Okay Mom?"

"Okay, I guess. We've been worried to death. All of us, especially Stan Jr. He got married, you know," she added.

"I'm glad. I gotta go now Mom but I'll write. I promise."

"Oh Reginald," she sighed.

"And Mom?" he wanted to tell her not to tell his father.

"Yes son?"

"Don't," he hesitated, "worry. I'll be in touch."

He did what he promised and wrote his mother a letter but he didn't get her all caught up. He didn't tell her about what happened in Colorado Springs or North Carolina but he did give her an address and told her it would only get to him if she addressed it to "The Champ." He claimed the guys with whom he was living would leave it alone if she did. After that Reg received regular correspondence from his mother and over the stern objections of Stanley Byrd, Sr. the correspondence almost always included money.

Life in the Haynes household changed very little after Hannah Hunt came to live there. Rampart actually discovered he liked having a "sister." They attended different schools throughout their childhoods which made family time when they got home even more interesting. Lucas Haynes founded and owned a distillery in town. The bourbons won awards in competitions all over the world. Beth Haynes was a professional photographer whose work was featured in magazines, newspapers and on museum walls. Life was good. Rampart came to realize his parents had kept their promise to him, nothing bad had happened to them. He also kept *his* promise to Hannah. He told her about Muhammad Ali and Oscar De La Hoya and Sugar Ray Leonard. They even watched their bouts on YouTube together. Hannah loved it. But when it came to Rampart's boxing Hannah sided with Beth. She did go to one fight but covered her eyes and screamed the entire time Ramp was in the ring. She never went again.

As for Rampart he and his friend Lee continued to enjoy the sport as they moved up divisions and weight classes. They were both good but Rampart felt Lee's style was more aggressive, too aggressive in his opinion, and coach Sarge agreed. They fought each other on several occasions and in the beginning Lee would get the better of Ramp more often than the other way around. That frustrated him but both Sarge and his dad told him to stay the course. Rampart did and it paid off. Before long Lee found it harder and harder to lay a meaningful glove on his buddy; all the while Ramp was scoring points with jab after jab, blow after blow. He'd come home and show Hannah how he "danced like a butterfly and stung like a bee!" "Like Ali!" Hannah would shout and giggle and beg him to "do it again." Over time the giggles turned to admiration. She also liked the fact that she felt like she had a protector and Ramp relished the role.

Both were good students. Mostly B's and sometimes A's at public schools for Rampart, all A's at private schools for Hannah. And through it all Ramp kept boxing. Thanks to Sarge and his own improving skills he caught the eye of the folks at USA Boxing, the group that picked the team that represented the United States for international competitions including the Summer Olympic Games. He was travelling to tournaments all over the region. There were times he'd have as many as six bouts at each if he kept on winning and he mostly kept on winning. He continued to move up in the amateur rankings and as he did, he became more and more interesting to USA Boxing. When he was sixteen, as his friends were learning to drive, he fought his way through a regional tournament against boxers from all over the Rocky Mountain West. Winning there meant he would qualify for the national tournament. Officials told him that if he won that he'd be considered "special." He did and he was. That victory meant he was chosen to be a part of USA Boxing's High Performance Squad which competed internationally. In less than a year he qualified for the 1999 Pan American Games as a middleweight by finishing in the top three at a tournament in Ecuador.

At the games in Winnipeg, Ontario, Canada he had a great tournament but not a golden one. He proudly stood on the podium, with a silver medal around his neck, listening to the national anthem of Cuba play for the gold medalist. He vowed he would represent his country again, this time in Sydney at the Olympic Games the next year. That dream ended when, at the Olympic Trials, he lost.

A National Golden Gloves Champion from Wisconsin beat him by a 14-8 decision. It made Ramp question whether he was good enough to keep going. A question that became easier to answer when the young man who beat him didn't even make the U. S. Olympic Team, losing at the USA Boxing National Championships. Rampart Haynes was seventeen and the next Summer Olympic Games were four years down the road.

He knew his heroes' gold medal stories by heart. He knew they all had climbed to the top spot on the podium before they turned 21. Ali was 18 when he beat Zbigniew Pietrzykowski for the light heavyweight gold in 1960. De La Hoya was 19 and a half years old when he won gold at the Barcelona Games in 1992 and Sugar Ray had just turned 20 when he walked away with gold in Montreal. Leonard was the oldest of the three and Rampart Haynes knew he was no Sugar Ray Leonard. One night, around the dinner table, he told the family he was done with the dream. Tears were shed, hugs given, sighs of relief were heard from Beth and Hannah. They all told Ramp how proud of him they were. That night while he was reading in bed, he heard a soft knock of the door.

"Come in, he called." Hannah opened the door and stepped in. She had a piece of drawing paper in her hand and Rampart could see it was his image. She had captured his celebration in the ring at the Pan Am Games. Arms thrust upward, a wide smile on his face. On the way to the edge of his bed she saw his silver medal. She picked it up in her other hand and put it around her neck.

"It always surprises me how heavy it is."

"I know," he replied with a nod. She smiled and sat. Neither said anything for minutes. Finally Rampart broke the silence.

"You okay?" He noticed a tear roll down her right cheek. She wiped it away.

"I drew this for you," she handed him the portrait.

"It's awesome Hannah," he admired her work. "Really, really good."

"You're my hero, Rampart," she said and she leaned in for a hug. He set the drawing to the side and held on to her tight.

Ramp decided to go to school at the University of Nevada in Reno for several reasons. The first was that it was only a two-day drive from Colorado Springs. Far enough away but close enough to come home if he wanted or needed to. The similar climate was a second reason and the third factor in the decision was that he could still box. Nevada was one of several schools in the Far West Collegiate Boxing Association. The school had won the national collegiate championship twice in the 1960s. While there he fought middleweights from USC, UC Davis, San Jose State, Oregon, Washington and others. Another one of the schools on the schedule was The United States Air Force Academy and one of the opponents Ramp fought from there was his old friend Lee who had modified his style. They squared off against each other four times in college, each winning two by close decisions. Ramp majored in Marketing and Communications and got his degree in three and a half years. His hope was to combine his love for boxing and the Olympic Movement with his diploma. He thought the best place to do that was right back in Colorado Springs at The United States Olympic Committee. With a little help from his friends at USA Boxing he got an interview at the USOC's downtown headquarters. Five days after that he had a job.

Hannah cried for hours the night her parents died but she could count on the fingers of one hand all the hours she spent crying in all the years since. Both Lucas and Beth Haynes made it a point to tell her she was in a safe place, a place where she could cry all day, every day, if she wanted. That just made her want or need to do it less. She was only seven when she first came to live with them but even at that age, she knew tears weren't going to bring her mommy and daddy back. She was also keenly aware that Lucas and Beth were not her parents, never would be, so she couldn't get comfortable calling them "Mom" and "Dad". The kids at school knew what had happened and Hannah felt that some of them looked at her differently, saw her as the poor girl with no parents, but the Haynes's helped her deal with that too.

Rampart was a different story. She always had felt a particular kinship with him and she had no problem saying he was her brother. They played in the yard and in the park together; Catch, tag, tetherball, hide and go seek. She liked the fact that Rampart never let her win although sometimes she did. She watched him practice his boxing in the garage, beating on a big, long bag he called "Buster Heavy" or pummeling the smaller speed bag that didn't have a name. Sometimes he'd dance around and scream that he'd just won "the heavyweight championship of the world." When he did, she couldn't contain her laughter.

She had started drawing. It started as doodles then advanced to tracing things like the characters in her favorite picture books. At some point the tracing stopped and the creating her own characters began. Hannah asked Beth to buy her drawing supplies and she obliged by bringing home pads of drawing paper and assorted pencils in different colors and with different point sizes. Sometimes Hannah would bring it with her when she watched Rampart practice. She'd sit on a bean bag chair and draw as he danced or threw jabs, uppercuts and hooks. She went to one of his fights. Once, because once was enough. She covered her eyes so she couldn't see him get hit and when they got home she begged Lucas to tell him to quit. When he said boxing was "Ramp's choice" she told him she'd never go again and she ran to her room.

Rampart told her stories about Ali, Oscar De La Hoya, and Sugar Ray Leonard and claimed he was going to win an Olympic gold medal just like they did. For a month she ended her nightly prayers by asking the Lord to "make Ramp's dream come true but keep him safe along the way." Even though she couldn't bear to watch him fight she also couldn't help but notice how good he was getting. The house was filling up with more ribbons, trophies and medals and her room was filling up with more and more drawings. Not just of her brother but landscapes, still life's and portraits of friends at school. Her favorite was a reimagination of the photograph her dad had taken of Rampart and her. She stared at it for hours at a time and drew an impressive recreation. Beth found it one day and loved it so much she had it framed and hung it in Hannah's room. The house was always full of love but it felt extra empty when Ramp was away at competitions.

Growing up she took particular delight in warning boys, and some girls, that if they messed with her they'd have to answer to her brother. The Haynes's asked her if there was anything she was interested in the way Ramp was in boxing. She told them what she had told her mom and dad about wanting to be a fighter pilot or a Rockies pitcher. They told her those were lofty goals. After giving it some more thought she added that maybe she'd like to learn to ice skate so they signed her up for classes at The Broadmoor Skating Club where she learned how to glide, turn and spin. Her teachers and companions were some of the country's most accomplished figure skaters. As she and Ramp got older, they spent less time in the yard or at the park and more time in one or the other's room. Reading, talking and listening to music.

"You're either a Beatles person or a Rolling Stones person," Rampart told her, "Dad and Mom are Beatles people." She didn't know what that meant but she nodded anyway.

Rampart would sneak in *A Hard Day's Night* and *Sgt. Pepper's Lonely Hearts Club Band* as well as records by Springsteen, Journey and Genesis from Lucas's collection. Hannah liked listening to Beth's country albums, particularly George Strait, Tim McGraw, Martina McBride and a new singer named Carrie Underwood.

"I like the words," she told him, "the stories the songs tell." Both agreed to occasionally listen to Green Day, Foo Fighters and U2 but neither liked heavy metal or rap. Hannah proved to be a better student than Rampart, prospering from the student to teacher ratio at her Colorado Springs private school. Somewhere along the way she realized her career goals had shifted. One night, as Rampart was passing by her room, he noticed her door was cracked open. He heard his sister talking to his mom so he stopped to listen.

"My mom and dad never laughed at me when I told them my dreams of pitching in the Major Leagues or flying a fighter plane," he heard Hannah say.

"Why would they laugh?" Beth asked.

"Because neither one is very realistic."

"They aren't impossible either."

"You sound just like they did."

"I sure hope so."

"The thing is," Hannah continued, "Ramp is *really* good at boxing." In the hallway Rampart smiled when he heard this.

"And you're getting good at skating," Beth replied.

"Thanks, I like it a lot but I don't love it like Rampart loves to box. Don't get me wrong I don't want to quit but…"

"But what honey?"

"But I'm never going to be a great skater, an Olympian like Ramp wants to be. And I don't think it's in me to try."

"I understand," Beth said, "you need to find something you're passionate about."

"I think I have," Hannah said as she looked around the room at her drawings. "One of my teachers said she thinks I have a gift." Beth noticed the art as well.

"She's right. You do." Rampart smiled for a second time and continued on the way to his room.

Hannah didn't know it at the time but she had money, plenty of it. Between her parents' savings, her dad's military pension and the two million dollar life insurance policies her parents carried, Hannah was set for life. Lucas and Beth had established an in-trust account for the girl and they used some of that to pay for her college education. She applied and was granted admission to the School of the Art Institute of Chicago and got her degree in painting and drawing. Then she came back home to Colorado Springs to live and work.

♪♫♪

The Seasons Changed

The seasons changed. After Allen arrested Garcia-Dawson he did the same with dozens of other Colorado Springs criminals. After a couple of admittedly rocky starts he got along well with colleagues and established himself as a hard-working, helpful, stand-up cop. He had never once been summoned to the Chief of Police's office except to accept congratulations, thanks or accolades. Remembering the Joe Kenda outburst during their first meeting he always made it a point to credit the uniformed officers and other detectives who made a difference. He *had* spent several additional hours in the office of the deputy chief. Each time he noticed the dog, "Sweetness" sitting by the desk but many times the painting on the wall was different. Once in a while he passed Officer Nobilo on the way out when he was heading in. He, Detective Paulson, and Lieutenant Danny Gutrich had become friendly and even played some golf together.

He also became a regular visitor to Larry "The Champ" Holm. Not every day, but coffee once a week and once a month he'd drop a case of canned goods. Sometimes tuna fish, sometimes soups and sometimes chili. He also gifted Holm some hand me down clothes, a Carolina Hurricanes cap or a couple of Raleigh P.D. sweatshirts that he no longer wanted or needed. On these visits he learned more about the Colorado Springs homeless population. It had grown in the past few decades thanks, in part, to an influx of former soldiers who found themselves with no place to go.

"Guys spent years, sometimes decades, with somebody else telling them what to do, where to be," Holm told him over coffee one morning. "Then all of the sudden they've done their time or got asked to leave. Nobody blowing reveille, ordering them around or cooking them something to eat in the mess hall. It's a shock to the system." Allen was a little surprised to find out that Larry Holm didn't consider himself one of the unfortunate souls.

"I got a bed, and a kitchen and a view when I want it," he told Allen one time.

"And a police force across the street that leaves you alone," Allen added.

"Except when they don't," The Champ said with a smile. "Thanks for the coffee, now get lost." It was his normal way of saying goodbye.

Allen read that in his new city there were somewhere in the neighborhood of 1,500 folks without a neighborhood. He discovered there were several pockets of homeless encampments or tent cities scattered around town. Some in city parks, some along the two miles of Monument Creek. He could sometimes see as many as a dozen folks with no place else to go from his own apartment's deck. One of the more populated areas was just south of Holm's van and police headquarters. The detective learned that it was the place where Holm occasionally went to the bathroom or cleaned himself up in the waters of the creek. To get there he had to pass a nursing home, a residential complex and a park with a small playground. The spot was usually occupied by people who didn't have a Dodge van in which to live.

On a different visit Allen discovered The Champ wearing clothes the detective had never seen before. A plain white tee shirt covered by an ill-fitting Green Bay packers zippered sweatshirt. Holm also had on a pair of cargo pants and Allen tried to think of a time when he had seen the man in anything but dirty blue jeans. He couldn't. On his feet were a pair of square toed, brown cowboy boots that had clearly seen better days.

"New threads?"

"Sorry, what?"

"Your clothes, "Allen pointed, "are they new?"

"Do they look new?"

"Not even a little," Allen admitted, "but I've never seen you wearing them."

"That's because I've never let you get a peek inside my walk-in closet, detective."

Allen continued to press the man about the wardrobe and Holm finally admitted that he had befriended an orderly at the nearby nursing home who sometimes gave Larry clothing that belonged to residents of the home that had passed on. Allen decided not to ask how the champ paid the orderly for the items. He started worrying more and more about Holm as the days got shorter and colder but he had to admit that the man had survived many more Colorado Springs winters than he had. Allen feared the combination of a rusty old van, a cold winter night and a jerry-rigged propane tank was cause for concern. When the days got particularly bitter the detective turned his thoughts from The Champ to another interest, exploring police department cold cases.

Teri was also settling into life in Colorado Springs. She had, indeed, made up for the unfinished first date with Jake. She frequented both the Rabbit Hole and the gun range until she ran into him again.

"Holler!" she said coming up from behind him as he occupied a stool at the Rabbit Hole bar. Jake turned and smiled; he couldn't help himself.

"You're," he peeked at his watch, "a little late for our date."

"Sorry about that," she was sincere. "I got cold feet," she wasn't. "But I'm here now."

"Yes, you are." He smiled again and rose to give his barstool to her. He looked her up and down and, like he had before, enjoyed the view but something about her had changed. She noticed him noticing.

"It's the hair," she said, "I changed it." He realized she was right. He remembered her having streaks of light purple, almost lavender, hair. Now it was a deep red.

"I like it," he said.

"Tito's? One olive, extra cold?" Dirk, the bartender, had joined them.

"Why not?"

"He knows your drink? So you have been here."

"A couple of times," she touched his cheek as she said it, "looking for you." She stood up and kissed him lightly on the lips.

"Well, you found me," he kissed her right back.

He spent a number of the nights going forward with her in the Monument Street condo, but not every night. She liked having him around but not all the time. She learned he, and his brothers, owned a full-service car wash in town. He was rarely there but it provided him with a decent income. He also said he did odd jobs around town because he was bored and he liked to. Among other things Jake helped out around the shooting range and worked, as a volunteer, at an animal clinic where one of his jobs was to come up with the corny sayings displayed on the exterior signage.

"If attacked by a mob of clowns, go for the juggler," was his latest and one of which he was particularly proud. She knew he wasn't the brightest bulb in the chandelier but he was fun to be around, he made her laugh out loud, he was good-looking and he was attentive to her needs in bed. If Teri fancied herself the type to get serious about a guy then Jake Holler might just be the type of guy she'd seek. But settling down with Jake Holler, or anyone for that matter, wasn't top of Teri's mind. He was a good guy, she surmised, but she knew from experience even good guys weren't always that good. She told herself she'd have to explore that further.

Jake mentioned he came from a family of mechanics starting with his great grandfather, then his grandfather, then his father. Even one of his brothers had taken up the family trade, but not Jake. He had learned how to take apart and rebuild most engines but he had no desire to follow in the Holler family footsteps. He did, however, out of the goodness of his heart volunteer his time to tune up or fix the vehicles in the motor pool of a local ambulance company.

"Gotta help keep the lifesavers on the road," he told Teri when she asked why.

On the days and/or nights Jake wasn't around Teri spent most of the time keeping an eye on Marc Allen. She followed him relentlessly, both when he was at work and when he wasn't, and kept a running log of his comings and goings. She kept the log in a safe with her guns and put that in a self-storage unit she had rented off 8th Street near the car dealerships on

Motor Way. Sometimes she saw Allen with other cops. A few times she watched him with Hannah and her brother. She also noticed him spending time with the other girl at the bar who Teri quickly learned lived across the hall from him.

She was most intrigued by his relationship with a homeless guy who seemed to live in a beat-up orange Dodge van parked near the police station. More often than not she watched Allen, alone with his dog, taking a walk, going to the grocery store or just hanging out on his balcony in the building a few blocks from hers. She thought each person and every situation presented interesting opportunities to torment the detective. Except the dog. She just wasn't sure she could harm a puppy.

♪♫♪

Best Buds

Rampart and Hannah were best buds as kids and they continued to be close into young adulthood. Both had gone their separate ways for college, pursued different careers, but they always found the time and a way, mostly personally but sometimes professionally, to get together. One such intersection was when a number of athletes arrived at the United States Olympic Training Center just east of downtown. The 150 acre complex included dormitories, a kitchen and dining hall, a state of the art gym, a shooting range and indoor facilities for volleyball, basketball and other Olympic and Paralympic sports. The U. S. Men's Gymnastics Team called it home. USA Boxing, USA Wrestling, USA Shooting, and more had offices and facilities on campus. USA Swimming had access to an incredible Olympic-size pool and the state-of-the-art training apparatus that came with it. Team USA athletes from across the sports spectrum came and went with visits increasing during the months leading up to a summer games.

One winter day Olympians and Olympic hopefuls from several disciplines had come to the training center and Rampart thought it was an excellent opportunity to get some images of America's most famous athletes to use in promotional campaigns, and to put on posters and drawings around the grounds. He pitched the idea up the chain of command and got approval from his department head. It didn't take much for him to convince Hannah to contribute her exceptional talents. Rampart only had to promise her a meal at their favorite brunch spot as compensation.

They arrived at the Training Center as the sun was making its first appearance in the eastern sky and made their way to the pool. Swimmers were starting to arrive for the first of three daily workouts and Rampart introduced Hannah to the women's National Team coach. He pointed out a number of his top medal prospects that included swimmers that had already won medals at multiple games. Hannah didn't need much prompting. She recognized most because she had watched them thrill the world on her television. She pulled a sketch pad out of her bag and got to work.

As Rampart watched Hannah watch the swimmers he was reminded of how amazed he had been by her gift. He often wondered how they could look at the exact same thing but she could see it in an entirely different way. He admired her as she worked, watching her eyes while her hand guided the pencil all the while translating her vision to the pages in her sketchbook. He also knew from experience that this was step one of her process. Hours of work would be added later to come up with a final, awe-inspiring product.

"It's like what happens when I look at you when you box," she had tried to explain it one time to him. "You don't realize how beautifully you move."

They spent several hours hanging out watching athletes prepare then go through the various stages of their workouts. Then she was finished.

“Hungry?” he asked.

“Famished. And I’d kill for a latte.”

“Then I guess it’s time for me to pay you for your efforts. What do you say we head over to Urban Steam?” They did and when they arrived they were surprised there wasn’t the customary line at the door. Rampart looked at his watch.

“It’s still early for the brunch crowd.”

“Let’s take advantage,” she said with a smile and they grabbed a table inside.

“Will you work more on those today?” he asked pointing to the sketch book.

“Nah. They need room to breathe and so does my brain.”

“Kind of like a fine wine.”

“Egggs zactly,” she said as the server brought their eggs. They both started digging in.

“The arena has open skating today,” he said after a full five minutes.

"Do they?"

"Yep. 10 AM until 4. Wanna go?" He could see her thinking about it as she sipped her latte.

"Sure, why not? I haven't laced the ol' skates up in a while."

"It'll be fun," he said.

They went to her condo so she could change and get her gear. She said she still had skates that fit, he said he'd rent some hockey skates when they got there. Ten minutes later Hannah came back out.

"That took a while," Ramp said.

"Saw someone, said hello. Remember the night in The Rabbit Hole? The night we first met Detective Allen?"

"Sure," Rampart said.

"I told you there was a girl at the bar who thought Allen was cute?" she prodded.

"Kind of," Ramp admitted.

"Well it was her."

"Who's her?" Rampart asked.

"The girl I just saw. Weird, huh?"

"Kind of," he said again and nodded.

Teri noticed the skate bag Hannah carried with her and wondered what that was all about. She decided to find out. When Hannah left the building to join her brother Teri rushed to her Land Rover and followed them.

The Broadmoor Arena had been a home away from home of sorts for Hannah as a kid. Now it served as a venue for concerts, shows and the Colorado College Tigers hockey team. After signing in, they put on their skates and joined close to a hundred others on the frozen surface. The moves came back slowly to Rampart, much more quickly to Hannah but soon they were both at ease on the ice.

Teri waited in the parking lot until she believed she wouldn't run into Hannah and her brother. Inside the building she noticed dozens of people lacing up skates and getting ready to hit the ice. Others had clearly just finished and were putting on their street shoes and getting ready to leave. There was a sign in desk but Teri walked right by it, telling a young lady she was just there to watch. She was craning her neck trying to catch a glimpse of Hannah and walked right into a boy who barely came up to her waist.

"Oh geez," she said, "sorry."

"It's okay," the boy said putting on his helmet. "I'm little."

"But I bet you're fast," Teri looked at him and smiled. The boy nodded. "How fast?" she asked him.

"Really, really fast."

"Show me," she suggested.

"Okay," he smiled from ear to ear. "Come on."

Rampart watched as his sister gracefully moved from place to place. He knew she could sense every bump, groove and imperfection in the rink and was able to make the needed minute adjustments with the blades. Her spins, turns and glides seemed effortless even though he knew that wasn't the case. His technique, on the other hand, was much less nuanced. He loved to attack the ice and gather as much speed as he could muster while taking care to observe proper etiquette. They went back and forth and forth and back meeting several times in the middle to share a story or a laugh. Rampart noticed he was working up a sweat while he thought Hannah looked as fresh as the second she first entered the oval. That's why it surprised him a little when she suggested they skate over to the side and take a break.

"I'm gonna be sore tomorrow," she confessed.

"Me too. And you're full of it, by the way."

"What?"

"I believe your exact words were 'I haven't laced the ol' skates up in a while'. After watching you out there I'm calling BS."

"I guess it's like riding a bike," she said with a shrug.

"Well whatever it is you looked great."

"Why thank you, my brother," she curtsied.

They both leaned against the boards and watched their fellow citizens of Colorado Springs skate. The group was made up of all shapes, sizes, and skill levels. Some as good or better than Hannah, others clearly on skates for the first time or at least for the first time in a long, long, time. A smattering of parents, siblings and friends hung out in the seats and watched too. They noticed several young kids, both boys and girls, in hockey jerseys and helmets speeding around the ice.

"Mighty Mites," Ramp said pointing at a couple of them.

"Was that you when you were a kid?"

"Sure was," he nodded, "but I'm not sure I was ever *that* confident."

"Or reckless," she added.

"Or that."

"Ready for a few more spins?" She asked as she pushed herself away from the boards. At that moment one of the youngest, smallest skaters came rocketing toward them. Rampart noticed and thought the kid couldn't be more than five or six. He was hauling with his head down, eyes on the ice.

"Hannah!" he yelled a warning. Startled by the sound she turned awkwardly and had to wave her arms a little to regain her balance. The kid, a boy for sure, had looked up when Rampart screamed but he hadn't slowed. He saw Hannah leaning one way so he went the other. But when she righted herself she slid a little further out than the kid anticipated and his right skate clipped her left sending her off balance again. This time there was no time for correction. She fell. Hard. The first thing that hit the ice was her head.

Teri watched it all from her perch in the arena. She grabbed her purse and left.

Rampart had watched in horror. He tried to warn his sister about the speeding bullet on skates but he acknowledged that his outburst may have made everything worse. He saw the skates make contact and the boy continue on as if nothing had happened. That's because everything happened to Hannah. Her left leg went out from under her and her right was ill prepared to compensate. Everything appeared to Ramp in slow motion as he watched his sister's arms flail in an effort to help her body find purchase. They failed and she went down. The trance he found himself in was broken by the sickening sound of her head hitting the ice.

“Hannah!” he screamed again. Her body lay motionless. *Thankfully,* he thought, *there was no blood.* “Somebody call 9-1-1!” he yelled as he fell to his knees next to her. “Call 9-1-1!” he cried. “Please!”

♪♫♪

Second Verse: After The Fall

Rampart lost all sense of time but he knew one minute he was kneeling next to Hannah's body and the next the paramedics were there. The police too. The medical professionals worked quickly, clearing the area of onlookers and stabilizing Hannah. Ramp tried to ask questions but they were ignored or quickly brushed aside. He could see his sister was still breathing so he sat back and watched them work. He looked on numbly as they lifted her onto a gurney and got her out of the arena and into an ambulance. She still had her skates on when they wheeled her away. The police were different. Their approach was much more methodical. They spoke to Ramp as well as dozens of other witnesses. Everyone's story was pretty much identical.

"A freak accident."

"Nobody's fault."

"An innocent collision that turned catastrophic."

"The kid barely touched her."

Rampart couldn't disagree with any of it. The arena people were understandably apologetic and he heard them tell the police they planned to immediately install signage to deter skaters from going too fast. They also said in the future they would post arena personnel on the ice and in the seats at the busiest times to monitor the situation. People Rampart didn't know, had never met, came over to offer their sympathies. Eventually the music started playing again and folks went back to doing what they were doing before the accident. Rampart asked the police if he could leave and they said yes.

"Which hospital?" he wondered.

"Beg your pardon?" an officer addressed him.

"My sister. Do you know which hospital they took her too?" The cop spoke into a walkie talkie.

"UC Health on Boulder," she said.

"Thanks."

He identified himself to a nurse at the registration desk and was told to have a seat in the waiting area. A doctor would be out shortly to speak with him. Shortly turned out to be almost an hour.

"Is she okay?" he asked when the man finally approached. The stitching on his white coat identified him as Dr. Thomas Christine.

"Not right now," he answered, "but we were able to stabilize her vital signs. She took quite a blow to the head."

"But there wasn't any blood, Dr. Christine," Rampart said thinking that was a positive sign.

"Call me Tom," he placed a hand on Ramp's shoulder, "and you are?"

"Rampart. Call me Ramp."

"And how do you know my patient?"

"I'm her brother."

"Okay Ramp," he said, thinking he'd never get used to seeing family members of patients look so distraught. "The lack of blood was actually not a good thing."

"It's not?"

"No. You see, the skull is a rigid box that serves to protect the brain. When there's trauma the brain can bleed and swell and that rigid box gives the swelling nowhere to go." Ramp nodded. "If it's left unchecked and the swelling continues the only place it has to go is down through the opening at the base of the skull. That could damage the brain stem and even result in death."

"But you made sure that didn't happen to Hannah?"

"We did. The paramedics that were first on the scene did a fantastic job and our team did the rest. We ran some initial tests, got her right into surgery, staunched the bleeding and alleviated the swelling. She came through all that with flying colors."

"But you said she wasn't okay when I asked."

"That's right I did because she's not. She's better than she was but she's still a long way from being okay. Are her parents on the way?" he asked, looking over Rampart's shoulder.

"Her parents are dead. Killed by a damn drunk driver, long time ago. She grew up in our house." The doctor nodded. "Can I see her?"

"Sorry to hear that," he said and Rampart believed he meant it. "Not much to see I'm afraid," Dr. Christine shook his head. "She's in a coma."

"Oh my God!" Rampart put his face in his hands. "This is all my fault," he said through his fingers.

"Not what we heard. Paramedics and the police said it was an accident, plain and simple." Rampart let that comment pass.

"So she's not okay now but is she *going* to be okay?"

"Unfortunately there is no clear answer to that question but there are some positive signs. Like I said she's stable now. There's a thing called the Glasgow Coma Scale and we use that to measure certain things at the time of an accident and during the initial stages of the hospital stay. Her numbers on that scale are encouraging."

"But she's still unconscious?"

"Yes but her brain is still working. It just seems to be taking a bit of a break."

"For how long?"

"Now that's the $64,000 question," the doctor said with a smile. "Experts say the average length of a coma is somewhere between eight and 41 days."

"41 days! Jesus, I can't believe this."

"That's on the far end of the spectrum," he tried to sound reassuring, "but truth is the longer it lasts the worse it tends to be for the patient when they come out on the other side. I know it's tough but keep the faith. It's way too early to tell in your sister's case." Rampart nodded. "A woman named Elaine Esposito holds the Guinness Book of World Records for the longest coma. It lasted from December of 1934 to November of 1978. Thirty-seven years."

"And what happened to her?"

"She died."

"Oh God, well that's just great Dr. Tom," Rampart tried not to sound angry. "You really need to work on your bedside manner."

"I've been told," he replied. "Look," he quickly added, "there's nothing you can do for her right this second. Go home. Try to get some rest. Grab something to eat and get cleaned up. She's gonna need you to be rested and strong." Rampart decided not to take his advice.

♪♫♪

Teri Trails Allen

Teri felt guilty for what happened to Hannah for about an hour then she went back to doing what she had been doing on many previous nights, following Detective Allen. She returned home to find Jake sitting on the ground next to the entrance gate of her condo complex. Next to him was a black plastic garbage bag. Teri pulled up in front of the garage gate several feet away from her boyfriend. She rolled down her window.

"I hope you don't think you're moving some of your junk into my place," she said. Jake got to his feet, picked up the bag and approached her car.

"Wait until you see what I have in here." Teri could tell he was excited.

"It better not be alive," she unlocked the passenger door. "Get in."

Upstairs Jake extracted the goods from the garbage bag and Teri saw that it was a bird made out of wire. It looked to her to be about a foot tall. She thought maybe she had seen it before.

"What the hell is that?" she asked.

"It's a bird."
"I can see it's a bird, Jake, but where did it come from?"

“Downtown,” he answered, “I took it.”

“You mean you stole it,” she took a closer look. “Is that the bird from the sculpture on Cascade?”

“There was a wire cat too but it was too big to take.”

“Good grief Jake what in the world do you think you’re going to do with it?”

“I don’t know,” he thought for a second, “sell it maybe?”

“To whom? For what? It’s a worthless piece of metal without the other part of the sculpture.”

“It is?”

“Of course. You can’t sell broken off pieces of art separately. They have no value.”

“I guess I never thought of that,” he looked at the bird in his hand.

“You could have ended that sentence after ‘I never thought.’ Go put it back.”

“Right now?”

"No, next week," she said shaking her head, "of course right now." While he started to leave Teri had a thought. "So, you like to steal stuff, do you?" she said as he headed for the door.

"I dunno," he shrugged. "Sometimes, I guess."

"Why?"

"Don't know that either," he said sheepishly. "For fun, for the challenge. Sometimes I do it just to see if I can. Personality flaw I guess." *I'd definitely steal for you*, he thought as he undressed Teri in his mind.

"Huh," Teri said wondering how she might take advantage of that aspect of Jake Holler's nature. "Get going," she added, pointing to the door.

Rampart sat in the chair in Hannah's hospital room, just a few feet from her bed. It was the third day of her coma. He was partially hidden from view thanks to the dozens of floral arrangements that had been arriving since day one. Flowers with balloons and flowers with teddy bears had come from her friends, her clients and even from the family of the boy who had accidentally knocked her over. There were also orchids, lilies and other plants sent by their friend Tracey, the Broadmoor Arena and the USOC. Detective Marc Allen had sent a succulent. Ramp watched a nurse as she stood at Hannah's bedside checking gauges and writing on his sister's chart. She looked his way.

“You’re here again?”

“Still.”

“Beg your pardon?”

“I’m here *still* not *again*,” he answered. “There’s no better place for me to be.”

“Are you her husband?” Rampart heard judgement in her voice like maybe she thought they were too young, too different or too something to be married. He didn’t like it, or her.

“I’m her brother.”

“Really?” she said as she looked him over.

“Yes. Really. Why do you sound surprised? Is it because I’m black and she isn’t?” he stared at the nurse.

“I’m not,” she started to stammer, “I didn’t—”

“Yes you are and yes you did.” Just then Dr. Christine entered the room. The nurse used his arrival to make her retreat. Both the doctor and Rampart noticed she couldn’t get out the door quickly enough.

“What was that about?” Christine asked.

“Have to ask her,” Ramp said and went back to reading. The doctor took the nurse’s place at Hannah’s side and stared at one of the monitors for a handful of seconds.

“Looks to be a healthy amount of brain activity,” he said. “More than before.”

Rampart looked up from his book. “Which means what, exactly?”

“Hard to say *exactly* but it could be a number of things. Maybe she’s dreaming. Maybe she’s waking up.”

“So that’s good, right?”

“Or it could be nothing,” the doctor added as he turned to look at Rampart. “You look awful. Are you sleeping here?”

“The increased activity is a good sign, right?” Ramp ignored the doctor’s question and asked his again.

“As far as I’m concerned it can’t be bad.”

Teri sat on her balcony with her feet on the railing, holding three fingers worth of 291 White Dog Colorado Rye Whiskey in a glass. She was bored and she knew when that happened her mind tended to drift toward thoughts of what it felt like to kill something. Or someone. She’d done it before, the killing someone thing, twice, and gotten away with it. She chased Marc Allen halfway across the country with the intention of rubbing his nose in that and getting away with it again.

Scott Ericsson had been right. She could usually hear both the train and the traffic from where she sat, but not tonight. For some reason there weren't many cars on I-25 and the train had rolled through the neighborhood hours earlier. She could hear one of the handful of homeless citizens rustling around in the brush and trees across the path just a dozen or so feet from the condo building. The activity had pissed her off for weeks and during that time she decided to do something about it. She had been formulating a plan and knew she needed Jake and his "personality flaw" as he had put it, to make it come to fruition.

She started telling him that she had been getting debilitating headaches and at first he chided her for using that as an excuse for not wanting to have sex. She convinced him that wasn't the case and asked him if maybe the altitude was the culprit. He answered by telling her that altitude sickness usually manifested itself when people first came to Colorado, not after they'd lived in the state for months. He suggested she see a doctor. She lied and said she would. A week or two later she claimed the headaches weren't improving and despite the medicine her doctor prescribed they were, in fact, getting more intense. She begged him to help her and set the hook after a particularly Jake-centric evening in bed.

"There's a lot of medical strength stuff at the ambulance service where you volunteer, right?"

"I guess."

"And I remember you said you liked to steal stuff, right?"

"Did I say that?" he asked. She rubbed his chest and kissed him lightly on the neck.

"I was reading about this drug tramadol," she said, "it's supposed to be really good for headaches."

"And you want me to see if there's any of it just laying around while I'm changing the oil in an ambulance?"

"Something like that," she kissed him again.

"That's not how it works."

"I know, it's just, I wouldn't ask if these damn headaches weren't getting worse." She rolled away and they both stared at the ceiling for a minute or two. "Never mind," she said, "me asking you to do that was selfish and stupid." She thought this was the point when she would find out just how far Jake would go for her.

"What was it called again?" he asked.

Jake had stolen the tramadol. Teri knew a few grams of it would take care of just about any headache. A much larger quantity would kill a 200-pound man. A man like the one that was making all the noise in the bushes beneath her. She had stepped up her reconnaissance of the homeless person and decided he weighed less than 200 pounds, not a lot less, but less. She also observed that he liked to sit on a metal bench close by and drink or sometimes smoke a joint. She didn't have any pot and knew buying it would create a paper trail that she couldn't afford. So, she bought both a fifth and a quart of Jack Daniels. At home, she changed into an old pair of jeans and a hoodie and took the smaller bottle down to the path. The stench of body odor hit her when she was ten feet from her target. She took a deep breath through her mouth and pressed on.

"Mind if I sit?" she asked but got no response. She sat. The man's head was lowered but she could see through the dirt and a beard that he was fairly young. Late 20's maybe mid 30's. *A shame to have wasted a life so young*, she thought. "Drink?" she asked.

"What do you want?" a gravelly voice emanated from the hairy mouth.

"Just to rest a bit," she answered. "Share a drink."

"Not thirsty," he said.

"Really?

"No," he grabbed the bottle of whiskey and took a long drink. He handed it back to Teri.

"Go ahead, finish it. I can get more."

“Now?” he asked as he sucked down the rest.

“Might take a few minutes,” she said.

“I’m not going anywhere,” he threw the bottle into the brush. *Gonna have to get that later*, Teri thought.

“I’ll see what I can do,” she said getting up.

She went back upstairs, opened the quart bottle and poured out what she figured was a slug or two. She had already ground up all of the tramadol tablets and she took the powdery substance and added it to the Tennessee whiskey. Teri swirled the Jack around in the bottle and watched the Tramadol dissolve. Then she pushed a pair of latex gloves in the back pocket of her jeans and headed back down to her new friend. He was prone on the bench, snoring lightly when she returned. She put on the gloves and shook him awake.

“I’m back,” she said.

“What took so long?” he asked even though Teri knew there was no way he could have been aware of how much time had passed.

“Takes a while to work for a quart of whiskey,” she said. He grunted in response.

“Here you go,” she pushed the bottle his way.

“You first,” he said. She thought he might say that and that was why she had already poured some of the Jack out.

“Cool,” she took the bottle and pretended to drink then gave it back to him. “Your turn.”

Two hours later he was dead drunk and well on the way to being dead dead. As quickly and quietly as she could she pulled him off the bench and rolled him across the dirt path. With both feet she pushed him down the hill and into the trees and bushes. He ended up face down which pleased Teri. *He looks like he’s sleeping one off.* Then she collected the fifth the man had tossed away earlier, smoothed the dirt where his body left tracks and jumped in her car to dispose of the bottles and gloves. Once back upstairs she peeled off her clothes and took a shower. As the hot water cascaded over her she wondered how long it would take the body to putrefy enough to make some jogger or dog on a leash notice. As science would dictate it was about two and a half days.

♪♫♪

Rampart Stands Vigil

Rampart stood and stretched. He pulled back the shade and looked out the window noticing a setting sun bidding farewell to another brilliant Colorado day. He shivered. He knew the doctors kept the room cool and the lights low because those conditions were said to be most helpful to coma patients. It was day four. Tracey and Detective Allen had stopped by. Allen had brought his dog.

"Hey Ramp," Tracey had said when the three of them came in the room. "Hope you don't mind but I brought Allen and Lettie." Rampart liked the detective but he really liked the dog. Lettie's tail clearly illustrated the attraction was mutual.

"Is she allowed in here?" he asked as he ruffled the pup's fur.

"Who's gonna stop her?" Allen replied showing off his detective shield.

"Go see Hannah, Lettie," Ramp instructed and the dog obeyed. He wandered to her bedside and sniffed. Hannah's arm rested by her side and the dog leaned in and gave it a lick. "Good girl," Rampart said.

"Need anything?" Tracey asked.

"Just her to wake up," he gestured toward his sister.
"Soon," Tracey nodded.

"Your mouth to God's ears."

"Come on Lettie," it was Allen, "time to go girl."

"Hey detective?"

"Yeah Ramp?"

"Thanks for the cactus," Rampart said with a smile.

"I thought it was a succulent?" Allen said shooting a look at Tracey, "and it was her idea."

"Hey, a cactus *is* a succulent you knucklehead," Tracey said defensively. "And it's a beautiful living thing that will last a heck of a lot longer than a bouquet of roses."

"Get out of here you guys," Rampart said and smiled, "I'll call if anything changes."

Rampart's parents had also stopped by to check on him and Hannah. They did that once a day. His dad brought him a bottle of his favorite tequila, his mom offered to relieve him for a few hours so he could go home, or see a movie, or take a walk in the park.

"It's not your fault honey," she reassured him for the hundredth time.
"I know, Mom."

He accepted the bourbon from his dad but not the offer from his mom. He did give her a key to the house so she could check on things for him and toss the things in the pantry and the fridge that had passed their expiration dates. His work had been more than accommodating telling him to take as much time as he needed. He thanked them but said he'd use his earned comp days instead. He took one last peek out the window. His stomach growled and Ramp realized he hadn't eaten lunch. He wondered what hospital cafeteria delicacy would be his dinner tonight.

"Hello?" It was Hannah. Rampart froze at the window. He wasn't sure if he'd actually heard her speak or if he was imagining it. "Hello, it's me," she spoke again. Rampart spun and stared at his sister.

"Hannah?"

"One and the same."

"My God! Thank you God! Hannah! Thank you Jesus!" Rampart cried and rushed from the room. "Nurse! Doctor Christine! Anybody! She's awake! Hannah's BACK!"

Within minutes the room was filled with nurses, doctors and Rampart. They were all business but he wore a smile from ear to ear.

"Welcome back Hannah," Dr. Christine said.
"Who are you?" she asked the doc.

"I'm Dr. Tom Christine. I'm the guy that's been looking after you. Well me, several nurses, and of course, your brother. We're all happy to have you back."

"Happy to be here," she looked at the doctor then at Rampart. "Where am I? What's going on?"

"Hospital", Ramp blurted out, "UC Health."

"How long?" she asked.

"Four days. There was an accident." Hannah just nodded.

During the next few minutes, the professionals asked her more questions and scribbled furiously on pads of paper. Then Dr. Christine took what looked like a pen from his pocket.

"Okay Hannah do me a favor and close your eyes. I'm going to poke a bit and you let me know when you feel something." She nodded again and did as she was told. A minute or two went by as the doctor touched different parts of her arms and legs with the instrument. Hannah's eyes stayed closed. She didn't say a word. Christine looked at the nurses and then at Ramp.

"Sometimes, when a patient comes out of a coma, it takes the nerves a little time to catch up with the brain." Rampart heard the words but he couldn't help but think the doctor was lying. He looked at Hannah. Her eyes were open and she was smiling.

“What?” he said to her. The doctor looked too.

“I feel it. I can. Feels just like it should.”

Allen returned to the police station after responding to an attempted robbery of a liquor store on Pikes Peak Avenue. The owner had described the assailant as a “young Hispanic kid, maybe twenty. Wearing a hoodie and jeans halfway down his butt. Scared to death. He wanted a bottle of Fireball and all the money in both registers.” Allen wrote it all down.

“What’s Fireball?” he asked.

“Are you serious?”

“As a box jellyfish,” Allen answered.

The man behind the counter chuckled at that then said, “It’s a combination of Canadian Whiskey, cinnamon flavoring, and sweeteners.”

“In one bottle?”

“Of course,” the liquor store owner answered with a shake of his head. “People say it tastes like the popular candy. You know the jawbreaker one?”

“Sounds awful,” Allen remarked.

“Don’t knock it until you’ve tried it.”

"I'll take that under advisement. So tell me what happened."

"Not much to tell. Punk kid comes in here, pulls out a gun and starts making demands."

"What did you do?" Allen asked while taking more notes.

"I pulled this out," he showed Allen a standard-looking, black 36-inch crowbar. "I told him he better hit the road or I was going to beat him over the head with it."

"But you said he had a gun."

"I did and he did, but he wasn't going to shoot me with it."

"And you knew that how?"

"I'm ex-Army, Detective. Three tours in Afghanistan, selected to the pistol shooting team twice. I know when the safety is engaged on a weapon, sir. Besides the kid was sweating and shaking like a leaf. Probably already high or involved in some dare or gang initiation. Even if he had mustered the cajones to fire he wasn't hitting anything but the shelf of airplane bottles behind me."

"Brave," Allen said, "or stupid."

"Don't consider myself either of those, sir. Fact of the matter is it wasn't the first time I've had a gun pulled on me in here and it won't be the last."

"Appreciate your time and your service," Allen said closing his notebook. "Now how about you sell me a bottle of Fireball."

"That's the spirit, Detective."

When Allen got back to the station he stopped at The Champ's van before going inside. He knocked.

"Get lost," was the familiar refrain.

"Special delivery, Champ," Allen said and the driver's door opened a couple of inches. Allen showed the bottle.

"What's that?" Holm asked.

"Fireball. It's supposed to be all the rage."

"Alcohol?"

"Says it's 66 proof. Not Everclear but I imagine it'll get the job done. Tastes like cinnamon candy I'm told."

"Thanks but no thanks," Holm said. "I don't drink."

"Really?" Allen said after having been surprised for the second time in an hour. "Since when?"

"Seven years, 142 days, 16 hours and 37 minutes," he answered, "but who's counting?"

"Well I'll be damned. Good for you Champ."

"Yeah. Good for me," he said and he closed the door.

Allen had two messages when he stopped by the watch commander's desk. One was from Tracey telling him that Hannah had come out of her coma and was going home. He felt relieved. The other message was from an old colleague at the Raleigh P.D. named Eliza Starz. That message was simple, "call me".

"Starz," she answered on the third ring.

"Officer Eliza Starz as I live and breathe. How the heck are you?"

"Not bad Allen and it's *Detective* Starz to you."

"To just me or to everybody?"
"B."

"Well I'll be damned. Congratulations Eliza. No one deserves that more than you."

"Thanks for saying so Allen. I guess they decided to give me your shield even though nobody can fill your shoes."

"So you called so I could tell you what a good cop you are?" he asked.

“Meeting of the mutual admiration society over?”

“For now. What’s going on?”

“You remember the Teri Hickox case?”

“Teri Hickox? Teri Hickox?” Allen tried to sound contemplative.

“Okay smart guy. Knock it off.”

“Of course I remember that case. Still sticks in my craw.”

“You mean you’re still not buying the old man confessing to killing two people and then blowing his own brains out? You continue to be of the opinion that he only did that so his daughter could get away with murder? Is that what sticks in your craw?”

“Pretty much nailed it there, Detective. No wonder you got that promotion. My theory at the time was she did it and it remains my theory now. If I remember correctly you thought I was trying to manufacture something that didn’t exist.”

“Yeah well, I’m not so sure anymore.”

“What changed? Pray tell.”

“Just the fact that there’s something else that isn’t there anymore.”

“What are you talking about? What’s not there anymore?”

“Teri Hickox. She appears to have flown the coop.”

Allen sat up straighter in his chair. “She’s gone?”

“Just like the Hall and Oates song, or the movie, gone like the wind. Gone as in not in Raleigh anymore. Old man Hickox left the property to her in his will and she sold it. There’s no sign of her anywhere.”

“She sold the estate?”

“Lock, stock and barrel.”

“Isn’t that interesting.”

“I thought so too so I decided to head over there and have a look around. Took the JW Fisher Pulse 8x Version 2 with me.” Allen could hear the pride in her voice.

“Don’t tell me that’s your new robot partner?”

“Something like that Allen, it’s a metal detector.”

“New owners didn’t mind?”

“Not only did they not mind, but they were also happy to see me with the unit. Some yuppie couple from New York. He’s a Wall Streeter and she called herself a ‘social influencer’ whatever that means. Said they were looking to reduce their carbon footprint and would be thrilled if I found and removed any metal from the ground."

"Left the big city and they bought a boatload of acres near the Raleigh, North Carolina city limits."

"Precisely. Anyway I fired up the Fisher—"

"Your little metal detector" Allen butted in.

"Nothing little about it, Allen. It cost the department 2500 bucks. Good thing you bolted so we could afford it."

"A man likes to know his worth. Find anything?"

"You could say that," Starz admitted. "Just a few buried coffee cans filled with cash."

"You're joking?"

"No joke. One had eleven hundred dollars in it. Eleven one hundred dollar bills. That one was a Folgers can I believe. Another one, this one was Maxwell House, had a big wad of cash held together by a purple rubber band. You know the kind you get wrapped around a bunch of asparagus spears at the Harris Teeter."

"Wouldn't know," Allen said.

“You’ve never bought asparagus at the Harris Teeter?”

“Not at the Harris Teeter, not at Publix, not at King Soopers.”

“King *Soopers*? Funny name. Is that the supermarket out there in Colorado?”

“It is but that’s not important now. Tell me more about what you found.”

“The wad with the rubber band contained thirty-seven hundred dollars. The denominations ran the gamut from tens and twenties to a five hundred dollar bill.” She heard Allen whistle through the phone. “But that’s not all.”

“What else?”

“There was a note. Had it analyzed and it turned out to be written in Hank Hickox’s own hand.”

“What did it say?”

“Thought you’d want to know. That’s why I called. Let me read it to you. Allen heard what sounded like Starz unfolding a piece of paper. Then he heard her voice. ‘Sweetheart,’” Eliza stopped. “That’s Hank talking Allen, don’t get any ideas,” she chuckled.

“Come *on*, Starz! Just read the damn note.”

"Sweetheart," she started again, "Lord knows I tried to be a good father, a good role model, but everything seemed to get so much harder after your mom left this earth. I know she wasn't your real mom and I wasn't your true dad but we always loved you like we were. Near the end Betty Lou said she was worried that there was bad blood in your genes. Some sort of evil born in you. I said that was the chemotherapy talking. Told her she was confusing her family history, her personal evil, with yours. But after what happened to that woman and Tanner Goochly I got scared too. Figured she might be right. I pray she's found peace in the afterlife and I'll do the same for you too. Sadly for me that peace is now forever lost. I Love You, Hank."

"Wow!" Allen said after a few breaths. "I *knew* it. Can you fax that over to me?"

"How about I scan it and email it to you? Like people do in the 21st century."

"If that's easier for you," he said.

"It's easier for everybody on the planet, Allen."

"Okay. Thanks."

"Look, Marc, Teri Hickox is in the wind and this note could lead one to think, like you did, that she killed two people in cold blood."

"I think that now more than ever, Starz."

"Figured you would. I'm just sayin' watch your six."

"Will do, detective."

"And if you need me, call me."

"I will Eliza. I promise. And thanks for this."

"You're welcome. Just remember we've got skin in this too."

"Copy that," Allen said, "and congrats again on the promotion. I'm proud of you."

"Well *now* my day is made," she said, "but seriously, I appreciate that."

They hung up and Allen sat there waiting for the email to come through. When it did he opened the attachment and read the note from beginning to end. Twice.

♪♫♪

Hannah Heads Home

They kept Hannah in the hospital overnight.

"Just for observation," Dr. Christine had said.

"I feel fine," Hannah argued.

"That's good but comas can be funny things. We just want to make sure you're okay."

"I wanna go home."

"I know you do and you'll be able to. Just humor me. It's for the best. Have something to eat. See if you can get up and go to the bathroom. Simple stuff. Normal stuff. Look, your brain went through a trauma. I'd like to make sure it's sending all the right signals."

"Well, alright. Okay. You win."

"Good, thanks."

"One more night," Hannah looked at him.

"That's it, I promise." He got up to leave but turned before he got to the door. "Do you need anything?" He asked.
"Pencil and paper," she answered.

Hannah did eat. She did get up to pee. And she did draw. At first the image she hoped to go from her imagination to the pencil to the paper wouldn't come. She worried whether the doctor was right, her brain wasn't a hundred percent. Then she closed her eyes and started to see what her mind wanted her to see. She'd seen it before. It was a room, much like the one she was in, and there were people lined up out the door waiting to visit with her. Familiar faces, famous faces. She started to draw.

The next morning Dr. Christine said she was good to go.

"As much as we all enjoy your company here at UC Health, I can't justify any more reasons to keep you," he told her. "Besides, we need the bed for actual sick people."

"Thank you for everything," Hannah said and she meant it.

"Pleasure," he smiled, "you take care of yourself. And if you don't mind I'd like to stay in touch."

"Bet on it."

A volunteer helped her gather the few personal belongings she had with her. At some point during the last evening Beth Haynes had brought by a change of clothes so she had those on. She placed a plastic bag, and her drawing, on her lap and the orderly wheeled her to the nurses' station. She used the phone to call Rampart.

"Come pick me up," was all she had to say.

They sat in silence most of the ride home. Rampart had given her a huge hug before she had gotten in the Jeep. They listened to the radio, Hannah stared out the window, and Ramp just smiled. He looked from the road to her then back to the road.

"Pay attention," she pointed out the windshield.

"It's just that I'm so glad to see you."

"I appreciate that."

When Rampart next glanced over he noticed the drawing. "What's that?"

"Just a dream," she said. He looked more closely.

"Carrie Underwood was in your dream?"

"She was."

"Lucky you," he said as he turned down Monument.

"Home sweet home," Hannah said and smiled. She grabbed her things and got out of the car.

"Call you later," he said as she walked away. He watched her raise her free right hand in a wave. Rampart drove home, fell into his bed fully clothed and slept like a dead guy.

As Hannah walked to her condo her mind was going a mile a minute. She played the conversation with the doctor back in her mind. Then the one with Rampart. Nothing she said either time was what she was thinking. She felt like the words carried the same meaning but they weren't the words she had intended to say. *What's happening to me*, she thought and then opened her mouth to say.
"What in the world," is what came out.

Allen walked to the break room to grab a cup of coffee. He was still processing the news from Eliza Starz. On one hand he felt vindicated, he had never stopped believing that Teri Hickox, and not her father Hank, was a murderer. But he also felt deflated. He couldn't shake the thought that he hadn't worked the case hard enough or well enough. And now Teri could be anywhere. He returned back to his desk but he wouldn't be there long. There was a dead body in Monument Park. Allen arrived at the scene and was greeted by Officer Stupples.

"Oh good, it's you," he said.

"What's that supposed to mean?"

"Don't get defensive Stupples. I meant it. It's a compliment. Where's Foltz?"

"Oh. Got it. Thanks. He's down there," she pointed over the edge of the hill, "securing the scene."

“What do we know so far?”

“One body. White male, looks to be early thirties, clearly homeless.”

“You mean unhoused.”

“What?”

“Unhoused, not homeless. Haven’t you been paying attention to our new liberal Governor? He wants everyone to say ‘unhoused’ instead of ‘homeless.’ Thinks it better humanizes our less fortunate.”

“That’s a bunch of crap,” she said defiantly, “I said homeless and I meant homeless. Not *unhoused.*” She put her hands on her hips. “Most of these folks *could* use the city shelters if they wanted to, there’s plenty of room.”

“But they don’t?”

“No, they don’t and they don’t because the shelters have rules like no pets, no grocery store shopping carts full of belongings.”

“Or no weed, booze, hard drugs or needles, I imagine?” Allen added.

"You *imagine* correctly," she agreed. "So they're not unhoused, they just choose not to take advantage of them. They're homeless."

"Take it up with Denver," Allen proposed.

"That's a hard pass."

Allen took a couple of steps toward the edge when a gust of wind hit him in the face, so did the stench from below.

"Jesus, that stinks."

"Dead bodies tend to do that," Stupples said with a laugh.

"Thanks for the heads up. I'll keep that in mind," Allen laughed too.

"A female jogger must have caught a whiff too because she decided to make the call to 9-1-1."

"That was only a matter of time," Allen said as he pulled a bandana from his back pocket and started covering his mouth and nose.

"Always carry one of those?"

"In the car. Usually put it in my pocket when I hear 'dead body.'"

"Smart," Stupples nodded. Just then her partner, Foltz, climbed up the hill.

"That was gross," he said then looked at Allen. "Nice bandana."

"Thanks. What's down there?"

"Some trash, bottles mostly, a few articles of clothing, several fast food wrappers, a couple of magazines. Oh, and a dead guy."

"How dead?" Allen asked.

"All the way dead, detective. I'd say he's been stewing in his juices maybe as long as 48 hours. Sarcophagi and some kind of scavenger already did some damage."
Allen knew Sarcophagi was the scientific term for a blowfly. Loosely translated it meant "corpse eater." Blowflies show up within minutes of death and one female can lay as many as 300 eggs. He was also aware that those eggs turn into maggots in anywhere from eight to twenty hours.

"Guess I need to take a look," Allen said unenthusiastically.

"Be my guest," Foltz said and he waved his arm like a maître d' showing a dinner guest to a table. "Like I said, the crime scene is a bit of a disaster."

"Do we know for a fact there's been a crime? Not just an accident or a suicide?"

"Don't know that yet," Foltz said.

"He always likes to assume the worst," his partner added.

"Probably not the worst way to approach the job," Allen said.

"My sentiments exactly, detective," agreed Officer Foltz.

Teri watched the scene below. She was happy to see the cops arrive and even happier when Marc Allen joined them but that didn't last long. Allen spoke with the female officer, then her partner appeared from the trees and the bushes. He spoke to the detective too. Allen then put on a pair of latex gloves and went over the side. She was disappointed that there was no urgency to any of their movements. It looked to her like business as usual, just another dead homeless person. Unlike the excitement she felt after pulling the trigger and sending bullets into Daisy Burns and Tanner Goochly, this time she was deflated. Sure, she had killed somebody again but she realized there was no danger in it. She was disappointed and angry. Disappointed because the death didn't cause more of a commotion and angry because she had missed an opportunity. She told herself that she wouldn't let that happen again.

An ambulance pulled up on the dirt path and she absentmindedly wondered if it was one that Jake had worked on. She watched as they carried the bagged body over the hill, loaded it onto a stretcher, put it in the back of the emergency vehicle and drove away. No siren, no flashing red lights. Just tires, kicking up a little dust, crunching on dirt and rocks. She tried to picture the homeless man she had murdered but couldn't. The only thing she could recall was his filthy beard. Then she went inside.

Allen pulled off his gloves and bandana and watched the ambulance drive away. He'd check with the coroner later but he suspected the cause of death would be an accident or an overdose. As Foltz had said there were plenty of empty liquor bottles around what appeared to be the man's encampment. Mostly whiskey, some vodka and they made Allen think of the bottle of Fireball he tried to give to Larry Holm. *There but for the grace of God*, he thought. Allen had also found a well-worn wallet with a VA card, a nude picture of Pamela Anderson and a Colorado Suicide Prevention Hotline card with an 800 number in big bold type. The name on the Veterans Administration card told Allen the dead guy's name was Daniel James Bowen and the picture was of him from better days. He wondered if Mr. Bowen had called the 800 number before.

Next the detective looked up at the condo building fronting the scene. He noticed large sculptures visible through windows in what he assumed were common areas. The building was about four football fields from his own but this one was newer, fancier. He realized it was the building where Hannah Hunt lived. He had walked by countless times with Lettie, he just hadn't stopped and given it a good look from this angle before. He guessed there were anywhere between 24 and 36 units, 6 or 8 on each of the 4 floors. If there had been suspicious circumstances around Daniel Bowen's death maybe somebody in one of the units saw or heard something. He decided to estimate high and went with 32 then immediately ignored 16 of them. They were east facing, away from the scene. He didn't discount them out of hand, just put them on the back burner for now, maybe forever. That left 16 more. All faced west with a view of any potential crime. 16 doors on which to knock.

Hannah sat on her couch, oblivious to the goings on at the other side of the building. Her unit faced east. That fact had saved her thousands of dollars on the purchase price and she was thrilled because she actually preferred the unit's location. Since her parents' death she hated traffic noise and facing east muffled the sound of the cars and trucks on the Interstate. She gave up the view of the park and Pikes Peak but her place did overlook a courtyard which she enjoyed. She wasn't thinking about the view at the moment. She was wondering what was going on inside her head. Hannah was coming up with things to say and then saying them. She had been playing the game for hours.

That's silly, she thought.
"Only a fool would say that," came out of her mouth.

I have to do something, her brain suggested.
"What can I do?" her voice said.
What's my next move? was the thought.

"What happens now?" were the words.

I'll get through this, thought.
"I will survive," words.

I can't stand this, she thought.
"It sucks," she said.
Are these all songs?
"Everything is a song. Everything is a song," she sang.

I need a drink she was thinking.
"I need a drink."

Rampart thought Hannah had acted a bit strange when he had given her a lift home from the hospital but he decided he couldn't blame her. She'd been in a coma for more than 72 hours. He was no medical expert but he had been around a few thanks to his USA Boxing experience. He remembered all of them saying, at one time or another, the most important thing he could protect was his head. Traumatic Brain Injury was the "real deal" they said and it was scary. He had read that humans only used about ten percent of their brain's capacity. He didn't know if that was true but he did know it was an incredibly complex organ and he should cut his sister some slack because hers had been in distress. But still some of her comments seemed particularly strange. He got an idea so he called Tracey.

"Hey Ramp."

"Hi Tracey. How's it going?"

"Good. Oh and great news about Hannah. I'm so relieved."

"I know. Me too."
"She's going to be okay, right?"

"Dr. Christine thinks so. He says nothing is a hundred percent certain but all the tests and all the indicators point toward normal brain activity."

"Normal normal? Or normal for Hannah?"

"Good point," he chuckled. "Hey, I called because I thought we could all get together in a bit to celebrate."

"Great idea. Can I invite Marc?"

"If, by Marc, you mean Detective Allen, sure. The more the merrier."

"Cool."

"See you soon."

♪♫♪

Song Girl Goes Public

Hannah decided the best place to have that drink was the bar at the Rabbit Hole so that's where she went. Dirk wasn't working and a bartender she didn't know was.

"Bartender," she said sitting down.

"Customer," the bartender said with a smile. "Day drinking?" she asked.

"Does anybody really know what time it is?" Hannah said. *This is kinda fun* she thought.

"Does anybody really care?" the bartender added.

"It's five o'clock somewhere."

"What can I get you?"

"One bourbon, one scotch, one beer."

"You having a record year?"

"You have no idea."

"I'll get your drinks, George Thorogood. By the way you're a riot." Hannah's phone rang; she saw it was Ramp.

“Hi there.” Rampart heard the background noise. “You in a bar?”

“You may be right. Everybody’s drinkin’.”

“Are you at the Rabbit Hole or in a Billy Joel song?” he asked.

“Both.”

“Go slow, we’ll meet you there soon.”

“I’m not going anywhere,” She said and hung up.

“What the heck was that?” Rampart said to his phone. Then he called Tracey back.

“We need to rally the troops,” he said after she had answered.

“Why? What’s up?”

“Hannah’s already at the Rabbit Hole,” he answered and hung up.

In short order Rampart and Tracey made it to the bar, greeted Hannah and ordered drinks. Allen arrived a few minutes after that.

“What’s your pleasure?” the bartender asked him as he sidled up next to Rampart.

"What's everybody else having?"

"Beer," she pointed at Ramp. "Ketel One Cosmo," Tracey was next. "And song girl there is all over the map." Allen looked at Hannah.

"Song girl?" he said. She just shrugged her shoulders so he turned back to the bartender. "I'll have a Mad Hatter," he indicated, asking for the establishment's signature Manhattan.

"My fav," she said, walking away. A minute later she was back and setting a glass in front of him. Allen picked it up.

"To Hannah," he said, "glad you're back among the living."

"Salute," Rampart said, lifting his beer.

"Kampai," Tracey added.

"Let's have a party!" called Hannah. They all clinked glasses. They shared some laughs and then some appetizers and about an hour in Hannah had had enough.

"I'm outta here," she said, standing up.

"So soon?" Tracey asked.

"No time like the present."

"I'll give you a lift," Rampart offered.

“Don’t be silly,” she declined, “I’m walkin’.”

“You sure?”

“I’m positive.”

“See ya Hannah,” Tracey said.

“Take it easy, young lady,” Allen added.

“I’ll call you later,” her brother told her as she started to walk away.

“I’ll be around,” Hannah sang as she headed up the stairs.

“Okay does anybody else think that was incredibly weird?” Rampart asked after Hannah had gone.

“What?” Tracey wondered.

“Hannah, that’s what. The way she talked, the way she acted, what she said. All of it. It was weird.”

“Well Ramp she did just come out of a coma,” Allen argued.

“I realize that and I said that to myself but something is going on.”

“Like what?” Tracey asked.

"You're going to think I'm crazy but she's talking in *song titles*! Didn't you notice?"

"I did," it was the bartender.

"You two are imagining things," Allen countered.

"Am I? Are we?" He pointed at the bartender. "She called her song girl. And when I spoke with Hannah on the phone earlier, she was here. She said, and I quote, 'You may be right.' And then she said—"

"End quote," the bartender said.

"Excuse me?" Ramp asked.

"You didn't say end quote after 'right.' You said 'and I quote' but you didn't ever say end quote."

"Seriously?"

"And you *were* right, she *was* here." Tracey chimed in.

"Just stop!" Rampart raised his voice. "When she left she sang 'I'll be around.' That's an old Spinners song!"

"Ooh, I love that song," Tracey smiled. "Joan Osborne sang it too."

"So did Hall and Oates, I think," the bartender added.

"You people are *impossible*!" Rampart threw up his hands.

"I'll have one more Mad Hatter," Allen told the woman behind the bar.

♪♫♪

Teri Buys a Car

Jake Holler pressed the button to get Teri's attention. She looked up at the monitor in her kitchen and saw him standing in the building lobby.

"Who is it?" she asked anyway.

"It's me, Jake. I told you I was coming over." She buzzed him up.

"Door's unlocked," she said into the microphone.

Jake rode the elevator to the top floor and opened the door to her unit. Once inside he saw Teri in the kitchen, standing near the refrigerator.

"Have you met the older woman who lives on the third floor?" He asked, closing the door behind him.

"The busybody that lives right below me?" Teri shot back.

"Is that where she lives? So you met her?"

"Met would be a bit of a stretch," Teri answered, "more like crossed paths in the garage a couple of times. Why?"

“I think she just hit on me in the elevator.” Teri laughed out loud. “Hey!” Jake said, “Don’t act so surprised.” Teri looked at him and saw that she had bruised his ego.

“It’s not that Jake. You’re a doll. It’s just she’s old enough to be your mother.”

“I know,” he admitted and smiled at her. His eyes went to the large island in the room where he saw a large, padded envelope with bundles of hundred dollar bills spilling from it.

“What’s that?” Teri looked.

“Money.”

“I can see that. Where did it come from?”

“Not sure it’s any of your business,” she said and remembered hurting his feelings just moments before. “An old law school buddy named Jimmy sent it to me.”

“An old friend just sent you a bag of money? What kind of lawyer is he?”

“Not a great one it turned out. He quit, moved to Las Vegas and became a professional gambler.”

“No kidding? Is he better at that?”

"Much. I send him some money around the first of every month and thirty days later he sends me back more. Most months."

"Do you want to make love?" Jake switched gears.

"Sure. As long as you promise to think of me and not the old bitty in the unit below us." She smiled.

"Are you trying to make me change my mind?" he smiled back.

"Not even a little."

"Can we do it on the money?"

"No."

Half an hour later they were still in her bed.

"Is that the reason you wanted to come over?" she asked.

"Not explicitly but I'd be lying if I said it wasn't always on my mind," he smiled when he answered. "The real reason was I just wanted to see you *and* the sign at the animal clinic needs changing. I wanted to run a few ideas by you."

"You could have done that over the phone."

"Kind of negates the whole wanted to see you part."

“True. Okay shoot.” Jake sat up.

“First one is, did you hear about the fire at the circus? It was in tents. Get it? *In tents,* intense.”

“Got it. It’s not bad,” Teri said as she sat up too. “Next.”

“Don’t spell part backwards. It’s a trap.”

“Good one,” she smiled at him, “anymore?”

“A couple,” he answered, “I’m reading a great book about anti-gravity. I can’t put it down.”

“Nah,” She shook her head, “too esoteric.”

“Agree,” Jake nodded. “Okay, last one. Why did the barber win the race?” He looked at Teri and she looked at him. “He knew a shortcut.”

“That’s pretty good too, “she said, “but I think I like number 2.”

“Then number 2 it is. Thanks.”

“Now get dressed,” she said rolling out of the bed and heading to the bathroom.

“Why? Are we going somewhere?”

"I'm going to pee and then we're going to Pueblo to buy a car."

"You have a car, a really nice one. And why all the way to Pueblo?" he called.

"If you don't stop asking questions, I'm going to tie you up and leave you on the busybody's doorstep," she shouted back. "Now, get dressed and put a few bundles of those bills on the island in a bag. Oh, and make sure you have your keys, you're driving."

Allen was heading back to the police station after grabbing lunch. There was a place on Nevada called The Bench, walking distance and good. Near it was the coffee shop that The Champ had said was good too so after a salad he treated himself to an iced vanilla latte for the stroll. It had been a slow couple of days but he knew from experience that things rarely stayed slow for long. As he walked east on Rio Grande he saw something that made him stop mid step and mid sip. Larry Holm was standing near the entrance to the cop shop. Allen was certain he was talking to Officer Selena Nobilo. He watched for several seconds. The exchange seemed pleasant, like the two knew each other, then Allen saw Nobilo hand Holm what appeared to be a letter sized envelope. The Champ slapped it on his thigh, nodded his head as if in thanks, and turned and walked away. Allen presumed he was headed back to his van. The detective picked up his pace and went inside. Nobilo was at the desk.

“Detective,” she said looking up.

“Officer,” he returned the greeting. “You got a minute?”

“Not really supposed to leave the desk,” she said.

“Just saw you outside with The Champ.”

“And?”

“You left the desk for that.”

“I did,” she admitted. “I was just giving the man his mail. He doesn’t like to come inside the building.”

“His mail? I thought the sign outside said P.D not P.O.”

“Don’t be such a hard ass, detective,” she admonished. “once a month he gets a letter. He either comes by to pick it up or somebody from here takes it over to him. Today it was the former.”

“The letter comes here? Why?”

“You’ll have to ask him that. I just know one does, every month, addressed to The Champ at 705 South Nevada.”

“For how long?”

"As long as I've been here." Allen pondered that for a moment. "Anything else, detective?" she asked.

"Maybe one thing."

"And what might that be?"

"Your relationship with Deputy Chief Paulson."

"My *relationship*?"

"From the outside looking in it seems to be more than professional," he stopped and thought about the words to use next. "I'm just saying it *could* look *unprofessional* to some."

"Is that how it looks to you?"

"Look, just be careful. From everything I've seen you're a good cop. Don't put your career in jeopardy by getting too close to the deputy chief."

"Is that your advice, detective?"

"It is, Nobilo." Allen could see by the look on her face that he was in a hole. He decided to stop digging. "You can take it or leave it," he ended.

"I appreciate the option," she said as he walked by.

He'd been at his desk about five minutes when his phone rang.

"Allen," he said without looking at the caller ID.

"You busy, detective?" He recognized the voice of Deputy Chief Paulson's gate keeper Jenny Mills.

"Not particularly, Jenny." *Oh boy*, he thought.

"Then why don't you *get* busy and head upstairs? The DC would like to see you."

"On my way," he said and hung up the phone. "That didn't take long," he said, grabbing his jacket from the back of his chair.

"Go right in," Jenny said without looking up when Allen arrived, "he's waiting for you."

Allen tried to parse the words 'waiting for' as opposed to 'expecting.' He thought it sounded more ominous. He went in. The office looked like it did the last time Allen had visited. The painting on the wall, conference table, dog next to the desk. But the desk was different. Gone was the handsome, ornate piece that had graced the room in the past. It had been replaced by what appeared to Allen to be a folding, plastic picnic table. The kind Allen remembered sitting at as a kid during family gatherings. Paulson was sitting behind it staring at his detective.

"It's temporary," he said. The words seemed to shake Allen from his trance.

"Sir?"

"The desk. It's temporary. My wife sold the other one right out from under me. Darndest thing." He shook his head, "anyway, the new one won't be here until next week. Come on over, have a seat."

"Hey Peyton," Allen said to the dog as he accepted the offer.

"You remember Detective Allen, don't you Sweetness?" Paulson addressed the dog. She wagged her tail. He turned his attention back to Allen, "Nice work on the Harvey incident."

Allen knew he was referring to a recent "shots fired" call to service. A man named Jason Harvey had come home from work early to find his wife with another man. He grabbed the gun he kept in a bedside table and fired three rounds into the wall above his wife's head. Somehow she had caught some shrapnel in her foot. Neighbors called the police who arrived to find Harvey holding the two at gunpoint. The standoff lasted about an hour as he threatened, at alternate times, to kill his wife, her lover, and them both. Allen was the detective in charge and managed to talk Harvey down and gain control of the situation without further harm.

"All in a day's work, sir. But thanks." He acknowledged the compliment.

"Is harassing an officer all in a day's work too, detective?" The question caught Allen off guard.

“Sir?”

“I’m talking about Officer Nobilo. Were you just sticking your nose someplace it didn’t belong?” He looked at Allen. “Think hard about what you’re going to say next.” Allen did.

“Deputy Chief I was in no way harassing her, I was just trying to be a good colleague. No harm intended.” Paulson leaned back in his big leather chair. It had apparently survived the sale. The juxtaposition between the chair and the desk almost made Allen laugh out loud. The deputy chief steepled his fingers in front of his face.

“Fair enough, detective.” Allen let out a sigh of relief, which he hoped hadn’t been too noticeable. “I like you Allen, think you’re damn good and because of that I’m going to let you in on something very few people know about.”

“Not necessary sir. I’m certain it’s none of my business and I do appreciate the kind words.”

“Be that as it may I’m going to tell you anyway.”

“Your call DC.”

“Selena Nobilo is also a good cop,” he started and Allen braced himself for what he thought was coming next, “and she’s my daughter.” *That* he did not expect.

“I’m sorry, what?”

"Officer Selena Nobilo is my daughter," he repeated.

"I don't mean to seem nosy sir and it really *is* none of my business but I don't recall ever seeing her wear a wedding ring and she seems awfully young to be married."

"Now that's first-class detective work," he answered with a laugh.

"Pretty lame, I admit."

"Not all that lame. Actually those are decent observations. She is young and she is *not* married. And Selena isn't her real first name."

"Now you've got me really confused sir," Allen shook his head. "Again, none of my business but you nor anyone else has ever mentioned you being married to somebody other than Heather."

"Haven't been."

"Then I've gone from confused to baffled."

"Understandable so let me clear it up for you."

"I'd appreciate that."

"You're focused on the last name."

“I was.”

“Remember the story of how I got my nickname?”

“Of course.”

“Well we just continued the golf theme with Dylan.”

“Dylan?”

“I mentioned Selena wasn’t her real first name.”

“You did.”

“Officer Selena Nobilo’s real name is Dylan Paulson.” Allen could feel his mouth drop slightly open. He closed it. “She wanted to follow in the old man’s footsteps and Heather and I were all for it but we thought being the daughter of someone of higher rank in the department might be a minus rather than a plus.”

“Makes a certain amount of sense, I guess,” Allen nodded.

“You familiar with the golfer Frank Nobilo?” Allen nodded. “He was one of my favorite players. I liked him when he was on the tour and later on TV. So we ran with it.”

“And nobody knew?”

"Of course *some* people knew, detective. We're not stupid. Some people *had* to know so we told them but they had to be the right people. And now for better or worse you are on that list."

"Copy that."

"Now get back to work."

"Yes sir," Allen rose to leave.

"And detective?" Allen turned.

"Sir?"

"Now that you know, don't you dare treat Officer Nobilo *any* differently. She *is* a good cop but she'll only get better with help from you and others."

"10-4."

He stopped at Nobilo's desk on the way to his own.

"Thanks for getting me sent to the principal's office, Dylan," he said softly.

"Just trying to protect my turf."

"Understood."

“No hard feelings?” she asked.

“Zero. Now tell me more about that envelope you gave to The Champ.”

“What else do you want to know?”

“Anything else you remember. That is if you remember anything else.”

“Of course I do. I want to be just like you when you grow up.” She smiled.

“You mean when *you* grow up,” he corrected her.

“No, I *mean* what I *said*.”

“Funny,” Allen smirked. “Aim a little higher, officer.”

“Detective, can we make a deal?”

“Depends. What sort of deal?”

“No more unsolicited advice, okay?” Allen thought about it.

“I can make that deal, officer. Now tell me about the envelope.”

“Standard letter size, white, addressed to ‘The Champ.’ Always thought that was kind of weird.”

"No name?" he asked. Nobilo nodded. "That is strange. Was there a return address?" Nobilo took a second to respond.

"One name. Byrd," she answered, "somewhere in Maryland. Rockland or Rockville I believe."

"Good, great. What else?"

"What do you mean?"

"Contents?"

"I didn't ask, he didn't tell. Not my business." Allen nodded. "But if you're asking me to speculate."

"I am."

"Then I'd say it felt like money."

"Money? Why do you say that?"

"When I turned ten my Gogga started sending me cash for my birthday. A hundred dollars, five twenty dollar bills."

"Your *Gogga?"*

"My Grandmother. We called her Gogga, family tradition."

"Cute," he remarked. "And it felt like that?" he asked turning his attention back to the envelope.

"It felt like that."

Jake and Teri looked at cars sitting on three different dealer lots before she found what she was looking for. A 1993 Ford Taurus and it was right under the sign for **Mort and Skinny Used Cars**. They pulled into the lot and were immediately greeted by a gregarious man in a short-sleeved shirt and too long pants.

"You Mort or Skinny?" Teri asked.

"Neither," the man said, "I'm Nate."

"Nathaniel or Nathan?"

"Neither," he said again, "I'm just Nate."

"Okay then just Nate," Teri said with a smile, "I'm just Teri and I'm interested in that Ford Taurus," she pointed at the car under the sign. Nate followed her finger.

"The blue one?" She continued to point as she pulled the salesman to her side.

"Do you see another Ford Taurus in the direction of my finger?" she asked.

"No ma'am," he said. "She's a beauty. Do you want to take her for a spin?"

"My friend Jake here does," Teri said. "He's a mechanic and I'll let him determine whether she's a beauty or not."

"I'll go get the keys and a dealer plate," Nate said as he hustled off toward the office.

"Take the car and put it through some paces," she said to Jake. "It doesn't have to be perfect, just smooth. And quiet. Quiet is really important." Jake nodded. "I'm planning to give Nate 11 one hundred dollar bills for it and I want to make sure it's worth it." Jake looked at the sticker on the windshield that indicated Mort and Skinny Used Cars thought this particular Taurus was worth $1,400.

"Okay Jake," Nate said returning, "let's go." He jangled the keys.

"Just Jake, not you Nate." Teri said.

"No can do ma'am," Nate shook his head, "law says I gotta go too." Teri pulled a wad of bills from the bag she was holding.

"I have a whole bunch of reasons why that's not going to happen. Besides," she smiled at Nate, "I'll stay right here as collateral."

"But I could lose my job," Nate protested.

“We both know that’s not going to happen either,” Teri countered. Then she took the keys out of Nate’s hand and tossed them to Jake.

He was gone for about 15 minutes and during every single one of them salesman Nate looked at Teri like he knew Jake was never coming back. At one point she asked Nate where the restroom was and he hesitated.

“Look *just Nate,* I have to use the ladies’ room. Do you want to show me where it is or do you want me to squat and pee right here on the showroom floor?”

Nate showed her the way. She chuckled the entire time she did her business and half expected Nate to knock on the door every ten seconds to check on her. He didn’t but when she left the restroom he was standing right outside the door. Exactly where he was when she went in. Then Jake came back.

“She’s perfectly serviceable,” he said tossing the keys back to Nate who caught them with one hand.

“But not exactly a beauty?” Teri asked.

“Not exactly,” he said to Teri, “but she’s quiet.”

“I’ll give you a thousand bucks for it,” Teri addressed the salesman.

"Sticker says fourteen hundred," Nate answered, "and I couldn't possibly let her go for less than twelve."

"Nice try Nate," Teri said as she started peeling hundreds from a wad. "Here's eleven hundred. We got a deal?"

"Deal," Nate said without a second thought. He took the cash. "Follow me back inside and we'll fill out the paperwork." He led the way.

"You know he's going to put a hundred bucks in his pocket and tell either Mort or Skinny that he sold the Taurus for a grand," Jake told Teri.

"That's exactly what I would do," she said reaching into her back pocket for her ID. Teri had grabbed her least favorite, the one that she would cut up into little pieces after the salesman took down its information. The license identified her as Teri Haroney and she liked it least because she no longer thought the nickname "Big Nose Kate" was funny. Then she and Jake followed the salesman toward the office.

♪♫♪

Making Discoveries

Allen went back to his desk with the information Nobilo had provided. As he sat he realized he hadn't asked her if the name on the return address was Byrd with a "y" or Bird with an "i." *I guess it could also be Burd with a "u,"* he thought but dismissed it and concentrated on the "y" and the "i" versions. He decided not to go back to Nobilo to find out and fired up his computer. He first punched the name B-y-r-d into a database then he replaced the "y" with an "i". He found more than a hundred thousand people across the country who spelled the name the first way and about thirty thousand who spelled it the other way. He suddenly remembered a kid in high school, Johnny Byrd, who was the star of the golf team. He took that as an omen so he started there.

A more refined search showed him the state of Maryland had more than a thousand Byrds while closer to home in the Colorado Springs area he found a few hundred. That's where he decided to begin his search. He made calls and went through the A's and B's with no luck so he started on the C's. As he got ready to dial another number a call came in for him instead. He circled the next name on his list, a Constance in Manitou Springs, and answered his ringing phone.

"Marc Allen."

"Detective, this is Paige Tomson. I'm one of two forensic toxicologists with the El Paso County Coroner's Office."

“Hello Paige. What can I do for you?”

“I hope I’m able to do something for you, detective. I’m calling because I have some information on your deceased, unhoused, victim Daniel Bowen.” Allen scribbled the word ‘unhoused’ on his pad and noted the coroner’s office had gotten the memo from Denver.

“That was fast,” he said because he knew it could take as long as a month to get a tox report back.

“I found this case very interesting.”

“Why would that be?”

“Do you know how many autopsies our office performed last year?”

“I do not.”

“More than a thousand and we’re on track to surpass that this year.”

“Okay.”

“Do you know how many of those deaths were drug related?”

“Again my answer would be no. Are we playing twenty questions Ms. Tomson?”

"133, to be exact," she said ignoring him. "78 of those involved opioids and four of *those* were attributed to the prescription drug tramadol."

"Okay." He said with the various numbers and reasons swimming in his head. "Are we getting around to the purpose of your call?"

"We are. Do you know how many unhoused person deaths we documented?"

"That would be another no."

"61 last year, detective. And your Daniel Bowen was our 58th this year."

"That certainly is a sad state of affairs."

"Yes, it is. Now, of the 61 last year and the 58 so far this year, drug intoxication was listed as the COD for 36." Allen knew COD was short for "cause of death."

"I'm guessing there's more info coming."

"You're guessing correctly. As I said we documented 36 drug overdoses as the COD for this subset of subjects."

"Subset of subjects meaning homeless people like my Daniel Bowen," Allen interjected.

"Yes, like him. Now, of those 36, 20 were pure methamphetamine, five were due to heroin, five more a combination of meth and heroin, three were meth and fentanyl and two were meth and cocaine."

Allen did the math in his head, "By my count that's 35 deaths Paige."

"That's correct. Very good, detective."

"So what about number 36?"

"Number 36 is your Daniel James Bowen and the drug responsible for his death was Tramadol."

"He's the *only* one?"

"That's right and he had enough of it in him, mixed with alcohol, to kill him at least three times over."

"And that's the reason you took a special interest in this case?"

"Detective Allen I've been doing this for a decade, six of those years here in El Paso County, and Daniel James Bowen is the first unhoused person I've ever seen or heard of to die from an overdose of Tramadol."

"Are you saying this is a homicide?"

"Not yet. Right now we've listed this death as undetermined."
"What exactly does that mean?"

"It means there may not be a determined cause or there may be *several* possible manners of death."

"How in the world would Daniel Bowen have gotten a hold of enough tramadol to kill him?"

"That, detective, is an excellent question and, my guess is, your job to find out."

Rampart couldn't get the thoughts about Hannah out of his mind. He had tried to remember everything she had said since "waking up" in the hospital bed. He couldn't recall all of it but what he did, he wrote down on a yellow legal pad. Then he googled each statement. He wasn't surprised to find every phrase was also the title of a song. He decided to put his theory to the test so he grabbed his phone and called her.

"Brother of mine," she said. He wrote.

"Hi Hannah, how are you doing?"

"Couldn't be better."

"Glad to hear it."

"You don't have to call me," she said.

“I want to,” he interrupted.

“Every day,” she continued. “Where are you?”

“At work, wrapping up. You?”

“Sitting in the sun.”

“You sure everything’s okay? Nothing weird going on?” he decided to press the issue.

“Everything’s coming up roses.”

“Okay, that’s it. Enough!” he raised his voice. “What the hell is going on?”

“I don’t want to talk about it.”

“Well that’s too darn bad. You have to realize everything that comes out of your mouth is a song.”

“Tell me you’re joking,” she said.

“I’m not. You know I’m not,” he yelled into the phone. “I’m dead serious. Just listen to yourself. It all started when you came out of the coma.” Hannah didn’t respond and Ramp wondered if she had hung up on him. “Hannah? You still there?”

"I'm still here," she finally answered. "I'm sorry I raised my voice, it's just," he stopped then started. "I'm worried about you."

"I know. Thank you for being a friend."

"Oh my God, Hannah!" he yelled again but this time she really had hung up.

Allen gave the tramadol mystery a little more thought. He scribbled on his pad, *Military? Nurse or other healthcare provider? Friend?* He made a mental note to circle back. Then he picked up his phone and started again on the list of Byrds. He remembered the next one was Constance Byrd in Manitou Springs. He punched in the numbers.

"Hello?" a woman's voice said. Allen heard a commotion in the background, some kids yelling, a dog barking. "Guys!" the voice said, "guys! Please take that outside, Mommy's on the phone. Hello?" she said into the phone again.

"Is this Constance Byrd?" Allen asked.

"It's Connie. My gosh I haven't been called Constance since my mother was angry with me when I was about 7 years old."
"Okay. Sorry. Hi, this is Detective Marc Allen of the Colorado Springs Police Department. Did I catch you at a good time?"

"That depends, Detective Allen."

"On what?"

"On whether or not someone I know is in trouble. Or are you just calling to ask me to contribute to the policemen's benevolent fund?" Allen decided he liked Connie Byrd.

"Neither ma'am and quite frankly I'm not even sure there is a policemen's benevolent fund."

"So then to what do I owe the pleasure of this phone call?"

"Are you, by chance, related to a Byrd family in the Rockland or Rockville, Maryland area?" He expected to hear the answer he had gotten from his previous calls. He didn't get it.

"So, this *might be* about somebody I know being in trouble." She said. Allen perked up, clicked his pen, and wrote Connie Byrd's name at the top of a fresh sheet of paper.

"Not necessarily ma'am."

"Please call me Connie, detective," she interjected.

"Alright. Sure. Connie do you know or are you related to anyone named Byrd in Maryland?"

"My Mam Mam and Grandpop live in Rockville," she said. "As far as I know there is no Rockland, Maryland. Are they okay?"

"I have no way of knowing," Allen said honestly.
"Again, then what's this about?"

"Honestly I'm not really sure yet Connie. I'm just trying to tie up a few loose ends," Allen stretched the truth.

"Loose ends that involve my grandparents?"

"Do you have any other relatives here in the Colorado Springs area?"

"All of us," she blurted out. "My brother Tripp, that's Stan the third. Tripp is short for triple," she clarified and continued, "and my mom and dad, Stan and Ginger. I'll ask one more time, what exactly is this about detective?"

"It's probably nothing," Allen said, "but it also might help me find the answers to a mystery I'm trying to solve. I promise it isn't anything more than that."

"Umm. Okay. My guess is that will have to do."

"For now at least, Connie. Now would you mind giving me the phone numbers for your brother and your parents? Or, if you're not comfortable with that I can just find them the way I found you."

"I'm happy to save you that trouble, detective, but Tripp's number isn't going to do you any good."

“Why is that?” for a second Allen feared the worst.

“He’s deployed. Somewhere in the Middle East I think,” she answered.

Army?”

“Delta Force. Tip of the spear,” Connie Byrd said. Allen could hear the pride in her voice.

“I appreciate his service and I hope he’s okay.”

“I pray for that every day,” she paused. Allen waited. “Anyway, here’s Mom and Dad’s number, you got a pen?”

“I do,” he said and he wrote down the digits. “Thank you.”

“You’re very welcome.”

“And Connie?”

“Yes?”

“One more thing if I may?”
“Of course.”

“Does your mom or dad have any siblings?”

“Mom has a sister, Gail. She lives in Connecticut out by where they make the submarines.”

"Groton," Allen thought out loud.

"Yep. That's it."

"And your dad?"

"He had a brother, my uncle Reg. But I've only seen pictures and heard stories about him."

"You said 'had.' I'm sorry to pry but is he deceased?"

"No idea. Dad never said."

"I can't thank you enough, Connie, you've been extremely helpful."

"Glad to be of service and I hope you solve your mystery."

I'm closer than I was ten minutes ago, Allen thought as he disconnected the call.

♪♫♪

Stalking Prey

Teri spent several weeks watching the guy in the orange van. She decided he was about 6 feet tall and probably weighed around 200 pounds. Both things would be important. He was older, probably in his 60s and seemed to wear the same clothes a lot. He also appeared to get a lot of visitors from the cop shop across the street and none more frequent than detective Marc Allen. Teri noticed Allen looked good, fit. Clearly the mountain air agreed with him. She wondered what his connection to the "van man" was. She came to the conclusion that it didn't matter. What did matter was that she felt Allen would react differently when something happened to *this* particular homeless person. She followed van man a few times at night when he left his vehicle to go down to the creek and do his business and she started to formulate her plan.

She had already purchased the Taurus. That was step one. Next, she bought a Daninject IM tranquilizer rifle along with a handful of S150 syringe darts and injection needles. She completed the outfit with a Sightron night vision scope because she knew she'd be hunting in the dark. After that she reached out to an old family friend in North Carolina. Dr. Charles Whitfield. He was a friend of Hank's and the veterinarian that tended to the family cows and sheep when the family cows and sheep needed tending to. After he told her how sorry he was about Hank she told him about her new life in Colorado that included a "coyote problem". A problem she estimated that 50 or 100 milligrams of the tranquilizer Rompun would fix. He said he'd get it right out to her and told her again how much he liked both Hank and her mother, Betty Lou. She offered to pay for the drugs but he refused.

Her next purchases were an 84 inch Frigidaire freezer and a Honda "whisper quiet" portable generator which she had delivered to the storage unit. With those plus the Taurus and the gun safe it was starting to be a tight squeeze but she was certain one more thing would fit. She felt it was all coming together and unlike the attack on the random homeless guy outside her condo this time the anticipation sent adrenaline through her body.

Rampart sat across from Dr. Christine who took a bite from a Jersey Mike's sub sandwich. Rampart had called and told Christine he needed to see him right away. The doctor answered by saying the only time he could accommodate Ramp was at lunch and *only* if he brought a "number 7, Mike's way" with him. Rampart had and now watched him chew a bite and swallow.

"What's the emergency?" the doctor asked.

"It's Hannah."

"I figured that. What about her?"

"She's different, acting strange. More specifically talking weird."

"That isn't that unusual. Sometimes the brain, after a traumatic event, takes a little longer to recognize and process speech and speech patterns. Both the temporal lobe and the parietal lobe can be affected," he took another bite of his lunch.

"It's not *how* she's saying something. It's *what* she's saying." He watched Christine chew. "I thought something was different the moment she woke up and then that feeling just got stronger every time I talked to her."

"Alright," Christine said as he set his sandwich down and picked a pen from his pocket. "Tell me more."

"She talks in songs."

"She's singing?"

"No, she's not *singing* songs, she's *talking* songs. She converses, answers questions, like normal but her answers are anything *but* normal. It's a song title every single time." He watched the doctor scribble something down. "Remember when she first woke up and you tested her?"

"I do."

"At the end she didn't say 'I can feel that doctor,' she said, 'feels just like it should.' That's a Pat Green song. When I took her home and dropped her off she blurted 'home sweet home.' That was recorded by Mötley Crüe."

"Among others."

"Yeah, among others. And when I called and asked where she was she said, 'sittin' in the sun.'"

"Louis Armstrong if I'm not mistaken," the doctor said.

"You're not."

"I see what you're saying but quite frankly even though those *are* titles of songs none of the responses seem out of the ordinary. What exactly do you want me to do, Rampart?"

"I want you to *fix* her. She's *broken*!"

"From where I sit, I see nothing to fix."

"*Nothing to fix*? She's speaking in song titles! Listen." He pulled out his phone and played the most recent conversation he'd had with his sister, pausing several times along the way. "That's a Buddy Holly song," he said. "That's Rod Stewart," he mentioned another time. "*Everything's coming up roses*?!? *Thank you for being a friend*?! I mean seriously? *You* don't think that's broken?"

"I agree it's a bit odd but you see broken and I see the miracle of the human mind at work."

"The *miracle*? She's reciting Ethel Merman songs for God's sake! The bartender at the Rabbit Hole called her 'song girl' the other day. It's crazy."

"Did you know Ray Lamontagne has a song titled *'Hannah'*?" the doctor asked.

"I didn't know that but what does that have to do with anything?" Rampart wondered aloud.

"Maybe nothing, maybe everything," Christine answered. "Let me ask you something else."

"Go ahead."

"Does she seem okay? Is she happy?" Now it was Rampart's turn to think.

"I don't know. I guess so."

"Is she physically okay? Motor functions, is she walking normally? Is she feeding herself? Drawing?"

"Sure. All of that, as far as I can tell."

"Look, Rampart, I know you're upset but please try and remember that the brain is a mystery to all of us and your sister has been on quite a wild ride. I'm guessing this is not what you want to hear but give it some time and it might just fix itself."

"And in the meantime, what? Brush up on my showtunes?"

"Don't worry, be happy," Christine said then he smiled and got back to his lunch. Rampart rolled his eyes, stood and left.

♪♫♪

Following Clues

Allen decided his next move was to call Stan Byrd, Jr. but first he thought he could use some fresh air. He drove home, went upstairs and knocked on Tracey's door hoping to pick up Lettie and take the dog for a walk. Tracey answered.

"Wow," she looked at the Apple watch on her wrist, "you're home early." The detective noticed she was dressed differently from the way he was used to seeing her. She wore a navy suit with a white blouse, and her hair was pulled back in a ponytail.

"You look…,"

"*Professional*?" Tracey finished the thought for him.

"I was going to say really good but I guess professional works too."

"I don't always look really good?"

"Not what I meant and you know it."

"I do, come on in." She turned to allow Allen enough room to get by.

"Why the suit?" he said once he had entered the apartment. He walked to Lettie's crate and opened it to let her out.

"Release the hound!" he said in a loud voice. Teri chuckled even though it was what he said almost every time. Lettie lumbered out of the crate and stretched. Her front paws went forward and her rump went up in the air.

"Good down dog," Tracey said as she joined Allen in the room.

"Is that why they call it that?" Allen asked referring to the yoga pose.

"You didn't know that?" Tracey asked as she scratched the dog's butt. "There's a 'cat pose' too," she added.

"Why the suit?" Allen asked again.

"Work. I'm juror number 7 today."

"And you have to dress up?"

"I don't *have* to," she answered, "I prefer to. It's serious business and I want the lawyers to know I'm serious about it."

"I bet they appreciate that."

"I think they do."

"What's the case?"

"Even though I'm just a mirror juror you know I can't discuss details about the case," she reminded him, "but I *can* tell you it's pretty big. Chief Judge Blaine's courtroom."

Allen whistled. He had appeared in the Chief Judge's courtroom on one occasion to testify for the prosecution and he had to admit it was intimidating. He was well aware of a big murder case working its way through the system. His old pal Carl Paulson had caught it and, by all accounts, was doing great work on it. The case involved a woman who had gone missing. She was last seen in a Colorado Springs mall store. As was almost always the case the police, this time Detective Paulson, suspected the victim's significant other and questioned him first.

As was also almost always the case the significant other, in this case that meant the husband, professed his innocence and begged the detective to find his wonderful wife. Paulson had told anybody who would listen that the guy "seemed a bit off" so he started digging and found inconsistencies in the husband's story. Inconsistencies that included a girlfriend that the man had failed to mention. It took Paulson a few weeks but he finally had enough evidence to convince the District Attorney to sign off on the case. The girlfriend flipped, the husband was arrested, and the case was now in the Colorado court system. He wasn't positive this was the case Tracey was working on but he knew he wasn't scheduled to be anywhere near the El Paso County courthouse any time soon so he wasn't all that interested professionally. Because of Tracey he was interested personally.

“Where does it stand?” he asked.

“Opening statements yesterday and this morning. Blaine recessed until next week when the State presents its case.”

“So you’ve got a few days off.”

“From that job, yes.”

“I’m headed over to Monument Avenue to knock on some doors. You wanna come?”

“Is that proper police procedure, detective?” Tracey asked. Allen didn’t answer right away because he was trying to figure out what Tracey meant. Then he did.

“Oh. No. I wasn’t asking you to join me for the door knocking part,” he smiled, “I just thought we could all walk over there together and then you could take Lettie around the trail.” Tracey smiled.

“Can we get ice cream after?”

“Don’t see why not.”

They walked the few hundred yards from their building to the condo building that fronted the spot where Daniel Bowen had died. Allen held on to Lettie’s leash as the dog tried to scramble after every squirrel in sight.

"She'll never stop thinking she'll catch the next one," Allen said with a shake of his head.

"Nor should she."

Just then another furry critter shot across the path and scampered up a nearby pine tree. The dog lurched after it nearly pulling her master off his feet.

"Lettie, stop!" Tracey said in a stern, controlled, voice. Lettie stopped. "Come girl," Tracey commanded and Lettie came. Allen stood watching, amazed.

"Wow," he said, "nicely done." Tracey curtsied and reached in her pocket pulling out a dog biscuit. She fed it to Lettie who gobbled it up.

"She is a super smart girl, Allen," Tracey said patting the pup on the head. "you just have to tell her what you expect from her. She wants to please you." With that Tracey took the leash from Allen and started walking. "Let's go girl," she said to the dog, "at Tracey pace and we're going to stay on the path." Allen didn't move as they walked away. After a few steps Tracey stopped and turned, "coming?" she asked.

Allen saw the name H. Hunt on the building directory next to unit number 310. He punched the button.
"Who's there?" he heard Hannah ask through the speaker.

"Hi Hannah. Sorry to bother you. It's detective Marc Allen."

“No muss, no fuss, no bother,” she said then added, “how are you?”

“Good. Good,” He started.

“Come on up,” she interjected and he heard the buzzer and a click that unlocked the door. Allen opened it but didn’t go in.

“Thanks but there’s really no reason to come up,” he said. “I just have one question.”

“Shoot.”

“Your unit, is it on the east side or the west side of the building?”

“East side,” was all she said.

“Okay, great, thanks a lot.”

“I’ll be seeing you,” he heard Hannah call as he stood holding the door to the building. For a second it made the detective think about what Rampart had been going on about. The whole notion of Hannah talking in songs but the thought didn’t last long. Thanks to her he now knew the even numbered units faced east so that meant the odd ones had windows looking west, out over the crime scene. Even though he had access to the inside he pushed a few more buttons to see if anyone else was home. The first three produced no results but the fourth was different.

"Who is it?" a women's voice called. Allen thought she sounded tired. Not out of breath tired or having just awakened tired, more like lived a long life and said a lot of words tired. He looked at the name and the unit number. C Schlamp, it read, unit number 401.

"Mrs. Uh, Schlamp?" he asked. He pronounced it like "lamp" and hoped that was correct.

"I used to be," the voice said.

"I'm Detective Marc Allen with the Colorado Springs police," he identified himself. "If you don't mind I'd like to come up and ask you a few questions."

"I don't mind at all," she answered quickly. Allen thought her voice sounded a little less tired. "It's been a while since I had a gentleman caller." *Oh boy,* Allen thought as he heard the buzzer. The door didn't click because he was already holding it open.

"Hello handsome," she was waiting in the doorway to her unit as he came down the hall. Allen saw an older woman who, in his humble opinion, had probably been quite the looker in her prime. She wore black slacks, a lime-colored sleeveless blouse with a high collar and open toed pink slippers. They had what looked to Allen to be a one-inch heel and pink feathered poms at the toes. Her hair was cut short and obviously colored a reddish brown with a few strands of silver. Allen got the immediate impression that the former

Mrs. Schlamp took very good care of herself and probably paid a pretty penny toward that end. He also guessed she had lied about the frequency of her "gentleman callers." In her right hand she held a small green glass, Allen figured it was crystal and it was filled to the brim with an amber liquid. She saw him look at her, then the glass, then back at her.

"Cognac," she said, "can I offer you one?"

"Oh no thank you, Mrs. Schlamp," he declined.

"You need to stop that right now," she scolded, "I haven't been Mrs. Schlamp in years. That bastard Myron took his secretary to the Caymans and I took him to the cleaners for half of everything. I don't think either of us ever looked back."

"Good for you Mrs. uh" he started to say but stopped unsure of what to call her.

"Tusi," she answered for him.

"I'm sorry, Tootsie?" he asked because he wasn't sure.

"No not *Tootsie,*" she said with a chuckle, "Tusi, no second t."
"That's an interesting name."

"Is it?" her smile stayed on her face, "I was quite the dancer in my day, detective," she shook her hips without spilling a drop of her drink. "The Watusi was my specialty. And I can still handle myself on the dance floor if I do say so myself." She ended the statement with a wink.

"I have little doubt about that," Allen said and winked back.

"I have been *so* rude," Tusi Schlamp said, "please come in."

It didn't take long for Allen to see on what else Tusi Schlamp spent Myron's money. The condo was exquisitely furnished and featured a large picture window from which the occupant could enjoy a spectacular view of Pikes Peak.

"Purple mountain's majesty," Tusi said from behind the detective.

"Beg your pardon?" Allen said turning.

"Purple mountains majesty, the words from America the Beautiful. I sit here often and imagine Katherine Lee Bates writing those words from a place not unlike my balcony," she pointed outside. Allen spent another few seconds admiring the vista and then decided it was time to get down to business.

"Were you home several nights ago?" he turned again and asked.

"I guess the pleasantries are over," Tusi answered and then drank half the brandy from her glass.

“Guess so,” Allen shrugged, “a few nights ago?” he asked again.

“Well, that doesn’t narrow it down much.”

“You’re right. I’m sorry. It was Tuesday the 12th,” he clarified.

“Tuesdays are book club nights,” she answered immediately. “Actually, it’s get together with a few friends, drink, and bitch about men nights but we call it book club nights,” she smiled and drained the rest of what was left in her glass.

“Where is book club and how long does it usually last?”

“Most nights we meet at Dani Tucker’s place and how long usually depends on the book,” she winked at Allen again. Then she turned and went to the nearby wet bar to refill her glass.

“Did you meet at Ms. Tucker’s place that Tuesday and would you, by chance, remember when you returned home?”

“We did and not exactly,” she said and he watched her pour Remy Martin Louis XIII. He recognized the distinctive, very expensive liquor because of the bottle. His ex-girlfriend Denise Clawsew was a fan of the same spirit. It made Allen wonder what Myron Schlamp did for a living.

“Ballpark?” Allen wondered.

"I would guess I returned home sometime between 10 and 11 PM, detective. We're energetic but none of us are spring chickens any longer." Allen expected another wink but didn't get one this time.

"And then what?"

"And then what *what*?"

"I'm sorry. After you returned home what did you do?"

"I took off my clothes, put on my nightie, brushed my teeth and went to bed. Alone."

"Did you happen to hear anything during the night?"

"Sure."

"You did?" Allen was suddenly more interested in the conversation.

"Always do, detective. I'm what you would call a light sleeper. I tried plugs but they hurt my ears so now I just go to bed with the understanding that I'm going to hear the traffic and the train and an occasional dog barking and the sirens."
"And you heard those things that Tuesday night?"

"Undoubtedly. With," she took a sip of the Louis XIII, "the possible exception of the dog."

"What kind of siren?" he asked.

"What?"

"You said you undoubtedly heard all the sounds except maybe the dog. Those sounds you mentioned included sirens. I was just wondering what type of siren you might have heard that night." He saw her looking at him like she didn't understand the question.

"I don't understand the question," she said, "I heard sirens."

"Here in the Springs, all over in fact, different emergency vehicles sirens have distinct characteristics. For instance my police vehicle can make different sounds."

"Can it?"

"It can. Sometimes I can make it go, 'whoop whoop'," Allen made the noise and Tusi Schlamp giggled. "Or I can make it sound like a loud, sustained wail but I'll spare you what that sounds like."

"It wasn't a 'whoop whoop' *or* a sustained wail," she answered not bothering to make the sounds.

"Good, we're getting somewhere," he said but he admitted to himself he had no idea where.

"What other noises do sirens make?"

"Well, let's see," Allen took a moment to think. "Here in town a fire department vehicle siren sounds like this," he made a long yell and followed it with the sound of a honking horn. Tusi's giggle was now a laugh.

"You sound like a sick goose," she said.

"I'm doing the best I can. Now an EMT vehicle—"

"A what?" she interrupted.

"An ambulance."

"Oh."

"That type of emergency vehicle siren sounds like this," and he let loose with a wail followed by another one but at a slightly lower pitch.

"That's the one!" she said excitedly.

"Great, an ambulance. And you're sure that's what you heard the night of the 12th."

"Not sure it was *that* night but that's the siren sound I hear most nights. You're not going to make me swear on a Bible are you?"

"No Tusi, I'm not. But I do want to thank you. You've been extremely helpful."

"It's the most fun I've had in years," she lifted her glass to Allen and drank down the entire contents.

Allen doubted that was true as he left the condo. An ambulance sometime after 11 PM on Tuesday the 12th. It might mean something but he had to admit that it probably signified nothing. Allen thought of something he forgot to ask and turned around. He knocked on 401 and Tusi Schlamp answered immediately.

"Change your mind, handsome?" she asked.

"No ma'am but I do have one more question."

"Go ahead." Allen thought he detected some disappointment in her reply.

"How well do you know your neighbors?"

"Pretty well," she said without thinking. "I was one of the first to buy in the building. There isn't much socializing going on but the owners do pass each other in the garage, or the elevator, or outside in the courtyard. There's a lovely girl who lives in 310 who likes to sit out there and draw. She's quite good." Allen realized she was speaking about Hannah Hunt.

"Okay. Thanks again," he turned to go.

"The lady upstairs is new," Tusi volunteered, calling after him. He turned around.

"Upstairs?"

"Right above me. She just moved in a couple of months ago."

"Single?"

"As far as I can tell but she does have a good-looking boyfriend. Spends the night sometimes."

"How do you know so much?" he asked.

"I pay attention, detective. Plus the previous owner was a baseball player. A real hunk!"

"But he's gone."

"Sadly, yes."

"And a single woman moved in?"

"With a fancy new Range Rover in the garage."

Allen thanked her again and decided to knock on a few more doors before leaving. There was no answer at any of them. He headed for the elevator and decided he could either go up to 501 or down to Tracey and Lettie. He checked his watch and realized he'd spent more time with Tusi Schlamp than he had planned and decided down was the best option. He could always come back to question the condo owner upstairs. He pushed the button for the lobby but before getting Lettie he pulled out his phone and took a picture of the building's directory. The name next to Unit 501 was Longabaugh, no first name or letter. He wondered why.

Teri had been upstairs watching the detective's friend walk his dog. "Another piece of the puzzle," she said through the window to them both.

♪♫♪

Allen Meets Jake

Marc Allen knew there were a number of ambulance services in the Colorado Springs metro area but one, in particular, did most of the city's business. That outfit's main office was north and east of downtown so, after leaving Lettie with Tracey again, that's where he headed. The detective instinctively checked his mirrors and noticed what looked like a late model blue Range Rover a few cars behind. His thought immediately went to what Tusi Schlamp had said about her neighbor upstairs. He started thinking about the name next to the number. It was his experience that Longabaugh wasn't a particularly popular or common surname. He knew that experience was limited but he had been a cop for a while, in cities across the country, and he had yet to meet, become friends with, question, or arrest, anyone named Longabaugh. He did however recognize the name as belonging to the notorious Sundance Kid. He checked the side mirror again and no longer saw the Rover.

It took him about twenty minutes to get to the headquarters of the American Medical Response company. He parked in the lot and went inside. A young woman sat behind a desk and greeted him as he entered.

"Help you?" she said. Allen thought she looked and sounded like they didn't get a lot of walk-ins.

"Hope so," he answered pulling his shield and showing her. "I'm Detective Marc Allen and you are?"

"Charlotte."

"Hello Charlotte. I'm here just looking for some information. Can you help?"

"I'll try." As he said it Allen realized he had made Charlotte nervous.

"Look this has nothing whatsoever to do with you Charlotte." He noticed that simple statement made her relax. It made him wonder if Charlotte, like most people, were automatically nervous around the police or if she had something to hide. "I assume you keep records of all the ambulance calls your company receives."

"We do, of course," she said as she tapped a few keys on her computer keyboard.

"Good. Good. I'm looking for one night in particular," he started.

"Um, do you have a warrant?" she asked. The question almost made Allen laugh out loud.

"Charlotte, did you watch Chicago P.D. last night?"

"I'm sorry, what?"

“Your question. It sounded like it came directly from a Dick Wolf script.”

“Dick who?” she asked. Allen leaned in and put his elbows on the desk.

“No, Charlotte, I do not have a warrant but I’ll get one if you need me to. And if I do it will be for a lot more than ambulance calls on one night. I just need a little information that, quite frankly, is part of the public record but if you want to play cops and robbers we can certainly do that.” He noticed Charlotte no longer met his gaze. “Would you like to call your supervisor and make sure this is the road AMR wants to go down?”

“Which night?” Charlotte asked. Allen smiled.

“I’m looking for calls from the night of the 12th or the morning of the 13th.”

“Of this month?”

“Yes Charlotte, this month.” Just then Allen noticed a door open and a man hold it open with his foot. The opening revealed an area that looked like a garage housing a couple of the company’s ambulances. Allen recognized the familiar red, white and blue paint scheme. There were several cabinets marked on the outside with labels telling the paramedics what was inside. Allen could read “Defibrillators” on one door, “Naloxone” on another. The man was younger than him, though not much, and he was wiping his hands on a rag. On the way out the door the rag was dropped into a large plastic container. The guy looked at Allen and Allen continued watching him.

“Hi Jake,” Charlotte said.

“Char,” He nodded. “Everything okay?”

“All good,” she said reassuringly.

“Cool,” he looked from her to Allen and then back. “17 is good to go,” he said. Allen assumed he was talking about one of the vehicles he had seen behind the door.

“I’ll let them know,” Charlotte said as Jake started walking to the exit. He gave Allen one last, long look and then a nod on the way out. Allen turned his attention back to Charlotte and noticed she was staring at the door, lost in thought.

“Who’s Jake?”

“Just a guy. Does some work on the ambulances. He’s nice.” Allen thought the way she said the last two words weren’t referring to Jake being kind or considerate. He tapped his finger on the desk breaking the spell.

“The night of the 12th?”

"Oh yeah," she said as she went back to her computer. "Let's see, there was a call around 8 PM. Looks like someone was choking at a restaurant up on Woodman."

"Anything else?"

"Yep. One more. Apparent heart attack in the Patty Jewett neighborhood a little more than an hour later. 9:07 PM to be exact." She looked back up at Allen.

"Thanks Charlotte. Nothing around the Monument Park area?"

"No sir. In fact we didn't get any other calls at all until 10:03 AM the next day. Someone having a seizure at the Quail Run apartments in Dublin."

"You've been a big help Charlotte. The CSPD appreciates it," Allen said as he turned and left the office. As he sat in his car Allen thought about checking with the other EMS companies but decided it wouldn't bear fruit. He fired up the engine and concluded that maybe, just maybe, Tusi Schlamp was pulling his leg.

Teri had put on a black turtleneck with black jeans over a pair of black boots. Everything else she needed to complete her look was in the trunk of the Taurus, safely housed in her storage unit. She stepped in the elevator and headed down to the garage. When the doors opened Teri stood face to face with Hannah Hunt who was on her way up. Teri felt another pang of guilt as she thought of the accident at the skating rink but that feeling passed as quickly as it came. Hannah held a yellow coated terrier in her arms.

“Well hello,” Teri said.

“Hey there.”

“Cute dog, what’s his name?”

“Mean Mr. Mustard.”

“Yours?”

“Hannah,” she said.

“That I know,” Teri laughed. “I was asking if the dog was yours?”

“Friend of a friend.” Hannah said entering the elevator car. Teri got out.

“Woman of few words,” Teri said.

“Nothing more to say,” Hannah announced as the doors closed. “She sure looks good in black,” she said to the dog. Teri, on the other hand, didn’t give Hannah any more thought, her mind instead turned to the job at hand.

Teri had everything she needed for her mission including a cooperative Mother Nature. The normally crystal clear, star-filled, Colorado night sky was forecast to be covered by clouds on this night. Teri was counting on that forecast to be true and it was. She had filled the tranquilizer darts with the Rompun and stocked up on Black Opal makeup, a pair of Freetoo rubber knuckle tactical gloves, and an Oakley fine knit black beanie. She had also been to the gun range more than a half a dozen times in the last two weeks. Teri made sure to go on off hours, times she knew Jake was otherwise occupied, and practiced her long-range rifle skills.

She had also spent the last week or so outfitting the trunk of the Taurus to accommodate the expected cargo. With the help of an online video Teri jerry-rigged a pully system, connected to a tarp, that would help lift approximately 250 pounds of dead weight. She knew her prey wouldn't be dead but if all went according to plan he would be unconscious and, in that state, would weigh more than normal. After a double, then triple, check she figured she was as prepared as she could be. Ultimate success would come down to timing. She couldn't know exactly how long it would take the tranquilizer to work but she had a decent idea. She pulled into the storage unit and parked the Range Rover. There were still a couple of hours until it would be dark enough to proceed.

Reg Byrd preferred to go down to the river after dark, at or around, the same time each day. The homeless folks were usually less active then and he had already established his bona fides with that group so they knew to leave him alone.

He had long since proved he could hold his own in any kind of a turf dispute and demonstrated he was only there to wash up and or relieve himself. He never stayed longer than he needed to. Reg didn't have anything for them and he didn't want anything from them.

Before leaving his van, he opened up a can of Hormel chili with beans and left it next to the empty pot on the hot plate at the back of his vehicle. He had joked to himself for the hundredth time that he liked to let the delicacy "breathe" before dumping the contents into the pot and heating them up. Over time he had convinced himself that the perfect duration for that was the length of time it took him to get to the creek and back. He wore a plain gray tee shirt and his Green Bay Packers sweatpants. He pulled the slightly too big cowboy boots over his tube socks and opened the door.

He noticed tonight was unlike most nights because of the clouds obscuring the moon and stars. That automatically made it darker than usual. He always enjoyed looking up at the night sky and seeing The Big Dipper, The Little Dipper, The North Star and on most nights the planets Venus or Jupiter. None were visible as he started his trek down to the creek. His disappointment reflected a lack of contentment. He certainly didn't need the heavens to guide him to his destination. He could navigate the route blindfolded. Just like most every other night, there was no one else was out and about. Weber Street was deserted.

Reg knew the problem with sweatpants was that there was no zipper so he had to pull them down a bit to do his business. But he also knew they were just so darn comfortable and it wasn't that big a deal, he just felt a bit more exposed. He had already washed his hands and face and only needed to do this one more thing before hiking back to his can of chili.

Teri looked through her night vision scope and couldn't believe her luck when she saw the van man leave his vehicle wearing a pair of sweats instead of blue jeans. *Less resistance for the darts* she thought. Her scope illuminated the nighttime scene and she clearly watched the man wash himself and then pull the pants down slightly to pee. She had left her Taurus on the street, next to the park about halfway between the creek and the van. She could only hope it was close to the right spot. After loading the rifle, she took aim, let out one long breath to ease the tension she knew was there and pulled the trigger. Once. She shifted her aim ever so slightly and pulled the trigger again. Both darts flew true and struck the man in the middle of each buttock.

Byrd started peeing. An act that, he had to admit, was becoming more and more uncomfortable with each passing day. He closed his eyes and was relieved that relieving himself this particular evening was a satisfying task. He allowed himself a small smile and then the first dart hit. Reg Byrd knew he'd never been bitten by a rattlesnake but he suddenly thought he could guess what that experience might feel like. He took in a surprised breath and then the second dart smacked into his ass. He dropped to his knees and tried to scream but no sound came out. Standing shakily, he reached behind him to feel his backside. His hands passed over not one but two darts, one lodged in each butt cheek. He pulled them out and felt almost as much pain as he had when they entered his body. He turned, trying to see from where the shots had come. *Were there kids out there? Was this some sort of sick prank? Had one of the homeless people gotten his hands on a dart gun?* He didn't see or hear anything that would help answer any of those questions. Reg started to feel nauseous and decided the best thing he could do was to head back to his van.

Teri watched the whole thing with a mixture of satisfaction and amazement. She was proud of her marksmanship. She knew her hard work had paid off when both shots hit the target. But she was equally impressed with the van man for the way he reacted to being slammed in the rear end by the two projectiles. She saw him sink to his knees but then get back up. Her hope was that he would manage to make his way back to his home on wheels, well halfway there anyway. Teri saw him turn and look around, at one point he stared at the spot from which she still crouched. A second of alarm overtook her but it passed because she knew she couldn't be seen. She also watched him grab at the darts and pull them from his body.

"Don't drop them van man," she said under her breath. She didn't want to expose herself any more than she knew she already would have to. She observed as he managed to start walking back to his van. He didn't make it that far.

In addition to feeling sick to his stomach, parts of Reg's body started to go numb. He had to concentrate on walking. He was losing the feeling in his legs but when he looked down, he could see he was still putting one foot in front of the other. Reg suddenly had no idea how long he'd been walking or how far he'd gotten. Everything was going dark and he knew he was about to go down. His last thought was the hope that he would pass out on the grass and not the sidewalk or the street.

Teri could tell that van man wasn't long for consciousness so she was on the move. *Get as close to the car as you can*, she thought as she hustled toward her victim. It turned out that he got within about ten feet of the Taurus before he toppled over onto the green grass of the park.

"Not bad," she said as she stood over the body.

She knelt down to check for a pulse and found one. She also found the fingers of his right hand still clinging to one of the two darts.

"Shit, where's the other one?" she said quietly to the man on the ground.

Teri knew she had to act quickly and find the second projectile. She replayed the scene in her mind, saw the van man go down, get up, look around and start to stagger. She headed in the direction from where he had come. Through the lens of her night scope, she surveyed the ground and she moved her head back and forth in a small arc. *It's got to be here somewhere*, she thought. Then a dog barked.

"Crap," she said slightly louder than she wanted to.

"Buster. Quiet," came a voice from the bushes down near the creek. The dog barked again.

Teri was acutely aware she was almost out of time. If the dog and its owner came out from the bushes and saw her, she was in big trouble. She hadn't planned for that contingency. She thought again about the dart and tried to remember if she had worn gloves when she filled it with the sedative and loaded it into the weapon. She was almost certain she had. Almost. A third bark. Teri knew any more noise might awaken some folks in the nearby apartments so she gave the grass one more look.

"There you are beautiful," she saw it sticking into the ground and quickly retrieved it.

"Buster. Hush!" called the homeless person.

Teri realized she was sweating as she took the projectile back and she still had to get the van man into her trunk. She ran back to where he lay in the grass and dragged him the rest of the way to the car. She popped the truck and hooked him up to her tarp and pully system. Buster had stopped barking. Van man went into the truck with room to spare and Teri gave herself a virtual pat on the back for the pully system and her choice of vehicle. She closed the trunk as quietly as possible and took stock of her situation. A quick look at her surroundings told her, despite the extra time and the barking dog, the mission had been a complete success. No lights came on in the nearby apartment buildings, nobody was in the park or on the street. She realized the dog's homeless owner might be watching from the bushes but she wondered who they would tell, what they would say and who would believe them. Teri already had the car painted a darker color to blend in and it still carried the temporary plates. She got behind the wheel and headed north on Weber.

"Whoo hooo!" she screamed as she passed between the police headquarters and the van man's former orange home.

♪♫♪

Teri's Prisoner Awakens

It was the worst night's sleep Allen had experienced since moving to Colorado Springs. He went from too hot to too cold. From opening the sliding door to his deck to closing it. From hearing every pant emanating from Lettie's lungs to not hearing any of it because the sounds from outside fluctuated from an eerie stillness to a cacophony of birds, squirrels, dogs and traffic. The only thing missing from the experience when the detective finally rolled out of bed at 4 AM was any semblance of a dream. He opened the dog crate door and Lettie bounded out, stopped, shook, and walked over to his side.

"Hey girl. Wanna go for a walk?" he asked even though he knew the answer to that particular question was always yes.

The cloud cover he had noticed during one of the night's sleepless sections had begun to clear, bringing Allen hope that the sunrise would bring another glorious Colorado day. He took the dog out the back door of the complex and through a gate that led to the path along Monument Creek. Once there they could either go south toward downtown or north along the creek up to the Colorado College campus and beyond. The northern route would take them past the spot where Daniel Bowen had met his demise. That's the way Lettie decided she wanted to go and Allen didn't try to convince her otherwise. Lettie sniffed and peed and looked like she was going to tear off after a squirrel a couple of times, but she didn't. He wondered if Tracey's training skills were paying off. As they wandered down the path Allen took a deep breath, sucking in the Centennial State's clean air. It smelled and tasted like moisture and the detective surmised that it must have rained, at least a little, overnight but through his stops and starts battle with sleep he couldn't remember hearing or seeing any drops. They got close to the spot where Bowen had been discovered which meant they were also across from the condo building that was home to Hannah Hunt, Tusi Schlamp, and dozens of others including the mysterious tenant in number 501. Allen thought again about the name next to the number.

"Longabaugh," he said softly. As the word rolled off his lips he couldn't help but think, for the second time in 24 hours, what an uncommon name it seemed to be. West Monument Street dead-ended at the bottom of a hill, 20 feet from where Allen and Lettie currently stood. He had noticed, on different occasions, cars parked there. It's where he stopped and dropped off Rampart Haynes so he could retrieve his Jeep. This morning there were three cars parked on the street near the dead-end and someone was sleeping at the wheel of one of them. The detective saw he could gain access to the vehicle through a path near a yard about 100 feet back the way he and Lettie had walked. He was curious about the sleeper and decided to have a look.

"Come Lettie," he called to the dog and they headed for pathway. When he got to the car and before realizing he had left his home without his CSPD shield or either of his handguns, he used a knuckle to rap on the windshield. The sleeping driver snapped to attention at the sound and looked Allen's way and the detective stared though the window at the ambulance mechanic, Jake. The window rolled down.

"Who the hell are you?" a still sleepy Jake Holler asked clearly not recognizing the detective.

"Allen. CSPD."

"Prove it," Jake retorted.

"Have to take my word for it. Sleeping one off?" Allen noticed Jake looking at him a little more intently maybe seeing a hint of recognition. "Well? Jake?" he revealed that he knew who he was talking to.

"You're the guy from the ambulance shop," Jake said and now they were even.

"I am. What's your last name Jake?"

"Holler," he said then he spelled it.

"What are you doing here Mr. Holler?" he watched as Jake stared out through his windshield, maybe trying to come up with his best response. Holler took in and blew out a breath and then he turned back to face Allen.

"Yeah, like you said, sleeping one off," Jake answered and Allen nodded slowly.

“You live around here?” the cop asked.

“Not far,” Jake replied. Allen had pulled over more than his share of inebriated drivers and rousted a lot of drunks in his time and the smell of alcohol was always present. This time, he thought, the unmistakable odor of someone having had too much to drink was conspicuously absent.

“Where did you do your drinking Jake?” he asked and noticed it took Holler more than a few seconds to respond.

“In there,” he finally said pointing to the condo building.

“Unit number?”

“Uh, I don’t remember. Fourth floor, I think.” Allen said nothing. He knew from experience that tactic was sometimes better than asking questions. “Look,” Jake sputtered, “I’m not trying to protect anybody or get myself in trouble. I honestly don’t remember. The place belongs to a friend of a friend. There was a party.”

“Okay, fair enough. Why didn’t you call an Uber?”

“I thought about it but I thought I could drive. But when I got out here I realized that was a bad idea.” Allen nodded. “I guess I dozed off.”

“What happened to your friend?”

“Who?”

“The friend whose friend was having the party in the unit you can’t remember.”

“Good question,” Jake said.

“Thanks.” Allen decided he had gotten all he was going to get. “You good to drive?” he asked.

“Think so.”

“Not good enough Jake Holler. Once more, you good to drive?”

“Yes,” Jake nodded, “I’m good.”

“Then go home,” Allen said as he tapped on the driver’s door and led the dog away. Jake let out another, longer breath and stared up at Teri’s balcony.

“Where the heck *are* you?” he asked as he started the engine.

Allen walked away knowing he had just been lied to about almost everything. He knew coincidences occurred in life but he thought that maybe running into Jake Holler twice in such a short period of time was a bit more coincidental than he liked. After giving it a little more thought he couldn’t chalk it up to anything other than coincidence. He didn’t dismiss it outright, just decided to file it away. Another thing he had filed away was the thought that Teri Hickox could have actually followed him to Colorado Springs. He had an idea and made a mental note to give Eliza Starz a call when he got into the office. His to do list for the day was getting longer because he had already planned to call Stan Byrd at some point. Allen added one more thing to the checklist, find out more about Jake Holler.

"H-O-L-L-E-R," he spelled the name out loud to Lettie as she wagged her tail and walked on.

Teri wasn't home because she had spent the night in the storage unit watching the van man snore. She had kicked him more than a couple of times to get him to wake up but with no luck. She had no idea how long it would take the tranquilizer to wear off and even less of an idea what kind of shape or mood her victim would be in when he came to. She had bound his hands together in front of him with zip ties and taped his legs together with Gorilla duct tape. She also used a strip of the tape to cover his mouth. Couldn't have him screaming bloody murder when he woke up. After applying the tape, she leaned in to make sure he could breathe through his nose. Van man wasn't going anywhere when he woke up so Teri had laid her gun on her lap, shut her eyes, and grabbed some sleep.

When she woke up, her Apple Watch told her it was 4:15 in the morning. Van man was staring at her. After realizing her prisoner was awake and looking at her, the next thing she noticed was that the man had removed the tape from his mouth but not his face. It hung from the edge still stuck to his left cheek. She offered up a slight smile and then put her right index finger to her lips in a "be quiet" gesture. He nodded in recognition so she crab walked over to him and delicately removed the rest of the tape.

"I'm awful thirsty," he said when she backed away.

"I bet," Teri answered getting to her feet. She put the pistol in the waistband of her pants and stretched. Then Teri let loose a huge yawn, cracked the knuckles of each hand, and walked over to a floor lamp. She flipped it on and a forty-watt bulb lit the space. She also opened a small cooler, reached in and pulled out a bottle of water. Teri unscrewed the top and drank about half of it without stopping then she brought the rest of it with her as she kneeled next to Reg Byrd. "Open up," she said. He did.

She poured the contents, a little at a time, down his throat. She saw his eyes roll slightly back in his head and it looked to Teri like the man had just gotten a taste of the elixir of the Gods. He finished the bottle and licked his lips.

"Appreciate that," he said, "and when you're feeling generous I'd like a little more."

"If," she said tossing the bottle into a corner.

"Ma'am?"

"*If* I'm feeling generous," Teri said.

"Of course. That's what I meant to say." Hearing that, she smiled.

Reg Byrd had slowly regained his faculties in the early hours of the morning. As he came to, he felt nauseous but fought the urge to vomit because his mouth was covered with duct tape. He lifted his hands and using the thumb and index finger of his left hand, peeled the tape from his mouth so he could more easily breath. He left it hanging from the left side of his face. Reg concentrated on his captor. She slept about 15 feet from him but she might as well have been a hundred miles away, behind a brick wall, with armed guards. His hands were zip-tied together and his legs were bound by duct tape. Both the left and the right one were asleep. On top of that his ass hurt like hell. It all brought him to only one conclusion; the woman asleep on the floor had shot him with some kind of tranquilizer darts, abducted him, tied him up and imprisoned him in what appeared to be some sort of storage unit. It was dark but as his eyes adjusted, he could make out, beyond the woman, two cars. One looked to Byrd like an older model Ford Taurus, the other was a newer SUV. He noticed a stand-alone freezer like the one his grandma kept in her garage when he was a kid. He hoped, like that one, it was full of food and water because he was hungry and thirsty. There was also a portable generator and a rather large gun safe.

He guessed the woman was probably in her thirties, early forties at the latest. Her hair was cut short and she wore black pants and a black turtleneck. It also looked to Reg like she had wiped dark makeup off her face. There was still splotches of it on her forehead and one cheek. He had no idea why she had decided he was worthy of capture. For a brief moment he wondered if she could be related to the cop he had killed all those years ago but that thought drifted off like so much smoke. There was zero chance he could have been tracked down after all this time for that. Since there wasn't much else to think about, he also fantasized about his captor being the child he fathered with Daisy Burns. He figured if Daisy even kept the baby to term, he or she would be about this person's age but again he decided that couldn't be possible. He left North Carolina in the middle of the night and nobody there knew where he had gone or who he had become. Or did they?

He didn't own much; couldn't think of anything he *did* have that anyone else would want and except for the long dead cop he hadn't done anything that would deserve kidnapping. He decided this capture was going to lead to one thing, and one thing only, his torture and eventually his death.

As he thought those thoughts, he actually was surprised by the sense of calm that washed over him. Save for his mother he couldn't think of one single person who would miss him or that he, in turn, would miss. Maybe this was the end he deserved. As he pondered this the woman slowly came awake. He told her he was thirsty and after a few minutes she offered half a bottle of water. He'd never tasted anything so sweet.

"What's your name, van man?" she asked after giving him another drink.

"Which one?"

"Ahh, a man after my own heart," she said. "What do your friends call you?"

"Wouldn't know. Don't have any friends that I can think of but the folks that know me a little call me The Champ?"

"You a fighter?"

"Hardly. Just happen to have a license that says my name is Larry Holm."

"You hungry, Larry Holm?"

"Famished."

After a quick shower and shave Allen dropped Lettie off at Tracey's and headed into the station. He liked the early mornings best because of the energy each day produced. He always thought his fellow cops were the best of the best. Sure he knew there were bad apples, he'd even worked with a few, but for the most part he found his brethren in blue to be optimistic, hard-working and ready and able to take on whatever each day brought. Allen knew he would be spending some of his time at his desk on this day, working the phones, but he also needed to make a stop or two. The first order of business was two hours east of Colorado Springs so he picked up the phone and punched in the numbers.

"Starz," the Raleigh P.D. detective picked up on the second ring.

"Allen," he was equally brief.

"Well hello Marc."

"Eliza."

"It's a little early out there for you isn't it?" she chided.

"I've come to find the mountain air is best in the morning."

"I'm sure it is," she answered. "To what do I owe the pleasure of this call?" she signaled the small talk was over.

"Teri Hickox."

"Did she find you or did you find her?"

"Neither. Not yet anyway but I've been getting a weird feeling lately. I remember you saying she might have headed west and I'm thinking more and more that you could be right."

"So, how can I help?" Allen had been thinking about the answer to this question for hours.

"Any of our old friend Tanner Goochly's associates still in business?"

"I'd be surprised if they weren't," she responded. "You thinking of anyone in particular?"

"Not sure," he said honestly, "maybe somebody good at forgery, fake ID's and new identities." He waited as Eliza Starz considered his request.

"Could be," she answered, "I'll check around."

"I'd appreciate it," he said.

"No problem. Anything else?" Now it was Allen's turn to think.

"North Carolina still has the death penalty, right?"

"Far as I know."

"Okay. Thanks Eliza."

"Talk to ya, Marc."

Allen hung up and turned to his computer. He fired up his search engine and typed in "North Carolina" and "death penalty". He found it was indeed one of 29 states that still executed its prisoners. He knew Colorado still officially had it on the books but the sentiment toward abolishing it was on the rise and conventional wisdom was that as soon as another Democrat was elected Governor it would be off the books entirely. Allen was also aware that the state hadn't executed anybody since Gary Lee Davis in October of 1997 and there were currently only three men on death row. By contrast he found there were 143 inmates who fit that category in North Carolina. Three of those were women. He shook his head, looked at his watch, grabbed his coat and headed out.

He walked back into the AMR ambulance service office. Charlotte was there again; this time she was painting her fingernails. Allen watched as she applied the polish to the pinkie nail on her left hand. Satisfied, she looked up.

“Back for more ambulance chasing?” she asked then smiled.

“Not this time,” Allen answered and saw her smile quickly fade and one ended up on the detective’s face. “Don’t worry Charlotte, you’re still not in any trouble,” he said, “at least none that I’m aware of,” he added.

“So what brings you back?”

“Is Jake here?” he asked knowing he wasn’t.

“Is *he* in trouble?” Allen couldn’t help but notice the concern in her voice.

“Is he here?” he asked again.

“No sir,” she said and this time Allen detected a little sadness mixed in with the worry.

"How much do you know about him, Charlotte?"

"Some," she admitted and looked down at her freshly painted nails, "but not as much as I'd like."

"Does he have a wife? A steady girlfriend?"

"No wife," she answered quickly, "and if he's got a steady girlfriend he doesn't talk about her to me."

"Hobbies?"

"Sir?"

"What does Jake like to do for fun?" he watched as Charlotte thought.

"Hmmm," she studied her nails again, "Oh! He likes to think up funny sayings. Does that count?"

"Depends," Allen said, "What exactly does that mean?"

"Well, he has to come up with them for the signs at the animal shelter. Sometimes he tests them on me."

"Really? Like what?"

"Oh, let me think," she thought then she smiled, "Okay, like this," she paused for effect, "If you're sleeping like a baby it's because you don't have one." She looked at Allen, "Stuff like that."

"He's a regular Shakespeare," Allen smiled back.

"Be nice."

"Anything else he likes to do?"

"Well," she thought again. "Yeah, as a matter of fact. He likes to shoot."

"Does he now?" All of a sudden Allen was even more interested in Jake Holler.

"Yep. He target shoots at the range out by the Air Force Academy, says he goes there all the time. He even asked me to go once." Allen could sense the pride in her voice.

"But you didn't go?"

"No sir. I'm not much of a gun person."

"Well, thank you Charlotte. Once again you've been extremely helpful."

"He's not in trouble, is he?" she asked clearly troubled again.

"I wouldn't worry about Jake," Allen said as he tapped on the counter, turned, and walked out the door leaving Charlotte to her nails.

♪♫♪

Closing In

Allen located the range Charlotte mentioned and put the address in his GPS. On the way he had another thought and dialed Hannah Hunt.

"Hannah," she answered simply.

"Hi Hannah, this is Marc Allen. You got a minute?"

"Anything for you."

"I appreciate that. I just have a question or two."

"Sure."

"Do you know the woman in unit 501?"

"What's her name?"

"The directory listed her as Longabaugh."

"We've met."

"Good. Great. Uh, did you ever happen to see her with a guy? Dark hair, thirty something, good looking?"

"I don't think so," she said. Allen waited for more but didn't get it.

“But maybe?” he prodded.

“Thinking.”

“Take your time Hannah.” She did.

“I don’t remember,” she finally admitted. “I’m sorry.”

Oh, no problem,” Allen said. “But please, if you remember anything give me a call.”

“I will.”

“Thanks Hannah.”

“You betcha!” she ended the call. Allen figured he got just about what he expected. As he replayed the conversation, he thought again about Rampart’s claims of Hannah’s recent speech peculiarity. He had an idea.

“Play ‘You betcha,’” he said to the sound system in his car. The digital readout told Allen a song by something or someone called Yung Gravy was about to play. “Huh,” Allen remarked, “what do you know.”

A few minutes later, and after other songs by The Beatles, Aaron Watson and Hall and Oates played, he exited Interstate 25 North at Northgate Boulevard and turned right on Meadowgrass Drive.

"The destination is on your right," his GPS announced. The building was impossible to miss. It was highlighted by a huge black cylinder above the entrance. The word "Magnum" was emblazoned in huge white letters. "Shooting Range" was directly below it is smaller, orange letters. There were two pickups in the parking lot along with a matte black Audi A7. He pulled in next to the Audi and killed his engine.

Once inside Allen thought the place looked like a giant sporting goods store that exclusively sold products related to firearms. Looking around the showroom he surmised all of the shooting was done in the back of the building. The guns, ammo, accessories and clothing were on prominent display. A counter sat smack dab in the middle of the space and a woman stood behind it talking to a man dressed in charcoal gray slacks and a navy sports jacket. His hair was salt and pepper and slicked back, *Pat Riley style*, thought Allen referring to the NBA coach. The detective pegged him as the owner of the Audi. He turned his attention to the woman.

He put her someplace north of 60 but admitted she could have been a decade younger if a few of those years had included some hard living. Allen guessed her height at 5' 6" or 5' 7" but without the knowledge of what shoes she had on her feet. He thought she probably tipped the scales at around 130 pounds, give or take 5, her hair was white and she carried herself like she was more than an hourly employee. Like she was someone in charge. She had apparently satisfied the needs of Mr. Audi because he turned and walked away, stopping at a Sig Sauer display to admire the pistols. Allen took the opportunity to approach the counter. The woman looked up as he did.

“Help you, officer?” she asked. He smiled.

“I sure hope so,” he stopped and looked at her name tag, “Abigail.” He saw her smile back as he continued. “I’m Detective Marc Allen,” then he showed her his shield.

“I’m pretty sure the CSPD has its own range,” she said without looking at his badge.

“It sure does,” he replied, “but I’m not here to shoot.”

“Just the breeze?”

“Ma’am?”

“You’re just here to shoot the breeze? Are you lonely, detective?” Allen thought her voice sounded like she had a gullet full of gravel. He imagined thousands of smoked cigarettes.

“Sometimes Abigail. Sometimes.” Allen smiled, “but that’s not why I’m here either.” Abigail smiled back. “Do you have a customer named Jake Holler?” he pressed on.

“Now detective,” Abigail shook her head slowly, “you must be aware that we are a private club, a member organization, and that information is none of your business. Unless, of course, you have a search warrant in your pocket."

"Look," he held his hands up in mock surrender, "I'm not here to get anybody in trouble. I'm just looking for information." Abigail's answer was to say nothing. "I think our mutual friend Jake might be mixed up in something, with someone, who might intentionally or unintentionally do him harm."

"So, you're looking to *protect* this guy Jake?"

"Exactly."

"By poking around in his personal and my professional business."

"Again, Abigail, I'm just looking for some answers. My hope is to head off trouble before it actually becomes trouble. Did Jake ever shoot here with a female friend?" he slipped in the question in case he caught her off guard. He didn't. Abigail just stared at him. "mid-thirties, tall, good with a gun." He continued then waited. Abigail shook her head.

"Get a warrant, Detective Allen," was all she said as she walked away.

"Thank you, Abigail. You've been very helpful," Allen deadpanned. She raised her left hand and waved.

Outside Allen noticed the Audi driver sitting in his car staring at his phone. He decided, since he was having such good luck so far, he'd take another flyer. He knocked on the window. It came down.

"Need something?" the driver asked.

"You shoot here often?" Allen asked. The driver looked the detective up and down then shook his head.

"Never. In fact, this is my first time to even visit this place. I'm new to Colorado Springs."

"Appreciate your time," Allen said and the window went back up.

"Strike two," the detective said as he climbed back in his car.

As Allen drove back to South Nevada Avenue he thought about Abigail. *Was she hiding something or just protecting her store and her customers?* Probably a bit of both, he decided. The detective knew Jake Holler was suspected of no crime and there was zero basis for a search warrant. He had hoped that Abigail would, out of the goodness of her heart or some sort of civic responsibility, cooperate. She didn't but she also never denied knowing Jake or any of his associates. That too, he surmised, probably meant nothing. He came to the decision that he wasn't going to spend another minute on Jake Holler this day. It was time to move on to the next thing and that next thing was Stan Byrd, Jr.

Teri pulled a peanut butter and jelly sandwich out of the cooler from which she had grabbed the bottle of water earlier.

“Any allergies?” she asked the champ.

“Sorry?”

“Are you allergic to anything?”

“Oh. Don’t think so,” he shook his head. “Maybe cats or bee stings when I was a kid. Why?”

“Just wondering if you had a nut allergy. Don’t want this peanut butter to be the thing that kills you.” She said showing him the sandwich. She opened the Ziploc bag and pulled out the food.

“A peanut is a legume,” he corrected her.

“What?”

“A peanut. It’s not technically a nut, it’s a legume. So even if I had a nut allergy peanut butter wouldn’t kill me.” She stood still for a moment staring at her prisoner then she slowly walked over and dropped the sandwich in his lap.

“Maybe I *do* want this to be the thing that does you in,” she said and walked away.

Reg Byrd grabbed the PB and J with his still cuffed hands and brought it to his mouth. He realized it had been hours since his last meal as he took the first bite. He thought it was delicious.

"Strawberry?" he asked with food in his mouth.

"Raspberry," she told him with a small smile. "Smuckers."

"It's really good," he added as he took another bite.

"The chef always appreciates a satisfied customer. I'm going to step outside for a minute," she said. "You stay put."

She left the storage unit, closed and locked the door behind her. Outside she sucked in a huge breath of fresh air and looked at the watch on her wrist. It indicated she had two messages; one of them was from Jake. She pulled her phone from her pocket, turned it on and waited as it powered up. She listened to the message and called him back.

"Teri! Finally! What the hell?" he skipped the pleasantries.

"Calm down Jake," she tried to sound sweet.

"Where have you been? What's going on?" Teri thought he didn't sound calm.

"I had some things I needed to take care of. I'm okay, in fact I'm flattered that you would be so worried. Thank you." Teri thought appealing to his “caveman” side might be helpful. It turned out to be.

“Of course, I’m worried.”

“Look, honey, I didn’t mean to upset you and I promise I’ll fill you in on everything.”

“Okay, but I went by your place last night and you weren’t there. I parked in the cul-de-sac to wait and I must’ve fallen asleep in my car.” Teri thought he sounded like a heartsick teenager. It was kind of cute.

“Jake,” she started but he wasn’t finished.

“This morning, at dawn, I was still there. A cop knocked on my window and woke me up.” Teri didn’t think he sounded so cute anymore.

“A cop?”

“Yep. Said his name was Allen. I also saw him over at the AMR office.” Teri froze. After a few seconds Jake continued. “Teri? You still there?”

“Oh, I’m here. Look I gotta go but I promise I’ll call you later and fill you in.”

“What’s going on?”

“I told you I’ll call you later,” she said disconnecting the call.

Back at headquarters Allen punched in the number Connie Byrd had given him for her mom and dad. After six rings it went to voicemail and Allen left a message. He was actually grateful because it gave him a little more time to figure out exactly how he wanted to approach Stan Byrd. While he was doing just that his phone rang.

“Allen,” he answered.

“Marc, it’s Eliza,” detective Starz replied.

“Hey Eliza, what’s new?”

“Hampshire, England, Brunswick, York,” she said.

“Ha ha,” Allen chuckled. “What’s up?”

“Cronies,” she answered.

“Cronies?” Allen asked.

“Well, one crony in particular. A *Tanner Goochly* crony.” Allen suddenly remembered asking about Goochly’s associates. He sat up a little straighter in his chair.

“And?”

"And, Luther Fisher," she replied. "Guy goes by 'Fish'. He was reluctant to talk to me at first but once I convinced him he may be in some hot water he decided it might be best to cooperate."

"What information did our fish provide?"

"As you suspected he was one of the folks who did some work for Teri Hickox."

"What kind of work?" Allen had his pen and pad ready.

"New identities. Five of them to be exact and guess what Allen?"

"What, Eliza?"

"All of the names were apparently old west outlaws. Fish said he thought it was weird but that's what she requested."

"Let me go out on a limb," Allen said then smiled, "one of the names was Longabaugh."

Teri paced around in front of the storage unit for several minutes. Before going back inside she remembered there was another unheard message on her phone. She punched it up.

"Hey, uh, Teri this is Fish," the message started. As soon as she heard the forger's voice, she paused the recording, pulled the phone from her ear and stared at it. *Why was Fish calling?* she wondered as she started the message at the beginning and listened intently. "Hey, uh, Teri this is Fish. I just got squeezed by the Raleigh P.D.. They asked about work I did for you. I didn't say nothing at first but then they put the screws to me pretty hard and I had to tell them. So, now I'm telling you." Teri had heard enough; she deleted the message and headed back inside. *Well this has escalated quickly*, she thought, going through the door.

♪♫♪

Confrontations

Still at his desk, Allen decided to try the number Connie Byrd had given him again. This time the call was picked up on the second ring.

"Stan Byrd here," a strong, steady voice answered. Allen thought it the voice of a busy man.

"Mr. Byrd, hello," the detective started.

"Hello," was all Stan Byrd said.

"Hi. This is Detective Marc Allen with the CSPD."

"Why are you bothering my family, detective? What's this about?" *Not only busy*, thought Allen, *but rude.*

"Well Stan, full disclosure," Allen said, "I'm on a bit of a fishing expedition trying to get some information about your brother Reg." The detective had rehearsed a couple of different ways to tackle this inevitable conversation and decided his best option was the direct approach. He wasn't sure what Stan Byrd's reaction would be and he half expected it would be to hang up the phone. He didn't.

"I'd rather have this conversation in person," Byrd said.
"That would be my preference as well," Allen was elated. "Where and when?"

"My office, 2 PM today."

This time Byrd did hang up.

"Hot damn," Allen slapped his hand on the top of his desk and then looked at his watch. He had a little more than an hour and needed to get something to eat. Then he realized he had no idea where Stan Byrd's office was located. He hustled out of the station and down the street to a grocery store that featured a deli. On the way he called Connie Byrd hoping she'd be home and agree to tell him where her father worked. She did. Then his mind wandered to Tracey. He wondered what she was doing, how her case was going, and whether or not his pooch, Lettie, was starting to like her more than him. At the deli he ordered a cup of sweet and sour soup and a bag of chips and headed back to the police station and his car. The entire way back he smiled to himself, realizing it had been a while since he thought about a woman the way he was thinking about Tracey. He plopped down on a bus stop bench, drank his soup from the cup, and ate the chips.

His thoughts drifted from Tracey Rice to Stan Byrd, Jr. The nondenial confirmed that he, indeed, had a brother named Reg. If, as Allen suspected, Reg Byrd was the orange van man he'd have to get Stan to open up about a relationship he apparently had no desire to perpetuate. Allen was an only child but he knew, thanks to friends, sibling relationships could be complicated, sometimes even destructive. He also knew he probably had one, and only one, bite at the Stan Byrd apple so he'd have to tread lightly.

When she reentered the storage unit Teri saw her captive seated against the wall right where she had left him. His head was down, chin against his chest. For a split second she worried that he had died while she was outside. But a soft snoring sound emanated from the van man alleviating her fears. She knew he was already a dead man, she just didn't want to miss out on the exhilaration of her being the cause. A few breadcrumbs and an empty Ziploc bag littered his lap, the only remnants of his lunch. Teri walked over to him and kicked the sole of his left shoe. His eyes fluttered.

"Wake up sleepyhead," she said softly and offered a smile.

"I was dreaming," the champ reacted lifting his shackled hands to his mouth to wipe some drool, "about a girl I used to know." He finished his thought.

"How sweet," she replied, her tone turned uncaring. "I just wanted to let you know this will all be over soon." She stared into Reg Byrd's eyes.

"You're going to let me go?" he asked. "Back to the van and my normal, boring life? So I can continue to be a bother to nobody?" Teri thought she heard the resignation in his voice when he asked the questions.
"Something like that," she answered, getting up and turning to leave.

"Any more peanut butter and jelly sandwiches?" he called out as she left the unit. The sound of the padlock clanging against the metal door was the only answer he would get for now.

So he sat in the dark trying to remember some of the good things he had done in his life. It came nowhere near countering all the bad. It led him to the only conclusion possible, if there was a heaven or a hell he was definitely destined for the latter. He decided not to bother with praying or apologizing, or asking for forgiveness, he'd just rely on what he believed: when you're dead, you're dead. Dust to dust, nothing more, nothing less. Eventually he realized his head now hurt worse than his behind. In the end he told himself his circumstances boiled down to damn bad luck. He just happened to be in the wrong place at the wrong time when some psychopath decided to go human hunting. There was no way he could have known he was a carrot on the end of a stick used to attract the attention of a certain CSPD detective. He also thought, albeit briefly, how his life would have been different if he hadn't been such a coward all those years ago.

Detective Marc Allen's stomach rumbled and he regretted the soup choice almost immediately as he drove from CSPD headquarters to Stan Byrd, Jr.'s office in the Penrose House on Mesa Avenue near the Broadmoor Hotel. He was happy to have his GPS because he had never heard of the place and had no idea where or what it was. A quick search on his phone showed him the estate was built in the early 1900s on land that was once an apple orchard. Spencer Penrose, one of Colorado Springs's early patriarchs, bought it in 1916.

As Allen read, he learned the city was founded by General William Jackson Palmer who built, among other things, the famous Antlers Hotel. The history, which the detective felt was also sprinkled with a heavy dose of urban legend, noted The Antlers (like much of Palmer's Colorado Springs) was "dry" meaning no alcohol was allowed to be served. Allen discovered that didn't sit well with one Spencer Penrose who, in search of a drink, went a bit south and west of The Antlers to something called The Cheyenne Mountain Country Club to have a libation. Several years later, as a thumb in the eye to his now rival Palmer, Spencer Penrose built The Broadmoor Hotel.

The Penrose House was a beautiful structure built just outside the grounds of the hotel resort. He drove through the gates and up the red brick driveway. He pulled into a parking place, killed the engine, got out and went inside. The foyer allowed a visitor views of the rooms to both the right and left of the entryway. Allen thought it looked much more like a museum than an office building. Directly in front of him was a staircase and he heard, before he saw, Stan Byrd, Jr. coming down it. When he finally did see him the one word that came to Allen's mind was "impressive". The younger Byrd was tall and trim. A straight jaw was the defining characteristic of a handsome face that was topped with a full head of silver hair. He came down the steps with a casual ease. His appearance was noteworthy because Allen couldn't tell if the man was in his 50s or 70s.

"Detective Allen," Byrd said as he reached the bottom of the stairs and headed toward his guest. He stopped about 10 feet short. Allen recognized that it wasn't a question and decided Stan Byrd didn't get many visitors these days.

"Mr. Byrd," Allen responded expecting his host to ask to be called Stan. He didn't. "Remarkable place," Allen added.

"It has its plusses and minuses."

"I've done some research on the estate," Allen embellished a bit, "and I would love a tour."

"Perhaps some other time," Byrd deadpanned. "What exactly do you want, detective? Why are you here?" It wasn't lost on Allen that Byrd knew exactly why he was there since he had told him on the phone. The detective couldn't imagine the man in front of him not being in full command of the details.

"No more small talk, I guess," Allen said, smiling, "I'm okay with that Mr. Byrd. As I said on the phone, I'm here to ask you a few questions about your brother Reg." Byrd didn't reply. He simply turned and started back up the stairs. Allen figured it was an invitation to follow so he did.

At the top of the second flight of stairs Byrd turned left and headed down a carpeted hallway with long, steady strides. Allen noticed Western themed artworks on both walls and thought they all looked old and expensive. At the end of the hallway a door on the right led to Byrd's office. Once inside

Allen came to the conclusion it was just as commanding as the man. The office was at least three times the size of his boss Dennis Paulson's space and ten times more imposing. The wood, the windows, and the atmosphere all told detective Marc Allen that an important man spent time here.

"Sit," Byrd motioned to a chair. Allen heard the word as something between a request and a command and complied. Byrd took his place behind the massive desk. He stared out the window for a few seconds and Allen took the time to retrieve a pen and his notebook from his jacket pocket. Byrd rocked ever so slightly in his chair and never faced the detective. "My brother Reg," he started.

"Mind if I take notes?" Allen interrupted.

"I'd mind if you didn't," Byrd retorted, 'I'm only telling this story once." And then he picked up where he left off.

Allen listened as Stan Byrd, Jr. laid out the story of his life. The detective knew he was there only by the good graces of his host and to make any attempt to delay the story by interrupting or try and speed the process along would not only be in vain but might actually slam the brakes on the entire enterprise. So, he listened and, when he thought appropriate or relevant, jotted down tidbits.

He heard, directly from the horse's mouth, a tale of a young man from the eastern United States who made his way west. An intelligent, athletic, self-starter who, after being accepted to and studying at Colorado College, worked to establish a foothold in the Colorado Springs community and forge a life. Byrd got a job as a bell hop at The Antlers Hotel, worked his tail off, and impressed people including the folks who ran The Broadmoor. They, in turn, recruited him away. He turned that into a career after graduation. He also met a girl with whom he would share his hopes, dreams, desires, and eventually his life. Byrd also described, with what Allen thought a blend of astounding clarity and a hint of nostalgia, a normal upbringing in an upper middle class family led by principled parents raising two boys.

"Shortly after I arrived, Reg came west too," Byrd said then looked at Allen for the first time since he started his story. Allen decided it was a good time to jump in.

"How did that make you feel?" he asked. Byrd stared at him, more like through him, Allen thought and the detective worried it might be the end of the meeting.

"How did it make me *feel*?" Byrd asked. Allen pressed his luck.

"Yeah, feel? Were you happy about it?" Byrd steepled his fingers in front of his face and looked past his questioner.

"I guess so," he answered, "at least initially."
"Why not later?" Allen wondered and Byrd leveled his gaze on the detective again.

"It appears we have come to the crux of this meeting," he said. Allen leaned forward in equal parts ready to start writing or put his notebook and pen away. "Detective," Byrd said coldly, "I don't know if your being here means my brother is in some kind of trouble or about to be given the key to the city. I don't know if he's alive or dead, in the Springs or in Paris, and quite frankly I care about all of that quite a bit less than you seem to." Allen scribbled as fast as he could.

"But while you're documenting this exchange please include this," he added and Allen stopped and looked up. "I loved my brother, detective." He paused to let those words sink in. "Surprised?" he asked. Allen said nothing. "Well don't be. Just because I couldn't care less about what's happened to Reg now doesn't mean I didn't love him then."

"What changed?"

"Reg changed, detective. Reg changed."

"In what way?" Allen asked. Byrd took a few moments to ponder Allen's follow up.

"We were pretty typical brothers growing up, I think. Competitive, supportive, combative, conspiratorial. I got the brains, Reg the brawn. I was a straight A student all through high school and college while Reg struggled just to get by. He was much more charming than I was and he was able to use that as a tool. I let my grades speak for me. He was captain of the hockey team, the basketball team and the football team.

While I also skated, my interests tended more toward the individual sports like wrestling and golf." He stopped and watched Allen write, letting him catch up.

"Reg was homecoming king one year, got most every girl he wanted," Byrd picked up the story, "My interest in the fairer sex leaned more toward the cerebral girls because they made great lab partners in chemistry and physics. But again, despite those differences, we loved each other, detective, we stuck up for each other. We were *there* for each other," he paused again. "Like brothers. Do you have any siblings Mr. Allen?" The detective stopped writing and wondered if the man across the desk really cared.

"No sir, I don't," Allen answered. "I'm an only child." He watched as Byrd simply nodded and then reach for a bottle of water on the desk. He unscrewed the top and took a long drink.

"Would you like a bottle of water, detective?" he asked after putting the top back on. Allen thought it and the previous question about his childhood were the two most human gestures Stan Byrd had offered since his arrival.

"Please," he answered. Byrd obliged and Allen took a drink from his own bottle.

"When I was offered an academic scholarship to Colorado College I honestly believed Reg was happy for me," Byrd continued his story. "But I also now believe in my heart he was also a bit envious. He tried to get our father to pull some strings so he could join me there but he couldn't get in. Back in the day CC had a national championship hockey team. They weren't that good anymore when I got there but I was lucky enough to get to join the team during some practice sessions. Sadly, for me, I had no chance of making the team. But Reg could have. He was a far better player than I and there's no doubt he would have been welcomed with open arms. But his grades just weren't good enough to get in."

"So why did he come out here?"

"That's a heck of a good question, detective." For the first time Byrd's facial expression changed but Allen couldn't decide if it was a smile or a smirk. "He got into a junior college in Pueblo but it was clear to me early on that he had zero interest in the education it offered."

"How often did you see him?"

"Quite a bit," he answered, "at least in the beginning. I had met Ginger, my bride, and I was hoping to introduce Reg to a nice girl, someone compatible, so he could feel as lucky as I felt."

"How did that go?" Allen asked.

"Don't be impudent, detective," Byrd scolded.

"That wasn't my intent," Allen said defensively, "please accept my apology."

"To answer your question," Byrd continued and Allen took that as apology accepted, "it didn't go very well. If a girl liked Reg, he didn't like her. If, on the other hand, he happened to like one of the girls it never amounted to anything. He usually seemed much more interested in drinking my bourbon and talking about the motorcycle gang he had fallen in with."

"Motorcycle gang?" Allen's ears perked up.

"A bunch of thugs," Byrd practically spat the words, "and they had clearly gotten their hooks in my brother. He seemed to find them quite appealing and that became more and more apparent each time he visited us." Allen watched as Byrd grabbed the water bottle again and drank what was left in it. It looked to the detective like the man was reliving one of the nights decades ago. "The last straw was the night before Thanksgiving." Byrd finally continued. "We had a fight."

"Thanksgiving?" Allen asked.

"As I said, it was actually the night before. Ginger and I always had Thanksgiving dinner with her parents. She and I were going to be married and it seemed the proper thing to do. But we wanted to spend the holiday with Reg as well. At least I wanted to. Ginger and I had planned to have kids one day and I hoped he would be a part of it all. But I told him that wouldn't be possible unless he severed ties with that pack of criminals. That bunch of Hells Angels." Stan grabbed another bottle of water, unscrewed the cap and drank. He put the bottle down and continued.

"I remember my brother was well into the bourbon that night and he didn't appreciate my demands or my characterization of his *friends*." Stan used air quotes when he said the last word. "There was an argument and he stormed out." Allen wrote furiously and then looked up.

"You seem to remember that night very well," he said. The comment was met with an icy stare.

"It was the last time I saw my little brother, detective, how could I forget?" The vitriol with which he said the final sentence let the detective know the story telling had come to an end. What Stan Byrd said next put an exclamation point on it. "Now, I'm fairly certain you can see yourself out."

Sufficiently chastised, Marc Allen did just that.

The detective drove east on Lake Street distracted by just about everything the conversation had revealed. He felt more certain than ever the man he knew as Larry Holm, The Champ, was in fact Stan's brother Reg. The timing, the Maryland connection, the discussion with Stan's daughter Connie was all, Allen thought, evidence of that. Something else was stuck in his head, like a blackberry seed between his teeth. It was Byrd's mention of the fight he and Reg had on Thanksgiving Eve. He couldn't quite put a finger on why that holiday was important, but something told him that it was. He drove by a Starbucks and decided to pull in and get a coffee while he looked over his notes.

♪♫♪

Making Other Plans

Teri sat on Jake Holler's lap. Jake sat on Teri's sofa. She had invited him over with the promise of coming clean. Where she'd been, what she'd been doing. She hadn't told him yet but she was going to and she knew his reaction would determine a number of things. She had both arms around his neck and kissed him softly on the ear. She knew Jake was still upset but she sensed, with every touch of her lips a softening AND a hardening.

"What's going on Teri?" he asked between kisses.

"I told you I'd tell you and I will," she whispered in his ear.

"When?"

"After."

"After what?" he asked.

Her answer was to get up from his lap, pull him to his feet and push him down the hall toward her bedroom. As he peeled off his shirt she admired the muscles of his back and thought if this was to be Jake Holler's last day on earth she was bound and determined to make it memorable.

The soup was definitely more sour than sweet and Allen evacuated what was left of it from his system thanks to a quick pit stop in the Starbucks restroom. He approached the counter and a smiling barista named Shayla took his order of an Americano and a pumpkin scone. He took it all and plopped down in a comfy chair in the corner of the room. Allen took a sip and a bite then pulled out his notebook and found the page on which Stan Byrd had talked about the Thanksgiving holiday. Why was it important? What was it that struck a chord? His hope was it would rattle loose the thought, feeling, thing, that was stuck up somewhere in his brain about that date, but it didn't. But what it did do was jog his memory about something else. He took another bite of the scone, wiped his hands on a napkin and pulled out his phone. By the time Carl Paulson answered Allen was finished chewing.

"Paulson."

"Hey there Carl, it's Marc Allen."

"Oh hi, Marc," Allen thought his fellow detective sounded cautious. "What's up?"

"Sorry to bother you but I'm looking for a little help," Allen said.

"No bother," Paulson replied, "help with what?"

"I remember hearing Lieutenant Gutrich say you worked in Pueblo before coming to Colorado Springs, right?"

“I did. Actually grew up there. My mom carried a badge. She was my hero.”

“That’s really cool, Carl. I’m sure she was proud.”

“Still is, I hope,” Paulson said.

“Listen, while you were there did you ever have any run-ins with the Hells Angels?” Allen heard Carl Paulson laugh out loud at the question.

“That’s funny,” Paulson said. Allen felt a little of his excitement drain away.

“How so?”

“Just the thought of the Hells Angels finding Pueblo, Colorado attractive is both odd and humorous. Anyway, the Hells Angels weren’t there when I was there and to the best of my knowledge they never were.”

“Huh,” Allen replied then pressed on. “So no motorcycle gang activity?”

“Now I didn’t say that,” Paulson countered and Allen started feeling a bit more energized. “I remember my mom having to deal with a couple of groups, one bigger than the other.” While the detective talked Allen grabbed his pen. “Pretty sure the main one called themselves The Silent Commandos and they held court for a while. Mostly small-time stuff like gambling and loan sharking but they *were* a presence."

"Interesting," Allen said because he thought it was.

"Mom always referred to a guy named C T Mascaro," Paulson went on, "as the head of the snake."

"You said they *were* a presence. Is the gang no longer there?"

"Nah. They all got old and the world around them changed. Why are you asking?"

"I just left somebody who said his brother was mixed up with a motorcycle gang in Pueblo years ago. That fact drove a big ol' wedge through their relationship. I'm looking for the brother and was hoping somebody down in Pueblo might remember something about him. But it sounds like no luck."

"I wouldn't say that," Paulson jumped in.

"Really?"

"Really. Mascaro, the one who I said ran the outfit?"

"Yeah."

"He's still in town. He's getting old but he's gone all legitimate now."

“He has, has he?”

“Yep. In fact he’s the starter at a golf course I occasionally play with some buddies. Walking Stick. Every time I show up C T gives me the hairy eyeball.”

“Walking Stick,” Allen repeated as he wrote it down. “And how do you spell Mascaro?”

“You need help with the C T part too?” Paulson chided. “M-A-S-C-A-R-O,” he said slowly. “Just like it sounds.”

“Thanks a ton Carl, “Allen said after writing down the name again. “I really appreciate it.”

“No worries, Marc. I hope it leads to something.”

“Me too,” Allen said and disconnected. He finished off his scone and headed to the register to request a refill on the Americano. He ordered decaf this time.

“It would be an honor if you allowed me to get that for you officer,” a voice from behind Allen said. The detective turned and saw a middle-aged man and his wife. Allen wondered how they knew he was a cop but a quick look down revealed he was wearing his shield on his belt.

“That’s awfully kind of you,” Allen said with a smile. He looked at Shayla and winked. She smiled back conspiratorially, both knowing his refill was free.

"We appreciate your service," the man's wife said. "Thank you for keeping us safe."

"That's my honor and my pleasure ma'am," Allen said, "you two have a nice day." He grabbed his cup and went back to his seat feeling better about things than he had for a while. He looked up Walking Stick Golf Course in Pueblo, Colorado and made the call.

"Walking Stick, gotta put you on hold," a grizzled sounding voice answered. Instead of elevator music Allen heard the receiver being put down on a desk or a counter.

"No problem," Allen said to thin air then in the distance he heard the same voice that answered the phone.

"Next on the tee the Fallin threesome and Jared single. This is the ten minute call for the Porter group. Fallin three and Jared you're," Allen could hear the man dragging out the word then he added with a flourish, "next on the tee." The rustle of the receiver being retrieved was the next sound Allen heard and then the voice was back. "Thanks for holding, how can I help you?"

"I'd like to speak to C T Mascaro please," Allen said hoping Carl Paulson's information was correct.

"Can I ask who's calling?"

"You sure can," Allen tried to sound friendly, "this is Detective Marc Allen with the Colorado Springs PD."

"And what can I do for you detective?"

"Well, like I said I'm looking for a gentleman named C T Mascaro. I was told he worked there."

"To be factual," the man replied, "you said you'd like to *speak* with this Mascaro person, *not* that you were looking for him and to continue down the factual path, I'm no gentleman." Allen realized he had indeed found the former motorcycle gang's head honcho. "Anyway, I'm a little busy here," Mascaro continued, "so if you'd mind getting to the point, I'd appreciate it."

"Sure thing Mr. Mascaro," Allen said, "Do you remember a guy named Reg Byrd?" Allen heard only the sounds of Mascaro breathing and the distant ringing of a cash register. "Mr. Mascaro?"

"I'm here,' the man said, "I always wondered if this day would come," he added. "Joey!" Mascaro yelled, "do me a favor and take over the tee sheet!" Then he addressed Allen again, "you got something to write with, detective?"

"I do".

"Then take down this number and call me in five minutes. I gotta have a smoke." Allen did what he was told.

"First off," Mascaro started as soon as he answered his phone exactly five minutes later, "I'm gonna need some assurances that what I say in NO way comes back on me." Sensing he was on the right path Allen thought it best to agree.

"Okay," the detective said.

"Not gonna cut it," Mascaro quickly responded. "I'm recording this conversation and I need you to say the words."

"Which words exactly?"

"Cop words. Legal words. Words that mean I can't get in any trouble. Words that hold up in court. Words like immunity and voluntarily cooperated. Words like not subject to prosecution and free and clear."

"Look, Mr. Mascaro, I appreciate your personal concerns but all I can do is promise you this is not about you. I am just trying to get a handle on a situation I have up here in the Springs that, I'm pretty sure, involves Reg Byrd. I'm doing my best to eliminate the pretty part. I don't know that I can legally give you the assurances you say you need." Allen paused for a sip of his Americano then he continued. "Look, I'm going to be completely honest here."

"Thanks," Mascaro interjected.

"I'm not all that concerned right now with what crimes might have been committed decades ago or how deep your involvement may, or may not, have been in any of them. I'm trying to track down Byrd and all I can do is give you my word that your contribution to that effort will stay between us. Speech over." Allen waited. He didn't have to wait long.

"I guess that will have to do," Mascaro said. "What, exactly do you want to know?"

"Everything you can remember about him."

Mascaro told Allen about first meeting a young Reg Byrd in the Pueblo bar. Taking him under his wing, having him do odd jobs like debt collection and what the biker boss described as "other muscle work." He said he grew fond of the boy. When Allen asked if Mascaro knew of the brother in Colorado Springs the man said he did and then referred specifically to a night before Thanksgiving.

There was that night again, Allen thought. "Why was that particular night significant?" Allen asked.

"Well, because that was the reason Tweety had to leave town."

"Tweety?" Allen asked a little confused.

"Yeah Tweety," Mascaro replied, "Byrd. Tweety. Tweety Byrd. Nickname I gave the kid."

"Oh, got it." Allen shook his head and then asked, "so, why did *Tweety* have to leave Colorado?" The question was met with another long silence. Allen waited.

"Look detective, I know agreed to talk to you but that doesn't mean I trust you. You're going to have to ask Reg Byrd that particular question."

"Fair enough," Allen decided to move on, "please continue with the story."

"Frankly there's not a whole lot more to tell. We set the kid up in North Carolina and I thought that was the end of it."

"Wait a sec," Allen said excitedly, "did you say he went to North Carolina?"

"I did. Raleigh to be exact."

"Raleigh, North Carolina?" he asked again, softly.

"Are you deaf detective or just dumb?" Mascaro asked.

"I'm neither, Mr. Mascaro. Please go on."

"Like I said not much story left. We sent him off to Carolina with a new life and figured we'd never see him again. But we were wrong. Several years later there he was, back in the bar, with his tail between his legs."

“What happened in North Carolina?”

“Don’t know. Didn’t care so I didn’t ask.”

“Why not?”

“Well, by that time I was pretty much,” Mascaro paused and Allen envisioned the man scratching a stubbled chin searching for the right words, “retired,” Mascaro said. “The kid, of course, was no longer a kid, but he was desperate. I was hell bent on leaving those days behind but I felt bad for him so I did him one last solid.”

“What was that?”

“I arranged for him to have wheels, some cash, another new identity and one last piece of advice.”

“Were the wheels an old orange and white Dodge van?” Allen asked.

“They were.”

“And was the name on the ID Larry Holm?”

“Could have been, detective. That was a long time and a lot of fake ID’s ago.”

“And what was the piece of advice?”

"Now that I *do* remember," Mascaro said with a chuckle. "I told the kid to stay the hell away from me."

"Got it," Allen chuckled too.

"That's all I got, Mr. Allen and now I have to get back to work."

"I appreciate your time, sir."

"You play golf, Detective Allen?" It was Mascaro's turn to ask a question.

"I do," Allen answered, "but I'm not any good."

"Nobody's any good, son," C T responded and they both laughed. "Why don't you come play my golf course some time. It's an Arthur Hills design and right now it's in terrific shape. Oh, and bring that ne'er do well Carl Paulson with you. My treat. That kid was a hell of a player growing up. Could've turned pro. He was that good. Decided he loved his Momma more than golf though and that's why he became a cop. Damn shame if you ask me." Allen could picture Mascaro shaking his head.

"We might just take you up on that Mr. Mascaro and thanks for your time," Allen said with a newfound respect for detective Carl Paulson.

"Take care, detective." C T Mascaro hung up.

“I thought there might be another guy, someone else,” Jake said as he lay in Teri’s bed. She straddled him. They had been talking for a half an hour, Teri doing most of it.

“Boys” she said dismissively, “you are all so insecure.”

“It’s not that,” he said defensively then stopped when he saw the look on her face. “Okay, maybe it is that a little,” he conceded, “but seriously I’ve had my share of girlfriends, some of them pretty serious relationships, and I’ve never felt the way about them that I feel about you. Teri, the last couple of days really bugged me. You were just,” he paused, “unresponsive. Invisible.”

“I know honey,” she rubbed his cheek with the back of her hand. “I’m so sorry about that. But I’m not unresponsive or invisible now.” He tilted from the waist and kissed her on the mouth. She kissed back. “So, are you in?” she asked then pushed him back down flat on the bed.

“I’m in,” he answered without hesitation.

“Good. Now I’ve got to attend to a little more business. Stay if you want but if you decide not to then meet me back here tomorrow around midday. I’ll make us brunch.” Jake smiled at that. “I *will,”* she said punching him softly on his chest. “Oh and pack a bag cuz we’ll be going on a little trip.”

“Trip? Where?” he wondered.

"It's a surprise. Trust me, you'll like it." They made love again before she left.

When she was gone Jake stayed in bed, Teri's scent enveloping him. He thought about what she told him. About the random dude she held captive in the storage unit. It scared him and if he was completely honest he had to concede *she* scared him a little. But she excited him too. Bottom line, he decided, was that Teri Hickox, and all that came with her, was worth it. He got up, made the bed, showered, dressed and left her condo.

For her part Teri was happy that she wasn't going to have to kill Jake Holler too. At least not yet. He was a good guy and she admitted she liked him a lot. She was actually glad he was her partner in crime. She knew he was head over heels for her, he was handsome, and he knew his way around both the bedroom and a handgun. In short, he was a more than adequate Clyde to her Bonnie. Teri had confessed to him about hunting down and capturing the van man but she stopped short of telling him about what was to become of her prey. She also neglected to tell him about the North Carolina murders, at her hand, of Daisy Burns and Tanner Goochly. She also left out the killing of the homeless veteran right here in Colorado Springs.

After all a girl is entitled to a secret or four, isn't she? Teri thought as she pulled her Smith and Wesson M & P .22 with the Genotech suppressor from the Land Rover's glove box and headed for the storage shed.

Allen Turns to Tracey

Allen drove home. On the way he marveled at the beauty that surrounded him. It was another remarkable Colorado Springs evening. The sky to the west was a palette of blues, yellows and pinks thanks to a setting sun and a few puffy cumulus clouds. His mind ran through the other cloud types. *Cirrus, stratos, altocumulus, cirrostratus, stratocumulus,* he thought. And his favorite as a kid, *nimbostratus*. The name made him laugh when he was ten and it elicited a chuckle now even though he knew that particular cloud always brought rain, sleet or snow. His mind wandered to his dad, his hero, a man who studied astronomy in college and constantly encouraged his son to look to the stars and reach for the sky. He was awed by the silhouette of the mountains including majestic Pikes Peak.

"You don't get this kind of view in North Carolina," he said to himself and thought the entire scene was worthy of the world's most accomplished artists. It had been a day filled with revelations and Allen suddenly felt exhaustion overtake him. He looked forward to picking up his dog from Tracey's and plopping down on his couch.

He rapped on her door. Through it he heard Lettie's tags and license jingle. He could picture her doing her usual shake from head to tail. Tracey opened up and Allen thought she looked as pretty as he had ever seen her.

“Hey,” she said swinging the door open to let him in.

“Hey back.”

“You look beat,” she added sympathetically as Lettie came between them and stuck her snout in his crotch.

“Well hello there, girl,” he said, “I missed you too.” Tracey laughed.

“Come on in,” she said.

“Can’t stay,” he said with a shake of his head, “you’re very observant. I’m exhausted.”

“Just one drink,” she offered, “I just picked up a bottle of Whistle Pig 18 year.” Allen remembered remarking one time that it was his favorite rye whiskey.

“That doesn’t come cheap,” he said, “did you win the lottery?”

“I wish,” was her reply, “but alas no. Just a paycheck. But it *did* come with a nice bonus.”

“Good for you, Tracey. I’m sure it was well deserved. I guess we should celebrate.” He stepped inside, “but just one. Otherwise I might just pass out on your couch.”

“That would be just fine with me,” she said with a wink. Allen looked around the room.

"Speaking of your couch I see you've rearranged the furniture." He noticed the piece was now facing the entrance to the apartment and by its side was a different chair. It looked new. She had also moved the television so it was visible to whoever took a seat.

"Needed a change of scenery," she said simply, "and I picked up that great chair at the consignment store. What do you think?"

"I like it," he said sitting down as Tracey headed to the kitchen and the whiskey. Lettie took her place at his feet and he reached down and scratched her head. Tracey came back into the room, a Whistle Pig, neat, in her right hand and a glass of red wine in her left.

"Music or TV?" she asked handing him his drink.

"Let's listen to some tunes," he said accepting.

"Sounds good. I just made a new playlist."

Thirty minutes later Allen was polishing off his second drink. Tracey had brought him up to speed on her trial and Allen had laid out everything that had happened during the day. Talking it through helped him put some more of the mystery that was Reg Byrd together but there were still aspects that nagged at him. He stared up at the ceiling and then closed his eyes, trying to let the music take away all of his thoughts. He sensed

Tracey take the whiskey glass from his hand then interlace her fingers through his. It felt good.

“I like this song,” he said, eyes still shut, “what is it?”

“When I Get Home,” she answered, “Post Animal. They’re a Chicago band.”

Teri had changed back into all black in her Land Rover. She thought the attire appropriate. As quietly as she could she unlocked the storage unit door and crept inside. It took a few minutes for her eyes to adjust to the darkness but when they did, she saw her prisoner curled up in the fetal position, his back against the wall, sound asleep. She checked the generator and noted the company was right to claim it was “whisper quiet.” Next, she tested the temperature of the freezer and noted it was nice and cold. She had brought along a few bags of ice and she placed them inside just in case. She located and carried the stepstool she had purchased and set it a foot and a half from the long end of the appliance. Then she woke Reg Byrd up.

“Rise and shine,” she said cheerily. The man came slowly awake and sat up. He moaned.

“Never thought I’d say I miss sleeping on the ratty mattress in my van,” he said.

“Thirsty?” Teri asked.

“Parched,” was his reply and she held a bottle of water to his lips and let him sip. “Thank you, Ma’am.”

“You need to stop getting all polite on me van man,” she said letting him drink a little more. “Let’s get you up on your feet.” He rose unsteadily and leaned against her for support. His legs and hands were still bound so it took some time.

“You gonna cut these off of me?” he asked holding his arms out straight.

“I’m afraid I’m not,” she shook her head.

“Hmph,” he nodded, “well at least you didn’t make them super tight and I thank you for that.”

“You’re very welcome,” she said helping him shuffle toward the freezer. “Right here’s good,” they stooped, “now turn and face me.” As he did what he was told Teri climbed up on the stepstool putting her about half an inch taller than him. She looked into his eyes and smiled. He smiled back. Then Teri put her left hand down Reg Byrd’s sweatpants and gently fondled him. Reg realized it had been so long since a hand, other than his own, had been in that place that he didn’t know how to react. At first Teri saw what she thought was a look of shock on his face which slowly transformed into what she could only describe as bliss.

“What are you doing?” Byrd asked, his words coming out in breaths.

"Just having a little fun. Why? Do you want me to stop?"

"God no," he pleaded. He looked her in the eyes. "By the way," he said softly, "my name is Reg. Reg Byrd."

"Couldn't care less," Teri said. Then in one practiced motion she reached behind her with her right hand and grabbed the gun that was tucked in her waistband at the small of her back. She brought it around while removing her left hand from his pants.

"Hey!" he practically shouted, his eyes still on hers. Then Teri shot him in the crotch. Reg Byrd's mouth opened as wide as his eyes. When he started to buckle forward Teri aimed the gun at his heart and fired again. The force of that sent his body angling in the other direction and within a second Teri put one last bullet right between his eyes. With her left hand she pushed the dead man over backwards and into the freezer. She jumped off the stepstool and walked around to the front of the machine and had a look inside.

"Nice fit," she said and wiped her left hand on her pants leg. Then she shut the top of the appliance, sealing Byrd inside. "Just like Mama," she remarked and walked away.

Allen woke himself up with a sound that was something between a snore and a snort. The room was dark and he was disoriented. *Where am I?* was his first thought. After clearing out a few cobwebs he remembered being at Tracey's and realized he was still on her couch. She was nowhere in sight.

He slipped out from under the throw blanket she had laid on top of him, stood and stretched. Lettie had moved from her spot at his feet to inside her crate. She saw Allen through one open eye and emerged, her tail wagging a mile a minute. Allen scratched the dog under her chin then stepped around her and headed for Tracey's bedroom. Peering in through the door he saw her on her side, sleeping. Her hands were together, as if in prayer, under her head. Allen turned and went back to Lettie.

"Let's go girl," he said. Before leaving he noticed a pad of Post-it notes, peeled one off the cube, grabbed a nearby pen, and wrote "Thank You" on it. He and the dog walked out the door and across the hall. It was already Saturday so Allen knew he could sleep in a little. With that thought in mind he undressed, went into the bathroom, brushed the stale rye whiskey from his teeth and hit the sack.

"Refill?" the waitress stood, hovering a pot of coffee over Teri's cup, ready to pour. She looked up at her and then glanced at the woman's Waffle House name tag.

"Sure, Val," she said. "I'll take a warmup." Val poured and then wandered away. Teri had devoured her sausage and cheese "hash brown bowl" and was considering a pecan waffle with chocolate chips for dessert. She had no earthly idea why putting three bullets into a complete stranger at point blank range made her so hungry. But it did. Thinking about something sweet to eat made her also think about Jake. She wondered if he was, right this minute, sleeping in her bed. She mulled over whether he was having second thoughts.

"Getcha anything else, hon?" Val had reappeared sounding and looking like someone straight out of central casting. She smiled and Teri noticed the waitress was missing a couple of teeth.

"You know what Val?" Teri answered, "you can. How about one of those yummy looking pecan waffles?"

"You want chocolate chips too?" It came out *chock-o-lot.*

"You know I do, *hon.*"

"My oh my!" Val exclaimed, "you eat like a truck driver," she added then giggled. "How *do* you keep your figure?"

"I work out," Teri answered and Val turned and walked a few steps away. "Hey Val?" Teri called after her.

"Yes, hon?" Val turned.

"You got any whipped cream?" The waitress shook her head.

"Where do you think you are? IHOP?" she said and started walking again.

Teri stared out the restaurant window. In the distance she could see a smattering of cars on I-25: headlights going north, taillights heading south. In less than 24 hours she knew she and Jake would join the flow. The only question was in which direction. But first she got busy cementing her plan for later that day.

As Val was setting a just off the griddle pecan waffle in front of Teri Hickox, Marc Allen sat up straight in bed, wide awake.

"Steven Churchfield," he blurted. Whatever was trapped in his subconscious had finally wriggled its way to his brain's frontal lobe while he slept.

"Officer Steven Churchfield, girl," he repeated this time to a yawning Lettie. Allen got out of bed and padded over to the cabinet in his living room office. His fingers ran over several files until they found the one marked "Cold Cases," the detective's pet projects. He had brought home a packet, filled with CSPD unsolved cases that captured his attention, from the precinct. The murder of Steven Churchfield on a Thanksgiving Eve decades ago was one of them. He refreshed his memory about the particulars of the case again and remembered that there were a number of personal items, belonging to the patrolman, that were never claimed by his family. They included his hat and badge.

Allen had an idea and tried to recall where he left his phone after coming home from Tracey's. He finally found it on the bathroom countertop next to the sink. He scrolled through his contacts and landed on the name he was after. Before hitting the call button, he pulled on a pair of pants and went back to his desk. Then he dialed.

"Hullo?" a sleepy voice answered.

"Larry," Allen had called Larry Green, the ballistics and forensics expert with whom he had worked in North Carolina.

"Yes, who's this? And *whoever* this is do you realize what time it is?!" Allen could tell Green was pissed.

"I don't," he answered honestly. "Larry, it's Marc Allen."

"Allen? Detective Marc Allen?"

"Yes"

"Don't you think you could have detected what time it is? Well I'll tell you," he answered his own question before Allen could. "It's 4 in the damn morning, Marc. Couldn't whatever you think you need have waited a couple of hours?"

"'Fraid not, Larry. Look I'm sorry but I called you because you're the smartest guy I know."

"While that may be true," Green interrupted, "sweet talk won't make me any less irritated with you right now."

"Fair enough."
"Now that I'm wide awake what the *hell* is so important?"

"How long can useful DNA stay on a surface?" Allen didn't waste any more time.

"Jesus wept," he said exasperated. "I haven't heard hide nor hair from you in more than a year and you call and wake me up in the middle of the night to ask me *that*? What's the matter, is your Google finger broken?"

"Come on Larry, help me out here," Allen said. He hoped he sounded sufficiently chastised.

"Oh, Alright. Simple answer is a hell of a long time. Some researchers estimate DNA, under certain conditions, can last more than six million years. But I'm guessing for your purposes a case like the Boston Strangler is a better bellwether." Allen listened hopefully. "They caught that sick creep," Green went on, "using 50-year-old DNA recovered from a god damn blanket." Allen had heard enough.

"Thanks a million Larry. Now go back to sleep."

"Fat chance of that," the expert complained.

"Good night Larry."

"Good *bye* Allen! And next time?"

"Yes, Larry?"
"Call at a reasonable hour. Or better yet, call somebody else." That's how Larry Green ended the conversation.

Like his friend in North Carolina Allen knew he wasn't getting much, if any, more sleep this night. He put on a sweatshirt and shoes and grabbed his car keys.

"Wanna go for a ride, girl?" Lettie reacted like she had never wanted anything more in her life.

The detective drove east on Bijou Street all the way to Weber. As he expected the streets were practically deserted. He did see a couple of homeless folks pushing shopping carts down the sidewalks. He felt a pang of sorrow for them but also honestly wondered what, if anything, could really be done to help. Driving south on Weber he passed eight blocks before going through the intersection at Rio Grande. He found a parking space three down from Reg Byrd's orange and white van. After killing the engine Allen and Lettie got out. Before he could check on the van the dog made a beeline for a grassy area across the street fronting the police headquarters parking lot. There, she did her business and started sniffing around one on the tree trunks looking for the squirrel that had left its scent.

"Lettie. Come!" Allen called. Lettie came.

He approached the van and noticed, as usual, all the windows were covered. Some from the outside, some from within. Allen was certain he was about to break the news to Byrd that he knew the man was a cop killer. He'd never considered Byrd to be much of a threat and the crime the detective was sure he had committed happened decades ago. Still, Allen couldn't, with any certainty, guess how Reg would react when confronted with the truth.

"Here we go girl," Allen said as much to himself as the dog. Then he pounded on the driver's side door.

Tracey opened her eyes. The condo was quiet and she thought her bed was *so* comfortable. Reluctantly she slid from under the covers and left the bedroom. Allen and Lettie were gone. The throw blanket was folded neatly on the couch and there was an orange post it note on top of it. Tracey walked over, grabbed the square piece of paper and read. She smiled, turned on a heel and went back to bed.

Allen had knocked on every one of the van's doors and windows. He had called out Reg Byrd's name as loudly as he felt comfortable and Lettie had even chipped in with a couple of barks. After rocking the van back and forth for a handful of seconds the detective arrived at the only logical conclusion. Reg Byrd, aka Larry Holm, aka The Champ, wasn't home. *But where was he?* Allen wondered.

"We're outta here, girl," he said as he opened the Tahoe's back door. The dog jumped in.

Allen felt the adrenaline rush dissipate on the drive home. Part of him was worried about Reg Byrd while most of him was suddenly looking forward to crawling back in bed and catching a few more hours of much needed sleep. He managed to do just that, fully clothed, on top of the covers, seconds after walking in the door.

♪♫♪

Teri Makes Her Move

Teri got out of bed having enjoyed several hours of sleep on a Waffle House full belly. She had come home to an empty condo and slept without Jake which suited her just fine. There would be plenty of nights ahead with him in her bed. She did have a couple of lingering doubts about the man's resolve but Jake had done his best to put them all to rest when she called to see if he was still on board. He was just in the process of loading up his car and getting ready to come over. She asked him to wait another half an hour or so and reminded him to grab some eggs before he made the trip.

She packed everything she figured she'd need or want in two large suitcases and decided to leave the things she knew she could live without. A separate duffle was loaded with a couple of handguns and about a hundred thousand dollars in cash. They would have to make one last trip to the storage unit on the way out of town to get her other guns. She knew she'd have to ask Jake to wait in the car when she went in just in case the van man had started to stink. One last look around the closet and the bedroom was all Teri needed then she stripped and climbed into a hot shower.

A few hundred yards away Tracey opened her eyes for the second time that morning. She felt content and a little guilty after a check of the clock. She got up and made her bed. It was a ritual drummed into her as a preteen by her late Army Colonel father. "If you want to make a difference in this world, Tracey," he had said again and again, "you can start by making your own bed." Satisfied, she walked out of the bedroom and toward the kitchen. As she passed the blanket on the Allen-less couch she smiled then headed into the kitchen towards her espresso machine. She filled one part of it with water, another section with milk, popped in a couple of pods and made a latte. While the black liquid and steamed milk came together, she found a small tub of coconut milk vanilla yoghurt in the fridge and a bag of granola and some raisins in the pantry. She dumped a handful or two of granola in the yoghurt, added the raisins, and mixed it all together. By then the latte was steaming and smelling delicious. She sat down at her kitchen table and had breakfast.

Jake had done as instructed. Along with the eggs he also brought bacon and a couple of bagels with cream cheese. While Teri dried her hair, he whipped up some cheesy scrambled eggs, cooked the bacon in the oven and toasted the bagels even though Teri had been the one who promised to make brunch. He poured them both coffee and set the cups on the island. He was just spooning the last of the eggs onto the plates when Teri came out of the bathroom.

"Smells good," she said as she sat down and took a sip from her mug. Jake joined her with the plates and started to eat. Teri picked at her food.

"Not hungry?" he asked. She thought she could hear the disappointment in his voice.

"Not really. Don't know why." But, of course, she knew exactly why having eaten like a pig at Waffle House hours earlier. She stared across the table at Jake and watched him eat. She realized it didn't matter anymore if he was "all in" or not on her plan. If he wasn't, he'd die right here in her condo. She knew it would be harder to accomplish her goal alone but she'd figure it out. She always had. Everything, however, pointed to the fact that they were still Bonnie and Clyde so she relaxed a little. She had assured her Clyde that the only person that had any chance of getting hurt that morning would be the detective Marc Allen. Teri concocted a story that Allen was a shunned suitor in North Carolina who had used his badge and his buddies on the force to make her life a living hell. That was the reason she moved to Colorado and now, she had embellished, it seemed the psycho had followed her to continue the harassment.

"We're just gonna scare him. Convince him that it's in his best interests to leave me, and us, alone," she told Jake as she sipped her coffee. "Then we're going to tie them up, gag them and get the hell out of Dodge." Jake didn't object.

Lettie's tongue on his face startled Allen awake. Still groggy, he decided the best way to get the blood flowing was a long morning hike. He fed Lettie breakfast and while she ate, he changed clothes, splashed some cold water on his face, brushed his teeth and grabbed a power bar for his meal. Then they both took off for Cheyenne Mountain and the Mt. Cutler and Mt. Muscoco trails because they were two of Lettie's favorites. It helped that Allen liked them too.

Showered and dressed, Tracey was reading the paper when she heard the knock on her door. She thought and found herself actually hoping it was Allen so she hastened her pace and opened up without looking through the peephole. It wasn't Allen.

"Well now don't you look happy," Teri said while pointing her Smith and Wesson at Tracey's head. "Mind if we come in?"

Tracey moved to shut the door but Jake had anticipated her action and blocked it with his boot.

"Nice try," Teri said. "I'll give you this one pass but as of now your dumb move bucket is empty. Next time I'm just going to shoot you. Now, get inside." They all went into Tracey's condo.

"Have a seat," Teri ordered and Tracey obeyed, sitting down on the couch.

"It's okay," Jake said, "we're not gonna hurt you."

"Hush!" Teri barked another order, this one directed at her partner.

"Who are you?" Tracey demanded, "What do you want? Look around, I don't have a lot but whatever I have you can take." Teri laughed.

"Oh girl, we're not here to rob you," at those words she saw Tracey recoil. A look of horror came over her face as she looked at Jake. "We're not here for *that* either," she said then she looked at Jake. "Unless you're into that, Jake?" He stared at her, speechless. She turned back to Teri. "Guess not," she added.

"Okay, here's what's going to happen next," Teri changed the subject. "You're going to call your friends, the three you're always hanging out with, and get them over here. Now, where's your phone?"

"Who are you?" Tracey asked again. "How do you know so much about me?" Teri didn't answer. Instead she found Tracey's phone and tossed it to her. "Start with the weird chick."

"And say what?"

"Whatever it takes to get her to come. And remember that empty dumb move bucket. If you try something funny or I don't like what I hear you get a bullet."

"Teri!" Jake raised his voice, "you promised." Her answer was to lift her index finger to her lips.

"Make the call," she commanded. Teri dialed Hannah.

"Speak," the girl said.

"Hannah, it's Tracey. I'm in trouble," she stopped when she saw Teri raise the gun and point it at her head.

"Tracey?"

"Yeah, it's me. I don't know what's wrong. My arm is numb and my chest hurts." She noticed Teri nodding her head in approval.

"Oh no!" Hannah exclaimed.

"I think I need to go to the hospital," Tracey continued, "can you come help me? And bring Rampart too."

"I'll get him."

"Hurry please," Tracey tried to sound desperate.

"Hold on," Hannah replied, "I'll be there." She hung up.

Twenty minutes later Allen and Lettie returned from their morning adventure up and down Cheyenne Mountain. It was another glorious day and the detective liked to think he could see all the way east to Kansas from the Mt. Cutler summit. Being 7,200 feet up tended to help you imagine that. He figured he was still on a bit of an endorphin high and thought about barging in on Tracey to share his experience. Then he looked at his dirty dog and his dusty hiking shoes and thought better of it. Instead, he went inside his own place. Lettie headed for her water bowl for a drink and her crate for a nap.

Allen shed clothes all the way to the bathroom where he fired up the shower. As the hot water cascaded over him washing away the sweat and dust, Allen thought about paying another visit to Reg Byrd. He figured that should be the first order of business, maybe get somebody at the station to help unlock a door if Byrd still refused to let him in.

Clean and dry, Allen put on fresh clothes. Still thinking of paying Byrd a visit he picked up his phone and found he had missed a call from Tracey. As he started to dial her number his phone rang. She was calling again.

"Allen," he said automatically.

"Hi Marc. This is Tracey, Tracey Rice." Allen's detective radar immediately went to Defcon 1. He knew she knew he'd recognize her voice. He also couldn't recall the last time she used her last name around him or on a call.

"Hello Ms. Rice," Allen answered hoping to signal that he knew she was trying to tell him something. "Is everything okay?"

"Everything is just fine," she said, "it's just that the gang is over here and we want to play Pictionary but we need a fourth. Hannah says she needs her expert drawing partner." Again, alarm bells went off in Allen's mind. Hannah Hunt was an accomplished artist and he knew the last thing she needed was him as a Pictionary partner. Besides, the four of them had never played the game as a group.

“I just got back from a hike with Lettie. Can I grab a quick shower?” He said, both hoping to buy a little time and to get a sense of the urgency of Tracey’s situation.

“We don’t care if you’re dirty and sweaty,” she shot back and Allen had his answer. “it would be great if you could come now.”

“Ok,” Allen responded.

“Oh,” Tracey tried to sound like she had just remembered something, “and could you leave the dog at home? You know how she gets when we play games.” Alarm number three, Allen thought. Allen knew Tracey had pretty much adopted Lettie and never referred to her as “the dog.” They both knew she couldn’t give a hoot about a bunch of silly adults playing a board game. He also knew Tracey absolutely loved Lettie and the only conclusion he could come to was that she feared the pup might be in danger if she accompanied Allen.

“I’ll be right there.” He hung up. Allen thought for an instant about calling the situation in but worried that the person or people threatening Tracey might be listening. Instead he gathered up a handful of sheets of copy paper and a black Sharpie. On one sheet he wrote 10-18, on another 10-31 and 10-78 on a third. They were police codes for “urgent matter”, “criminal act in progress”, and “need assistance”. He added the words “across the hall” on another piece and then plastered them at different places around his apartment hoping Tucker Booth and his band of CSPD spies at 705 Nevada Street were still keeping an eye on him. He thought about writing one more message, "10-999" but that was reserved for the most dire police circumstances. He decided against it because it might be an overreaction and he knew he'd never live down calling in the calvary because of a game of Pictionary.

He took one more look around his home. Satisfied that he had communicated the situation as best he could, he checked on Lettie and found her sprawled, flat on her back, sleeping soundly. He grabbed his 9MM, made sure it was loaded, chambered a round, and headed across the hall and knocked on Tracey's door.

"It's open," he heard her say. Allen turned the knob and entered. He saw Tracey and Hannah on the couch, Rampart Haynes in the new chair. They weren't alone. Standing over Tracey was a man Allen recognized as Jake Holler who had a gun in his left hand. He was placing duct tape over Tracey's mouth with his right. Her hands were on her lap and Allen could see they were bound together by a plastic zip tie. His eyes then went to Hannah. He could have sworn he saw her mouth the words, "smooth criminal" while she glanced to his right. Then he looked back at Jake.

"Into kidnapping and torture now Mr. Holler?" he said spelling out Jake's last name. Allen raised his gun.

"We haven't tortured anybody," Teri Hickox said and she pushed the door shut behind the detective. "Yet."

He realized she had been there the entire time, directing the process, and that was who Hannah had referred to as a "smooth criminal". Teri had her own gun drawn. Allen couldn't help but notice the silencer at the end of the barrel pointing directly at his head.

"Hello Teri," Allen said, "is it still Hickox or do you go by Longabaugh now?"

"Did you miss me detective?"

"Like a toothache," he replied. "How long have you been in town? Did you follow me right after I left Raleigh or did you wait a while?" He noticed Jake looking at Teri.

"Before we continue this fascinating question and answer session why don't you drop Mr. Smith and Wesson," she said. Allen did as he was told. "I've been here long enough," she told him.

"Long enough to murder a homeless veteran by pumping him full of booze and Tramadol?" Allen decided to swing for the fences.

"What!?" Jake called from the couch where he had started binding Hannah's wrists, "you said that stuff was for your headaches." Allen felt he had his admission of guilt.

"You're so adorable Jake," Teri said.

“Hit me with your best shot,” Hannah said because Jake hadn’t gotten around to taping her mouth. Allen noticed that as she said it, she gave a sideways glance to Rampart who slid ever so slightly down toward the edge of the chair.

“What?” Jake said again, this time looking at Hannah.

“Fire when ready!” she said as a response. The back and forth distracted Teri and Allen noticed her gun was no longer pointed at his head.

“Shut her up, Jake! Now!” Teri yelled.

Allen turned his attention back to Ramp who was watching Teri. It looked to the detective like he was ready to be shot out of a cannon. Then, for a brief second, he and Rampart Haynes locked eyes. Ramp gave an almost imperceptible nod.

“I LEFT my heart in San Francisco,” Hannah shouted next, emphasizing the word ‘left’.

When Rampart heard it, he bolted from the chair loading up his best left hook. His fist caught Teri directly on her right temple and she went down like a sack of stones. At that instant, Allan launched himself at Jake. He caught him full in the chest and rocked him backward. Jake’s head slammed against the wall. He dropped both the gun and the roll of tape when he fell to the ground. Allen put his boot on the man’s neck and set to tying him up with his own restraints. Then he

dragged Jake Holler across the floor and laid him next to an unconscious Teri Hickox.
"That was a hell of a left," Allen said to Ramp.

"Hey, I may not be as good as I once was," he shrugged as he looked at Hannah and not Allen.

"But you're clearly as good once as you ever were." Allen added. The three of them laughed.

Just then the door to the condo burst open and officers Stupples and Foltz came through, guns drawn.

"Police!" they said in unison.

"I see somebody got my message," Allen said. Foltz and Stupples surveyed the room.

"What the heck happened here?" the female officer asked.

"So many questions," Hannah said from the couch.
"Mmmphh, mmmphh," it was Tracey. Mortified, Allen realized in all the excitement he had forgotten to free her. He went to her, pulled out his pocketknife and cut the ties that bound her wrists. Then as gently as he could he peeled the duct tape from her mouth.

"Nice work with the phone call," he said with a smile. She threw her arms around his neck and kissed him on the mouth.

Allen found her sticky and thought she tasted like adhesive but he didn't care or stop.

"Looks like we made it," Hannah exclaimed.

"So, where should we start?" It was Stupples.

They took pictures of the scene and then statements from the group. After a couple of tries Foltz gave up on Hannah, unable to make hide nor hair of what she was trying to say. An ambulance came and the EMTs took Teri to the hospital; Stupples went with them. Foltz escorted Jake Holler to jail.

"You were really brave," Allen said to Tracey. "You all were." They were still in Tracey's place sitting around the scene of the crime.

"Hannah and I knew something was weird from the get-go," Rampart said. "I mean, Tracey acted like she was having a heart attack but she called Hannah and *not* an ambulance. Who does that?"

"I'm lucky I have such perceptive friends," Tracey said, smiling at Ramp and Hannah.

"Aw shucks," Hannah shrugged.

"What the hell was her deal?" Tracey addressed the question to Allen.

"Old friend," Allen said simply.

"You need better friends," Tracey said.

"I think I've got them," Allen responded.

"Glad it's over," Hannah said and they all nodded in agreement.

"Wilco," Rampart said to his sister. She smiled.

A couple hours later Allen stopped by the hospital to see Teri. The doctor said she had a concussion but was awake.

"Can I see her?" Allen asked.

"Guess so but she's still got a killer headache," the doc answered.

"Good," Allen said as he turned to walk toward her room.

"Oh, detective?" the doc called after him.

"Yeah?"

"Don't be shocked if she vomits all over you. She's still nauseous."

"I'll take my chances."

He found her lying in bed, her upper body propped up, her head on a pillow. He asked if she had been read her rights knowing she had.

“Lawyer,” she said, “asshole.”

“Why would you want a lawyer who’s an asshole?” Allen asked before leaving the room.

It didn’t take the detective long to get Jake Holler to flip on his girlfriend. Throwing out charges like accessory to murder, kidnapping, assaulting a police officer and reckless endangerment in rapid succession tended to be great motivation. Then adding the corresponding Colorado prison time for each sealed the deal.

♪♫♪

Science Doesn't Lie

A week later they moved Teri to the El Paso County jail on Las Vegas Street in the Springs. It was about 10 miles from CSPD headquarters and it took Allen about 20 minutes to get there. He had made special arrangements to meet with Teri in one of the facilities private conference rooms. The folks at the correctional facility weren't too keen on the idea but after some not so gentle prodding from Deputy Chief Paulson the request was granted. A guard walked Allen to the room and opened the door. Allen, carrying two file folders, looked around. There was a table, he figured about six feet across, and three chairs. Two were on one side of the table and they were occupied. Allen's seat waited for his butt. The guard took up his position near the door.

Teri Hickox sat in one of the chairs, bound at the ankles and the wrists by a length of chain. She stared down at the desk, refusing to look at Allen. Next to her was a burly man in a three-piece pinstripe suit. Allen recognized him.

"Detective Allen. I do declare, I haven't seen you in a coon's age," the big man said with a thick southern accent.

"Dolly Madison, it hasn't been long enough for my liking," Allen replied. The detective knew the man as a big time, blowhard, attorney who spent more time on cable television than in the courtroom. Teri had utilized his services when Allen had suspected her of two murders in North Carolina. He offered a phony smile to Madison and turned his attention to Teri.

"I see you're spending Hank's inheritance wisely," he said. "How's your head?"

"Up yours," Teri responded, eyes still down.

"Now you just hush, young lady," Madison said as he reached his hand and patted Teri's right forearm. "Not another word."

"That's okay with me, Dolly," Allen told the attorney. "Can I call you Dolly?"

"Mr. Madison will do just fine, son. Thank you."

"That's great, Dolly," Allen smirked. Then he placed the file folders on the table and sat. "The two of you can just listen," Allen added and slid one of the folders toward Teri.

"What's that?" Madison asked.

"Science, Dolly. Science."

"Whatever," Teri interjected, "can we go now?"

"Shhh Shhh Shhh," Madison scolded his client. "What's this all about, Marc?" the attorney said Allen's name like it left a bad taste in his mouth.

"For starters it's about your client killing her mother," Allen answered.

"Jesus!" Teri started.

"Teri," Madison touched her arm again. "Be quiet! Now I don't want to have to tell you again. You're not doing yourself any favors." She nodded and slumped down in her chair. "Now detective," Madison addressed Allen, "*that* accusation again? You appear to be barking up the wrong tree. Have you forgotten Hank Hickox *confessed* to that crime? But do go on."

"I will, thanks. Did Hank confess? Are you sure about that?"

"Sure as sugar," Madison said, "I saw the note." He looked at Teri, "we both saw the note."

"I saw it too," Allen agreed, "but I've seen another note since."

"Bullshit!" It was Teri.

"Maybe, maybe not," Allen said, "but it really doesn't matter does it Teri?"

"You are going to have to explain yourself, young man," Madison shook his fat finger at Allen. "If not, I'll kindly ask the guard there to take my client back to her cell."

“You’re not going anywhere,” Allen stared at the attorney. Then he turned back to Teri. “Killing two people in North Carolina wasn’t good enough for you was it, Teri? You had to come to Colorado and kill two more.”

“*Dee Tec Tive,”* Madison shouted. “That’s enough! You have no proof of any of that and if you do I suggest you fish or cut bait.”

“I have all the proof I need, *Mister* Madison,” Allen countered and slid the other file folder toward to man.

“What’s *this*?” Madison asked as Allen looked at Teri.

“Your boy toy Jake Holler told us everything,” he said. “That, among other things, is his voluntary confession.” Madison opened the folder and started reading.

“That’s interesting,” Teri defied her attorney by speaking again. “How could he tell you *everything* when he doesn’t know *anything*?”

“He knows you asked him to get you Tramadol.”

“Never happened,” she countered.

“And he knew the two of you talked about being the modern-day Butch and Sundance right Miss *Longabaugh*? Or was it you were Bonnie and he was Clyde?

"You tell me," she sniggered. Allen couldn't help but notice the esteemed attorney had stopped scolding his client for talking too much. "That boy is such a romantic." Teri went on. "There's no telling what he had made up in his pretty little head. Don't you just love him, detective?"

"You bet I do," Allen said, "and do you know when I *really* fell head over heels for him, Teri?" She didn't say anything. "When he took us to your storage shed." Teri's mouth opened but nothing came out. She looked at Madison for support but got none. Allen leaned back in his seat and expelled a breath before continuing.

"Like I said I *know* you killed your birth mother. I'm pretty sure you whacked Tanner Goochly too," Teri just looked at him, "and now I also know you murdered your father."

"Enough, detective!" Dolly Madison had rejoined the conversation. "These accusations you're throwing around are heinous, beyond reproach, and at least for the last one not based in fact. You know as well as I do that Hank Hickox, God rest his soul," Allen watched as Madison crossed himself and looked up at the ceiling, "died by his own hand."

"I'm pretty sure even though she didn't pull the trigger, this monster," he pointed at Teri, "is responsible for Hank's death. His dog too but I'm not talking about Hank Hickox, Madison."

"Then what the hell *are* you talking about?" Teri asked.

"Your *real* father," Allen replied, "Reginald Byrd."

"Who?!" both Teri and Dolly Madison said in unison.

"As I said," Allen continued tapping the first file folder, "science. The dead guy in your freezer? Remember him?" Allen asked Teri. "And by the way," Allen added as an aside, "it's illegal to have a gas-powered generator in a Colorado Springs storage shed. Might just add that to the charges."

"So, arrest me," Teri blurted out.

"You're already under arrest here but I know my old pals in North Carolina are interested in talking to you again too," Allen said. "And I'm sure your esteemed attorney knows they still have, and use, the death penalty there." He saw Teri's face lose a little color. "Anyway, back to the guy, with three bullet holes, taking a forever nap in the freezer inside your storage shed." He used the index finger and thumb of his right hand to mimic a gun and pointed at Teri. "One in the head, one in the heart and one in the privates, *just* like your mother Daisy Burns. You know *that* guy?" Teri said nothing.

"Why him?" Allen asked.

"Don't answer that," the attorney warned.

"Was it just for fun or did you see going after Reg Byrd as a way of getting to me?" Teri opened her mouth to answer but stopped when Madison touched her arm.

"It doesn't really matter because, as it turns out, you made a huge mistake," Allen tapped one of the folders.

"Meaning what, exactly? The attorney wondered.

"It just so happens that this particular victim wasn't just some drifter living out of an orange van."

"Bless your heart, detective, but enough already." Allen recognized the subtle southern insult as Madison tried to go back on the offensive. "Let's pretend, for one second, that my client knows what you're talking about," he leaned forward, "so pray tell, who was this freezer man of whom you speak?"

"Went by the name of Larry Holm, in fact called himself 'The Champ' but, like I said, his real name was Reginald Byrd."

"So?" Madison asked.

"The *same* Reginald Byrd who ended up in North Carolina more than three decades ago," Allen said then looked at Teri. "How old are you anyway Miss Hickox?" She stayed silent. "The *same* Reginald Byrd who got a young girl named Daisy Phillips pregnant and then ran like a rabbit because he couldn't come to grips with being a dad. He left young Daisy high and dry. Her only recourse was to put the baby girl up for adoption. And do you know who did the adopting?" Neither Madison nor Teri answered so Allen did. "That would be Hank and Betty Lou Hickox."

"You're out of your mind," Teri said without much enthusiasm.

"That means the freezer man," Allen looked at Dolly Madison, "*of whom I speak* is Teri's real father. Deoxyribonucleic acid don't lie." Teri said nothing but looked at her attorney.

"DNA honey," Madison returned her look and answered, "DNA. Chromosomes, genes, science, Teri, and the detective is absolutely right, science never lies. It can't" Then the attorney turned back to Allen. "Well, I guess even a blind hog finds an acorn now and then, detective. Now, about jurisdiction," he started to ask.

"Not up to me," Allen interrupted. He grabbed his file folders and got up to leave but before he got to the door he turned back around and addressed Teri.

"What?" she snarled.

"You know you like to think you're some sort of evil genius but, to my way of thinking, you're just like those dumb bad guys I see in almost every movie I watch and most of the murder mysteries I read."

"Meaning what exactly?"

"Meaning you should have shot me in Tracey's condo." He walked back to the desk, placed both hands on top of it and leaned in. "Why all the histrionics? What were you trying to prove? I mean if you wanted me dead you should have just pulled the trigger as soon as I walked through the door. Left me bleeding out on the floor while my friends watched. Then hightailed it out of town with your boyfriend. The dumb bad guys never just get the job done." He looked at Dolly Madison. "They get too big for their britches and then end up getting the short end of the stick," he said in a theatrical southern accent. "Did I get that right counselor?"

He straightened up and this time he did leave the room. Teri and her lawyer sat in stunned silence.

♪♫♪

Just Rewards

“Nice work, Marc,” Allen was in the deputy chief's office sitting across from another new desk. He accepted the praise from his boss’s boss, Dennis Paulson.

“Thanks sir, “Allen said. “A little luck, a lot of help and some decent breaks that went our way.”

“You’re much too modest, detective,” the Chief responded, “which, by the way, is an attitude I endorse wholeheartedly. But I gotta tell you solving two murders and a years old cold case usually boils down to damn fine police work.” Suddenly uncomfortable with the compliments, Allen decided to change the subject.

“Who gets her, Chief?” he asked about Teri.

“Well?” Paulson took a second or two to think, “They want her bad,” he said. Allen knew he was referring to their colleagues in North Carolina. In fact, Eliza Starz had already told Allen that. “And our guy,” the deputy chief continued, “is a bleeding heart liberal so my guess is he’s conflicted.”

“How so?”

“I think he’d like nothing more than to keep that murdering bitch away from the gallows but that’s bound to cause a boatload of headaches for him. The ol’ Gov is probably doing some kind of dance as we speak deciding if trying to save her soul is worth it." Allen simply nodded sensing there was more. There was. "If you ask me, and I know you already did, I'd say five will get you ten that your friend Teri Hickox has her butt on North Carolina's death row sooner rather than later."

"Hope so," was all Allen said.

"That's not to say Florence would be a life of leisure," the Chief added referring to Colorado's Supermax prison that was currently home to some of the world's most notorious murderers and terrorists.

"I know," the detective agreed, "but, in my humble opinion even Florence is too good for her." Chief Paulson nodded and looked at his watch.

"Don't you have a party to get to?" he asked. Allen knew the chief was aware of it because Tracey had told him she extended an invitation.

"Oh, crap!" he said and he got up to leave.

"Detective," the deputy chief called before Allen got to the door, "I almost forgot."

"Sir?" the detective turned and asked.

"This is for you."

Allen recognized the distinctive shape of the box. He knew contained Whistle Pig's most expensive rye whiskey, The Boss Hog. The box was in the shape of a small coffin. He had seen it in his favorite Springs liquor store going for $575.00 a bottle.

"Really?" he asked his boss. Then he walked back to the desk to grab the gift. Paulson handed him a note and Allen saw it was from the chief of police.

"Go ahead and read it here," Paulson implored. Allen pulled the note from its envelope.

Detective,
Great work! I am happy to let you know you have now solved more of this department's cold cases than that windbag Joe Kenda ever did. Don't let it go to your head.

He smiled and nodded to the deputy chief, certain the man had read the words. Then he slipped it into a back pocket, took the bottle of booze and left. Buoyed by the praise, Allen was looking forward to having a cocktail with friends, especially Tracey. He walked out of the station and almost ran right into a reporter from one of the local television stations.

"Got a minute, detective?"

"Not really," he said honestly as he looked the reporter up and down. Allen realized he was looking at a kid, a twenty something year old, and he suddenly felt a little guilty. "What's your name?" he asked, "and how old are you?"

"Dalton Toledo," the reporter responded, "and I'm 26."

"Real name or TV name?"

"Real, sir." Dalton smiled.

"Call me Marc, Dalton. Is this your first job?"

"No sir, uh Marc. Out of college I got a job at the ABC affiliate in Bakersfield, California. This is number two."

"Sure, I've got a minute," Allen said. After answering the questions he felt he could, and deferring the ones he couldn't to higher ups, he reached into his pocket and handed Dalton Toledo one of his business cards.

"Take this and call me if you think I can be of service." Then he walked to his car, climbed in, and headed to The Rabbit Hole.

"My hero!" Tracey called, spotting Allen on his way over to their booth in a back corner of the restaurant and bar. He smiled widely at her then waved to Rampart, Hannah and a man sitting very close to Hannah who he recognized as Dr. Tom Christine. Glasses with dark beer were in front of Ramp and the doc. The ladies had martini glasses filled with a pink tinged liquid which Allen assumed were cosmopolitans. The space left for him was fronted with what he could tell was a Mad Hatter. The scene looked quite inviting. As Allen got closer, he noticed again the proximity of Dr. Christine to Hannah Hunt. The detective figured he'd be hard pressed to slide a sheet of paper between them.

"Hi Marc," Tracey said getting up so he could slide in and sit between her and Hannah. Before he could she grabbed him and gave him a kiss. *No adhesive this time*, thought Allen. He tasted cranberry juice and vodka instead.

"It's a love thing," Hannah said and then she grinned. Allen sat. "Raise your glass," Hannah added grabbing hers, "Let's celebrate."

Rampart looked at her and then the doctor.

"See," he said, sounding exasperated, "It's *still* happening." Allen and Tracey took sips from their glasses. Hannah did too then she set it in front of her and looked at her brother.

"What's still happening, Ramp?" she asked him. His mouth fell open. It was the first time he had heard his name pass her lips since the accident.

"Oh. My. God! Hannah is it really *you* again? What happened? What changed?"

"No idea," she said honestly. "I was really tired this afternoon so I took a nap. Had another weird dream like in the hospital but this time the singers and songwriters weren't coming *in* to see me, they were leaving. When I woke up it felt like my whole world was different. I don't know, normal."

"That's fantastic," Tracey chimed in. They all nodded.

"The first person I called was Tommy." She put her hand on top of the doctor's.

"Like I told you before," Christine said to Rampart, "it's a miracle."

"It's like magic," Tracey said softly.

"Abracadabra," Hannah said looking at Tracey and winked. Then she turned her attention to the bartender. "Beer for my horses!" she yelled.

"You got it, song girl," the barkeep called back.

The whole group laughed. Then Hannah leaned over and kissed her doctor boyfriend. Allen and Tracey stole a kiss as well. Rampart Haynes didn't have anyone to kiss so he polished off his first beer. He couldn't remember a time in his life when he had been happier.

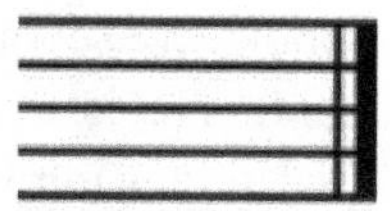

THANK YOU FOR BEING A FRIEND

As always everything begins and ends with Sarah. She is my True North. Despite all that is on her plate on a daily basis she always finds time to encourage me to find the good in others and the best in me.

In my prior life I worked in sports, mostly producing golf tournaments for television. I was involved in thousands of broadcasts and wrote the words used to come on the air for nearly everyone. They were 30 to 45 second intros and we called them "teases". After penning platitudes and words of praise then editing dramatic pictures to match the words for one, I had one of our talented on-air personalities provide the voice over to the video. When it was finished a dear friend and colleague on the crew named Bob Swanson said, "another nice tease, Keith" to which I replied, "you know Swanny, they practically write themselves." That was close to the truth because I was dealing with world class athletes, chasing dreams, and staring at outcomes that could be life changing. Writing books is different. They most certainly DO NOT "write themselves".

As is the case with each book, my second set of eyes and ears belonged to Jake Hirshland. He is my most trusted editor. Among all the corrections and suggestions, (and there are always many) he never failed to offer praise and encouragement. He has always made my work better and he did it again this time.

So did Susan Green. She is my "first-read master" pouring over sheets of 8 & ½" by 11" paper in a binder to tell me everything she liked, and more importantly, didn't like about Song Girl. Thank you, Susan. I hope you never tire of reading what I write.

A legal thanks to my older, wiser, brother David. When I first had the idea for **Song Girl** I thought of a character who, after awakening from a coma, could only speak in song *lyrics.* As the work progressed, I thought I better find out the proper way to get the clearances necessary to use the words from songs. My brother, who's well versed in those things, immediately advised me to change tack. It turns out using song *lyrics* in a book is a huge no no but song *titles* are fair game. Changing Hannah's dialogue made the work a little more difficult but no less fun.

Then there are my wonderful friends. The people that allow me to attach their names to my characters. When I call in the favor, they never make demands or ask if the character is going to be "a good guy or a bad guy?" They just say yes. So, thank you Dana, Marc, Elizabeth, Tracey, Dan, Dennis, Carl, Chris, Tom, Karen, Jerry, Jamal, Tucker, Danielle, Frank, Christine, Dalton, Wes, Selena, Lucas, Daisy, Michael, Larry, and Larry. Regardless of how your character "turned out" I hope you don't regret your generosity.

An additional "hat tip" to Mike McAtee at USA Boxing. He spent a great deal of time with me on the phone explain the long, hard, road the special athletes who represent Team USA in International competitions must travel. And to my dear friend Matthew Laurence who told me of his son, Lee's, own boxing experience. I hope he understands why the Lee in the book had to lose a few bouts.

For the third time in this second career journey the fantastic team at Beacon Publishing Group have found my work worthy of their fine name. The editorial team makes sure all the I's are dotted and the t's are crossed. The artists take my concept and turn it into an eye-catching book cover. The social media and website folks are always there to promote my efforts. I am forever grateful for all the support.

Finally thank all of you for going on this journey. If you're still here you're like me… the kind of person who sits in the theatre, after the movie has ended, to watch the credits. I hope you liked Song Girl. Now get ready for what's next.

Keith